A MURDER IN CONCORD

ALSO BY CALEB WYGAL

Mytle Beach Mystery Novels
The Brass Key (Short Story Prequel)
Death on the Boardwalk
Death Washes Ashore
Death on the Golden Mile
Death on the Causeway
Death at Tidal Creek

Lucas Caine Novels
Moment of Impact
A Murder in Concord
Blackbeard's Lost Treasure
The Search for the Fountain of Youth

A Murder in Concord

*A Lucas Caine
Mystery*

CALEB WYGAL

Grand Strand Publishing

Published by Grand Strand Publishing, LLC

Author photo by Pamela Hartle
Printed in the United States of America

THIRD EDITION
ISBN 979-8-218-30251-1

Fiction: Amateur Sleuth
Fiction: Southern Fiction

"She has misled him by the abundance of her persuasiveness. By the smoothness of her lips, she seduces him. -Proverbs 7:21

PROLOGUE

An influential man was about to die.

For over twenty years, Trent Simon Mahoney II held the same pattern of being the last person to leave the Mahoney, Incorporated office building located on Copperfield Boulevard in Concord, North Carolina. He and his father, also named Trent, were the co-owners of Mahoney's Restaurants, and two of the richest men that lived in the state of North Carolina. Trent the younger was one of the most driven and indefatigable restaurateurs in the business.

This pattern would ultimately lead to Trent's death.

His murderer hid behind a row of tall, thick bushes that lined the sidewalk in front of Trent's shiny, new Lexus. The sun had set, leaving a picturesque sunset behind. Soft phosphorescent lighting bathed the parking lot from elegant streetlamps reminiscent of the streetlamps on old cobblestoned streets. The lamps decorated the sidewalk and parking lot of this otherwise thoroughly modern structure.

The night was dry and sticky, as it had been for the past several months. The entire southeast was amid a hard drought.

Trent was the last person to leave the building on this day. An hour had passed since the previous person left.

The murderer waited patiently that entire time. He had an excellent view of Trent leaving the building and locking up. The killer remained hidden.

Mahoney, Incorporated was the holding company of one of the largest restaurant chains in America, but did not have security to watch the building during the night hours. This was part of the family's belief of keeping the base of operations simple and small. However, there was a state-of-the-art security system installed that the Mahoney family thought eliminated the need for anyone to watch the building in during the night hours.

The killer knew this.

From the killer's vantage point, Trent looked tired and beaten as he walked the short distance to the primo CEO parking space at the front of the building. The killer thought Trent looked disappointed.

The killer knew why Trent had that look on his face.

The killer did not have to fear any random cars coming into the parking lot, nor anyone driving by on Copperfield Boulevard to see the deed that was about to be committed. The building was set behind an automatic locking iron gate where a person could only get in by inputting a security password. The three-story glassed structure was set off the road, behind a line of tall oak trees, obscuring any view of the parking lot from the road.

The killer knew this and had planned upon it.

Trent looked around, as though searching for something or someone. He looked hopeful. The killer knew for whom Trent was searching.

When Trent pushed the button on his keychain to unlock his silver car, the parking lights flashed, the security alarm chirped, and the killer took that as good a time as any.

CHAPTER ONE

The next day . . .

Lucas Caine awoke at the same time he had every Wednesday for the past year and a half: 5:40 a.m. He rolled over in his lonesome bed and quieted the buzzing alarm clock. He stretched and tried, unsuccessfully, to stifle a yawn.

God, this is getting old, he thought. If it were not for the pay and the benefits that went with his job, he would have quit a long time ago. He was in his second year on the job. Every Monday through Friday, he had to be at the office at around six in the morning. He was one of the first people to arrive, and one of the last to leave every day. It almost killed him those first few weeks. They hired him right out of college. He had to adjust from college life to working life in the course of two weeks.

He rolled out of bed and repeated the same routine that he did every morning; shave, shower, brush teeth, put on coffee, read the headlines on the Charlotte Observer paper, eat waffles, and leave.

The headline on the front page of the Observer read, **'Charlotte Area Muggings Up 500%.'**

The article stated that the reported muggings were in Mecklenburg, Iredell, and Cabarrus—the county in which he lived. Over the past year, there had been many more muggings than had ever been reported in those areas. These muggings seemed to occur primarily at night, but there was the occasional daytime, broad daylight mugging. The police suspected the same person, or persons were perpetrating the crimes. Usually the assailant threatened the victim with a knife or gun. Sometimes it was just a purse-snatching. The muggings happen so randomly, the paper reported, that the police have been unable to catch even one of the muggers. The people who were robbed said the crime happened so fast they did not get a good look at the mugger other than it could have been a white or possibly a black man. Further investigations were pending.

The muggings worried Lucas, but he was not going to let them keep him at home. The victims were mainly women and a few older men. Lucas stood nearly six-three and weighed a shade over two hundred pounds. Not the typical target for a mugger. Lucas had read these reports in the paper over the past couple of months. He did not know what the crime rate of Concord was before he moved to Spring Street, but the police kept a visible presence in his neighborhood, giving him a sense of safety.

When he moved to Concord, he bought a small house on Spring Street, which was just off Union Street. Union leads to the small, historic part of downtown Concord. The small house was located just one block from the historic section, which included many, old, breathtaking, Victorian-style houses. It was a quiet part of town. He appreciated that fact, having grown up in a small West Virginia town where one rarely heard a siren of any kind breaking the silence. His home was a small, one-story white house behind two, towering oak trees. The grass in the front yard is a nice color of burnt brown from his neglect and from a long, lasting drought.

He kept telling himself that he was going to hire someone to tend to his lawn. It was a decent starter home, but with the money he made, he knew he could afford better. At the time that he moved here, it was the best that he could do.

Lucas backed his brand new Scion TC out of the driveway and pulled away. The sky was starting to brighten with some high cirrus clouds in the sky and a burgeoning sun turning the clouds different shades of blue, violet, and orange. It was a stunning sunrise. The air was already muggy, as it had been for days. Usually the high humidity combined with the heat brought along afternoon thunderstorms, but not in recent weeks, contributing to his dying lawn.

Lucas worked at Mahoney's main office. He labored along-side the owner's son as his personal assistant. He dealt with public relations for the company and their restaurant chain. Not a position many would accept, fresh out of college with a degree in business administration. The truth was that they offered him truckload of money to take the position. He had a huge amount of debt left over from his college loans, and with this job, not only could he have that paid off quickly, they also promised him an even higher position if he remained employed there for two years. He was more than halfway to that promotion.

Much of what he did as Trent Mahoney's assistant was man-age his time, keep butt-kissers off his personal schedule, arrange public appearances, issue press releases, grant interviews, and otherwise try to keep the family's name out of the public eye.

Lucas was young and still learning the nuances of his job. It was exciting and fun.

He pulled onto Copperfield and soon pulled up to the huge wrought-iron gate guarding Mahoney Incorporated's parking lot. Two huge crepe myrtle trees flanked it on both sides. Lucas could see the building from where he was at the gate, but passersby couldn't see the building from the highway. This spot at the gate was the exception as a line of thick fir trees running along the property line concealed the building.

Once in the parking lot, the building looked similar to other large buildings in the area with one exception. The façade of the building. All three stories of it, is comprised of a huge, glassed-in atrium housing a full-sized, live palm tree.

There was no guardhouse at the gate, although a few cameras had their lenses directed at the entrance from either side. The Mahoney's didn't want for their employees to feel as though they worked at some minimum-security prison. A brushed nickel number pad with black plastic housing, firmly attached to a heavy-duty black steel post sat beside the gate. A driver came to the number pad, rolled down their window and input their code. If successful, the gate would open.

All a person needed to get into Mahoney's main building was a password. The password changed daily and was unique from person to person. It was not a difficult password to crack if a person had the time to sit at the gate it and knew an employee's personal info. It was a ten-digit number that consisted of the last four digits of the employee's social security number and the current date. It seemed simple, but no one ever got in the gate uninvited. The Mahoney's wouldn't call the SWAT team or the cops if that ever happened. They would simply tell someone to turn around and go away. If an argument ensued, then the intruder received vouchers for a free meal at one of the Mahoney's restaurant.

Lucas posed the question on his first day of work of how they received deliveries by UPS or Fed-Ex. Trent smiled, and said that they had a Post Office Box, and did not receive any deliveries of any sort at the office. They had a person whose job was to pick up and deliver the mail for the office. Only on rare occasions did a delivery driver or technician need to come through the gate. When that happened, they gave a temporary password to the driver that only worked one time.

Lucas then asked about the unique, in his opinion, way in which they had their security set up. They told him they liked to keep the number of people coming out of the main office to a minimum. That hiring security was unneeded for an area in which the Mahoney family felt relatively safe. Lucas wondered if they wanted to keep workers to a minimum, why have such a large office, and why hire him. He did not voice this thought to Mr. Mahoney, however.

He punched in his code and proceeded through the gate. He saw Mr. Mahoney's Lexus already sitting in his parking spot near the entrance. This was normal. He was supposed to be here before Trent, to arrange his day, and get other affairs in order. For Trent to be here first was no surprise. His work ethic was legendary.

All members of the Mahoney family had parking spots near the main entrance. Trent and his father's parking spot were side-by-side. The leading women of Mahoney's spots were next to them. They remained vacant most of the time. The last two spots belonged to the two grandsons, Simon and the younger Brian. Also vacant most of the time. Particularly Simon's parking spot. Brian came about once a week. Lucas's parking spot, while not anywhere near as glamorous, was still closer than some who have been working for the company for far longer than he has.

He pulled into his reserved spot on the second row back from the entrance, all the way to the right of the parking lot. He grabbed a Brooks Brothers leather messenger bag from beside him and got out of the car.

He almost missed it as he passed by the front of Trent Mahoney's Lexus.

Trent's body lay crumpled on the pavement next to his car. He was on his back, feet facing Lucas, legs askew. Trent's right arm was extended from his side, and his left arm pinned underneath him.

Lucas thought he yelled, "Trent!" In an instant, he was kneeling next to Trent's body.

It was obvious the instant Lucas got close that Trent was dead. He smelled bad, not in a B.O. way either, and his trouser pants landed in a puddle of blood that seeped from the neat bullet hole in the middle of his forehead, and meandered in a trail to a nearby sewer drain. Lucas looked closely and saw no other obvious bullet holes. From his cursory examination, he thought Trent had been here for a while. This did not happen recently.

He looked around to see if the killer was still hiding somewhere in the parking lot. Lucas did not panic. He gathered his wits and tried to slow his pulse. He pulled the cell from his pocket and called 911 although he knew this was no longer an emergency.

Trent was long dead. The killer, long gone. Hopefully.

He explained to the operator who he was, where he was, and what he found. She said that she would dispatch the detective and the crime scene investigators right away, for him to wait where he was and not disturb the crime scene. He thanked her and hung up the phone. This was the first time he had ever seen a dead body that was not already in a coffin, much less the dead body of someone he knew and worked closely with.

Lucas knew the operator had told him not to, but he took a closer look at the body. He had read many books and watched dozens of murder mysteries on TV. He had seen what detectives look for at a murder scene, which this was. He examined the hands. There were no scratches on his hands or anything under his fingernails to tell him that there was a struggle involved. Trent felt cool, again leading him to think the murder was not recent. Either the killer got the drop on Trent, or, a ghastlier thought, he knew the person.

In the distance, Lucas heard a siren. He stood up, careful to leave Trent the way he found him. Lucas did not want to leave his fingerprints on the crime scene. He already knew that they were there, but he did not want his prints to show up on Trent's clothes or briefcase, which stood next to the driver's side door of the car. He walked over to a nearby row of bushes that lined the front of the building, sat down at the edge of the sidewalk, took out his phone again, and dialed a number that he knew well.

After a few rings, someone picked it up. "Hello," said a tentative female voice.

"Hey Carly," Lucas said in a low tone. Carly was Trent's wife.

"Oh Lucas. How are you?"

"Umm, not too great," he replied.

"What's the matter? Does it have anything to do with my husband? Have you seen him? He didn't come home last night. That sometimes happens, but he didn't call, but I tried not to worry," she said, stacking the sentences on one another.

"No, I know he didn't come home last night," Lucas replied. "Are you sitting down?"

"Yes."

The nervousness in her voice told Lucas she suspected what was coming.

"Listen," Lucas said, pausing before he broke the news. "Trent's dead. I found him here in the parking lot when I pulled in a few minutes ago."

There was no reply, she did not ask him how her husband died. Lucas could hear her sobbing through the phone.

He looked up and saw two police cars, one of them unmarked, with a single flashing red light perched upon its dome, pull up outside the gate. "Listen Carly, I've already called the police. They're here now, and I need to go let them in the gate."

She sniffled. "Okay. Thanks Lucas. Who else have you called?"

"You were the first after 911."

"Thanks. I'll be down there as soon as I can."

She seemed to have regained some composure. That made sense. Carly Mahoney was much like her mother-in-law, Laura Ann: a very strong woman. As much as Carly would not admit to it, she knew she and Laura Ann were a lot alike, though at times they acted as though they were mortal enemies.

"If I don't see you before I know more, I'll call your cell."

"Okay, and thanks again Lucas," she said breaking the connection.

Lucas was halfway to the gate when the call ended. He doubted that the police had received the emergency code so soon. He would have to let them in.

As Lucas walked to the other end of the parking lot, he wondered who would do such a thing. Trent Mahoney did not have any enemies who would do this. Lucas shook his head and wondered, as he looked at the pass code box, the security cameras at the top of the lighting poles and the ten-foot wrought-iron fence ringing the property, *how did this happen?*

The only conclusion Lucas could draw was that it had to be someone that worked for the company.

But who?

CHAPTER TWO

After Lucas let the police in the gate, he followed their cars on foot back to the crime scene.

Crime scene. He could not have pictured when he left work yesterday that he would return to one.

The previous day had been a successful one for Lucas and Trent. The contract they had with one of the food vendors in the northeast was ending. They managed to negotiate an extension with the company that would save around one hundred thousand dollars per year over the next four years for the same service as before. Lucas received kudos from Trent before he left because Lucas happened to mention to the vendor's rep that they were in talks with one of their competitors. It was not a lie when he said that, Lucas spoke on the phone with one of their competitor's reps for about five minutes a couple of weeks prior to see what they had to offer. They were overpriced.

The two police cars screeched to a halt, even though they only had to travel a hundred yards from the gate to Trent's body, and there was no real emergency. Two officers got out the marked cruiser, while only a single person got out of the unmarked car. The first two officers wore full uniforms. Before the officers examined the body, they put up yellow crime scene tape around the lighted poles near Trent's car. They ran the tape back to the columns on the portico above the front entrance, effectively marking off the crime scene. The other officer was wearing a rumpled blue sport coat, red shirt, khaki pants, with white tennis shoes. Lucas frowned in distaste at the choice of wardrobe. He wondered if this guy's significant other would let him out of the house dressed that way. If he had one.

After stringing up the yellow tape, the officers went over to the body, while the guy in the suit walked straight to Lucas and stuck his hand out.

"Hello," Lucas said, shaking his hand.

"Hey," the plainclothes police officer said, "I take it you're the one who called this in?"

Lucas nodded. The investigator gave Lucas a hard look. The cop had penetrating blue eyes which made Lucas feel as though the man could peer into his soul. The eyes made Lucas nervous.

"I'm Greg," the detective said, "Greg Hanover, and I'm the lead homicide investigator for the city of Concord."

"Lucas Caine. I am, was, Mr. Mahoney's personal aide."

"Give me the short of it, starting with what all that you touched before we arrived," Greg said, getting down to business. Lucas told him what he found and how he found it. Greg listened with rapt attention, occasionally nodding or muttering something.

When Lucas finished, Greg turned to look at the body lying ten feet away from where they were talking. He let out a low whistle. "Whew, this is going to be big," he said. "The chief of police, maybe even the mayor of Charlotte is going to come out and see this."

Lucas did not know what to say, this was all new and surreal to him.

"This is going to be one of the biggest murder investigations in this town's history, maybe even in the state's history. All the big-wigs are going to come out for this," Greg said.

"Do you have a partner?" Lucas asked. Greg eyed him like he was going to pounce. Lucas explained, "I thought that detectives usually had a partner."

"No, no partner for me. I work better alone, and when I have had partners, they usually end up asking to be reassigned." He shrugged. "I don't know why."

"Oh," Lucas said.

Greg stood a full head shorter than Lucas but seemed larger than that, as though he could destroy Lucas at any minute. "Is there somewhere you could go, close by, while we do an initial examination of the scene and body?"

"Yeah," Lucas replied.

"I'm going to inspect what we have here. The forensics people should arrive shortly to really get their investigation under way," Greg explained. "After that, I would like to talk to you more."

Lucas had already told him what he found and how he found it. He did not know what more Greg could want from him. He looked at his watch. People would not start arriving at the office for another hour. He figured some of his coworkers were already awake, preparing for a normal day at Mahoney's home office. This was going to be a day unlike any other and Lucas made the decision that no one needed to be here to see it. He needed to make some calls and tell people not to come in today.

"That should be fine," Lucas said. "Anything you need, I'll try to help as much as I can."

"Thank you son," Greg said, clapping Lucas on the shoulder. "Listen, it's never fun finding a dead body, much less someone that you work with or for. I've seen it all before. I'm desensitized. We get about five or so murders a year here in Concord, so I don't see it that often, but over the course of twenty years you get used to it," he admitted. Lucas nodded in understanding. "Go do what you have to do, but don't go far. Also," Greg continued, pulling a pair of rubber gloves and some paper shoe covers from the pocket of his jacket, handing them to Lucas, "Put these on so you don't get your prints everywhere."

"Yes, sir."

"Please, call me Greg."

"Okay, Greg."

Lucas gave Greg a code to unlock the gate so that his other people could get in. He gave Lucas another penetrating stare before he turned and retreated to the sanctuary inside the building.

Lucas had the eerie feeling that Greg considered him a suspect. Lucas was the last known person to see Trent alive in the police's eyes. Lucas preferred to think of the killer as being the last known person to see Trent alive before pulling the trigger.

Lucas hoped that the police would eventually come around to his point of view.

Lucas did not need to go past the reception desk after he walked inside the building. All of the information he needed to make the appropriate calls was at the desk. Besides, he wanted to be near the front where he could observe the investigation.

When people asked why they were not coming to work today, Lucas gave a vague response by saying something had happened that the family needed to deal with that would take their full focus, and all corporate operations were closed for the day. One or two people asked about missing a day of pay and he told them that they would consider today a paid holiday.

While Lucas made the calls, he saw Greg head out to the gate and let a couple of big vans with 'Concord Forensics' emblazoned on their sides through the gate. Within minutes, a dozen men and women were crawling over the scene, taking pictures of the body, pictures of Trent's Lexus, and pictures of his body in relation to the front door. A woman, who Lucas assumed to be the medical examiner, poked and prodded at the body. Lucas noticed that everyone wore the same rubber gloves that he had on.

It was a ghastly thought to think of someone who as late as yesterday as his friend and mentor as 'the body.' It made Lucas shiver.

He saw the examiner also put bags over Trent's hands. Lucas assumed this was to keep anything under his nails intact.

A few people came into the lobby and asked where Trent's office was. He led them to third floor where his office was located, unlocked the door, and let them in. Ten minutes later, they came back downstairs with the mainframe of Trent's computer tucked underneath one guy's arm. They were going to see if there was any evidence stored in Trent's computer. Lucas doubted there was. Trent was almost computer illiterate, and the computer on his desk was mainly for show for any important person who might come and visit. Lucas often had to help Trent navigate through Ebay.

After Lucas made the last call, he put his head down on the desk. He knew it was an odd thing to do, but he felt compelled to do so. He felt completely drained and needed to clear his head.

When the Mahoney family first hired Lucas, one of the first things he did was write a short history of Mahoney's Incorporated, and the rise of Mahoney's as one of the premier dining destinations in the nation for use on their website. He had some fun with it, and learned a lot about the family in the process. He tried to put in some personal info about the family to make the release more appealing.

It read as follows:

"Quinn Simon Mahoney and his wife, Laura Ann, opened a small blue-roofed diner in the mid-1950s in downtown Concord, named simply, Mahoney's Diner. The diner specialized in offering quick homemade style lunches meant to feed the politicians, bureaucrats, and the executives who were looking for a quick bite to eat on the lunch hour.

"The restaurant was popular because the food was excellent, and Laura Ann was an especially striking, raven-haired beauty who offered a pleasant distraction for her clientele. She was not above flirting with every man that walked through the door. Most of the men who were her regular customers were of the over-fed, balding variety that rarely received the kind of attention that Laura Ann Mahoney provided them. Most of the middle-class wives of that era from around Concord were of the kiss-on-the-cheek, "yes dear, no dear" variety that could not quite get their husband's motor running quite the way that Laura Ann could.

"The men of Concord during that era looked forward every day to receiving a well-cooked meal from the beautiful woman working behind the counter of the Mahoney Diner. One day, the wife of a low-level bureaucrat decided to drop in on her husband and surprise him by taking him to lunch. The man was not thinking with his head when he suggested that they go to the Mahoney Diner.

"While his wife, Susan, told her husband how wonderful that she thought the meatloaf was, she also watched how often her husband's eyes wandered over to the woman with too much makeup standing at the counter. She noticed just how friendly the girl seemed to be towards every man who came to the counter. Susan also noticed that she seemed to be the only other woman in the diner. As she and her husband waited to pay for their meal at the register, she noticed the man in front of them. It was Arthur, of an older woman, Martha, in Susan's bridge club. He did not notice her. He was too busy flirting with Laura Ann.

"At one point, Susan saw the woman rest her hand on Arthur's wart-spotted wrist.

"After Susan and her husband left the diner and walked back to his office on Church Street, she went straight to Martha's house to tell her what she had seen. Martha, of course, did not believe Susan. Arthur had been faithful to her for thirty-five years. Besides, Martha joked, they both knew that never, even in his younger days, could Arthur have attracted such a beautiful woman. Susan saw the logic in Martha's point, and was relieved.

"At the next Bridge Club meeting, Martha and Susan told the other two women in their club the funny story about Martha's husband. They laughed and saw how far-fetched the idea was of the beautiful woman and Arthur. Susan made comment about how great that she thought the meatloaf was at the Mahoney Diner and mentioned that her husband loved the food as well.

"The next week, the four met for lunch at the diner. The other three members of the Bridge club loved the food and the speed with which they received their meals, and decided to recommend the Diner to all of their friends. So overjoyed by the food they were they failed to notice how friendly Laura Ann was with the male customers. Quinn knew what his wife did with the male patrons, even encouraging it to some extent.

"Quinn Simon Mahoney knew how to sell a product, and if it meant using his wife's sex appeal to keep their diner busy, then he could live with it. Not one time in the five years that Laura Ann worked at the Diner was she unfaithful to her husband.

"Susan, Martha, and the other two women in the Bridge club told their friends and neighbors of the great new diner that had opened up in downtown Concord. The busiest time of the day for the diner was usually around lunchtime. Soon after the women from the bridge club ate there for the first time, the diner started to stay busy throughout the day thereafter. It overjoyed Quinn at how busy his diner had become. He and Laura Ann lived in a small two-bedroom house on Burrage Road. near downtown Concord. With the influx of money they were now receiving, they soon moved into a four-bedroom home on Union Street, four blocks from their diner.

"They planned to have a large family and bought a house they figured would accommodate all the children that they planned to have.

"In addition, with the influx of money coming from the restaurant, the Mahoney's could afford to hire some more help, so Laura Ann could stay home to concentrate on having that big family they had hoped to have. With Laura Ann leaving the diner, the male patrons were heartbroken, but continued to come back almost every day. The diner stayed busy enough that Quinn soon opened a second diner in nearby Salisbury.

"This new blue-roofed diner depended mostly on word of mouth to attract new customers. Quinn Mahoney did not believe in advertising to promote his diner. He believed that an excellent reputation was better than any sort of advertising.

"Not long after the new diner opened, Laura Ann gave birth to their first of what would be many children. They hoped. However, Trent Mahoney would be the only child the couple ever had.

"During the next eighteen years, the Mahoney Diner expanded to ten new locations in the rapidly growing cities around Charlotte, Winston-Salem, Raleigh, and three other towns in the North and South Carolina area. Over those eighteen years, Quinn groomed his son to help run his small empire. Trent proved to be an intelligent and ambitious young man with maybe a keener business sense than that of his father. He encouraged his father to begin advertising in some of the newspapers that were popular in the towns and cities in which they had diners. His father could see the ambition in his son's eye's, and decided to take Trent's advice.

"With the help of advertising and traditional word-of-mouth, Mahoney's began a rapid expansion. When the Mahoney's opened up a blue roofed diner in a new town, they would advertise in all of the newspapers and take advantage of advertising on the radio stations. They would use these means to draw new customers into their new diners, but it would be through word-of-mouth of the great food and service recommendations that would keep the customer base growing. The Mahoney's would then withdraw most of their advertising in those towns to help boost revenues and open up new diners elsewhere.

"Over time, the name of the diner changed. They shortened the name from 'Mahoney's Diner' to simply 'Mahoney's.' They felt that the shorter name would give their restaurant chain more prestige without 'Diner' in the title. The decision proved to be beneficial. Profits increased greatly in the first six months with the shortened name. Now, the Mahoney Diner chain is poised for unprecedented growth and profits almost unseen in the dining industry."

Lucas thought the bio was good. When he submitted it to Trent Mahoney, he loved it. He said he could see right then he made the correct choice in hiring Lucas. It allowed him to receive his own education on the Mahoney business and family. He had eaten at their restaurants before, the food was great, but before they hired him, he knew little of their history.

Lucas left a few personal details about the Mahoney family out of the release.

Before Trent's two boys, Brian and Simon, entered high school, they were golden. Simon always had the highest scores in his private school's class, and Brian, a year younger, was never far behind. They never got into trouble, had clean records, and were a good representation of the Mahoney family in the community of Concord and around Charlotte.

However, as soon as Simon made it into high school, his spotless record went downhill. He did some minor stuff such as cutting class, but then it escalated quickly when, at sixteen, the police arrested him for drinking and driving. It was a PR nightmare for the family and their former publicist. She was unable to control the disaster in the media and unable to face the pressure of actually having to do some real hard work for the first time with the family, so she quit. A media crisis had never happened to the family before. Quinn and Laura Ann were pillars in the community and in their local church. The community respected Trent and Carly for what they did, though there were not as active in the community as the elder Mahoney's were. The community highly respected Quinn in particular.

At least the company's profits didn't suffer. As Mahoney, Incorporated was a privately held company and not publicly traded on the stock market, they had no stock that could slip. People still came to the restaurant in droves no matter what trouble the founder's oldest grandchild got into.

The former PR person left, literally, in the middle of the night. She had been in the business for years, and was with Mahoney's for almost that entire time. When she left, Quinn and Trent got together and decided that they were going to go for a PR person much, much younger. Someone with a fresh perspective and a thorough understanding of social media marketing. They were going to do an extensive search for the youngest and brightest person possible and find someone they could mold. They did not hold open interviews for the position. In fact, they did not post the position anywhere. Meanwhile, while the search transpired, there was still the matter of what to do with Simon. The solution came in the form of a trust fund, a two million dollar trust fund to be exact.

The thought of that number made Lucas ill.

Quinn and Laura Ann sat down with Brian and Simon one evening soon after Lucas arrived to tell them about the massive trust fund that had been set up for them. Simon and Brian were ecstatic. They already knew that they were going to be well off just by being a member of the Mahoney family, but now they knew they were going to be set for life.

When their grandparents told them of the terms, their expressions soured. Each of them had to maintain a certain level of grades through graduation. They had to attend church regularly and they could not get into any trouble that Quinn and Laura Ann considered grossly immoral. Then they would go to college and take courses that would help the family continue to run its business. After they graduated college, they would join the family at their headquarters and take up a position within the company. Then and only then would they receive the two million dollars. They told the boys they were going to be watched to make sure that they were doing the correct things and staying out of trouble.

Sure enough, Simon straightened up, and to this point, has stayed out of trouble. Brian just kept doing what he was already doing. No changes needed.

Much of that occurred before Lucas arrived. He was glad no disasters arose to take care of in his year and a half of employment with the company. Quinn seemed pleased by Lucas's work. Trent did not show pleasure the same way his father did, and was sometimes hard to get a read on. Trent had not fired Lucas before his death, so he assumed Trent liked the job Lucas was doing.

The Mahoney line of restaurants was growing at a rapid pace. They had plans of expansion forecasted five years into the future. The Mahoney family sat on one big, fat, giant cash cow that showed no sign of slowing down and Trent Mahoney was a big reason that was the case.

Now, someone chopped the head of the giant off. Lucas wondered how the corporation would cope. Who would lead it? And an even worse thought: if the person who he was personal assistant to were dead, would he still have a job?

He looked up from the desk and shook his head. A great man had just died and all he could think of was dollar signs. Lucas came from a lower middle-class family in West Virginia. He grew up knowing what the value of a dollar was and how to hold on to it. Never in his entire childhood did he envision that one day he would be around the amount of money he was today.

He knew the Mahoney family personally. Quinn and his wife Laura Ann, the two founders of the business, were devout Christians. They gave much of their time and money to their church. Their church was the biggest and grandest in Concord. The Mahoney family was behind that. They devoted their life to serving God's purpose, whatever that was. The entire family preached family values, humility, and being humble, but if you were to take their money away, Lucas thought that most of the six in the family, well five now, could not live on.

Not that he had close, personal relationships with the entire family. They can be reclusive and limited their contact with Lucas. He didn't know what the two sons, Simon and Brian, do for fun, nor did he know what Carly did in her spare time. He assumed she was a frequent shopper at the many area malls. He was familiar with them, but did not *know* them.

Money was a huge part of the Mahoney's lives, whether or not they admitted to it. They all drove luxury vehicles. Both sides of the family used to have eighteen thousand square foot Victorian mansions. Trent's parents sold their mansion a few years ago because of their failing health to move in with their only son. The Mahoney family had a summer home on Edisto Island in South Carolina, complete with a million dollar yacht tied up at the dock. They frequently traveled around the world.

Lucas did not, however, stop to think about who could have possibly killed Trent. He did not know Trent Mahoney to have enemies of any kind. He was a peaceful, personable man who would do anything for anyone. That he received a bullet to the head was a complete and absolute surprise to him. Lucas had the hunch that it had to be someone he worked with. There was no one in particular Lucas singled out and thought, "Oh, yeah, *he* is the person who killed Trent."

Every person Lucas worked with was handpicked by the Mahoney's. They did not pick disgruntled, grumpy people, no matter their qualifications.

Lucas was staring off into space when Greg walked through the front entrance. The penetrating gaze was on and he felt the need to hide under the desk.

"Is there someplace that we can talk?" he said without preamble.

Lucas looked around at the completely empty atrium. "This is as good a place as any."

Greg handed Lucas a clipboard and asked Lucas to sign it. He explained it was a crime-scene log. It listed everyone who entered the scene. Lucas signed it while Greg walked over to a row of seldom used upholstered chairs lined up in a row serving as the waiting area for the building. He grabbed the one on the end, pulled it over to the reception desk, and sat down heavily.

He rubbed a hand across his eyes and muttered, "Oh, God." Lucas sat in silence, studying him. After a few seconds, Greg pulled out a small notepad and a pen. "I'll just ask you a few questions for now and then probably ask you some later on, but I want to get to a few things now while all of this is still fresh in your mind."

"Okay," Lucas said.

"Umm, first, when was the last time you saw Mr. Mahoney alive?"

"I saw him yesterday evening before I left work at around seven."

"In what kind of state did he appear when you left? A good mood? Distraught? Upset?"

"He was happy when he left yesterday. We completed a deal which was months in the making. Going to save the corporation a ton of money."

Greg grunted and scribbled on the notepad. "Had he been having any problems with someone, such as a business rival or a family member?"

Lucas did not even have to think about this one. "Trent, er...Mr. Mahoney did not have any enemies. He got along with everyone. I'm not extremely close to his family, nor have I done much with them outside of the office here, but he was always in a good mood."

"Okay, what about anyone he may have done business with?"

"He also had good working relationships with all the vendors and contractors that worked for us. He tried to treat everyone as though they were the most important people he had ever met. I can't think of any reason someone would do this."

Greg jotted something down. He laid the pen down and sat back in the chair.

"I met Mr. Mahoney one time," he said. "I took my ex-wife and our two kids to the Mahoney diner in Harrisburg for my son's sixth birthday. After they showed us to our table, I excused myself and found one of the manager's on duty. I mentioned it was my son's birthday and wondered if they could do the thing where the staff brings out a cupcake or something and sings the birthday song. The manager smiled and said he would see what he could do.

"I went back to the table. We ordered and ate our food. Towards the end of our meal, I saw a bunch of the uniformed workers come out from the kitchen in a group. I tapped my son on the elbow so he'd look up. I think he knew what was coming, because surely he had seen it before in a restaurant. When the workers arrived at our table, the person who had the small birthday cake in his hand was none other than Trent Mahoney. I think I was the only person who recognized him from my family. He led his workers in singing "Happy Birthday" set the cake down on the table, and went back to the kitchen with the rest of the workers."

"I'm not surprised," Lucas said. "He does, did, things like that from time to time. It was normal for him to visit a restaurant to make sure it was running up to his specifications. Sometimes he would even help in the kitchen."

Lucas thought about Greg's story and the reason he told it. Here Lucas was, so saddened by Trent's sudden death, he did not stop to think how this affected others. Trent was a pillar in this area, and through his business and charity, touched the lives of many of the area's inhabitants.

They sat in silence for a few moments, lost in thought.

Greg shook it off first and held up his notepad. "Just one more, small question Mr. Caine. I'm sure you have a lot of work to do yourself." Lucas nodded. "What time was it when you left last night?"

"Around seven."

"Right, you mentioned that." Greg made a notation. "Okay, that's all I need for now. I noticed there are cameras in the parking lot, I'm going to need you to pull those feeds for the previous twenty-four hours and have the recordings sent over to the police department. Plus, I'm going to need any feeds you have from that camera," he said, pointing at a security camera directly over the reception desk. "Then I'm going to need a list of all the people Trent met with over the past few days. I'm sure you either have a list already available or you could put one together fairly quickly."

"Yes sir. The camera feeds will take time to pull, but I could have them to you by this afternoon, along with the list of contacts."

Greg stood and stretched his legs. "God, this is going to be a long couple of days," he said.

"Tell me about it."

They shook hands. Greg's eyes bore in on Lucas. "This afternoon sometime?"

"Yes, sir, that'll be the first thing I work on after making a few calls."

"I understand," Greg said, handing Lucas a business card. "If you think of anything else, call me immediately. I've got my home, cell, and office number on there."

Lucas took the card, studied it, and slipped it into his jacket pocket. Lucas pulled a card of his own out of his back pocket and handed it to Greg.

They turned towards the door upon hearing a cry of anguish spring from outside the building. Lucas presumed this was Carly announcing her arrival. Greg took one questioning look at Lucas, then rushed out of the building. Lucas followed into the blinding sunlight.

When they arrived outside, to where Trent's body lay, Lucas and Greg saw the two uniformed police officers trying to restrain a persistent Carly Mahoney, Trent's wife, from approaching the body.

"No!" she screamed, reaching a hand out between the two police officers, as though she could touch the body while still being over ten feet away. "You have to let me go to him!"

The officers made no reply. They grunted in the effort it took them to restrain Carly.

"Hey!" Greg yelled at the two officers. "Let her go!"

Without question, the officers released her from their grasp. She lunged for her dead husband. She cradled his head in her arms, not caring about the remaining blood flowing all over her yellow designer blouse. "No, no, no," she sobbed.

Greg and Lucas stood quietly side-by-side, content to let her live this moment by herself. This was not the place for someone to separate from the former lovers.

When composed, Carly was an elegant middle-aged woman, always clad in designer clothing. She had short, curly, red hair and a full set of lips that usually bore an extensive amount of bright red lipstick on them, revealing a stunning smile. There were pictures of her from twenty years ago where she flashed the same infectious smile. Lucas could see why Trent fell in love with her. Even today, physically, she was still a knockout. However, her personality left something to be desired.

Although beautiful, Trent's parents, especially his mother Laura Ann, considered Carly nothing more than a haughty gold-digger. Carly and Laura Ann had a personal feud going back before Trent and Carly wed. Lucas heard stories of some of the fighting that went on during the early years of their marriage between the two women. He was glad he never had to be in the middle of any of them. They seemed to have set aside some of their differences after Simon and Brian were born, and now existed in restrained harmony.

A big reason the feud existed was simply that Carly liked to shop. A lot. Lucas could not remember seeing her wear the same set of clothes twice, and he saw her several times a week. She had little to do with the company's running. She came around the office several times a week to see what was going on, or to ask Trent if she could buy this or that. Trent usually agreed to her requests.

Lucas was sure she found some way to show her appreciation to him.

Greg nudged Lucas to break Carly away from her former husband. Lucas went and kneeled beside Carly and Trent. Trent was beginning to smell as a wet puppy does in the heat of the morning. Lucas had heard of people throwing up because of the smell of a dead body. Carly did not seem to notice any smell, and the body was not ripe enough yet for him to give that sort of reaction. The sun was heating up, and he figured if the body lay there much longer, the odor would get to that point.

He put his hand on her elbow and said softly, "Carly."

Tears flowed between clinched eyes. "He's dead," she cried. "He's dead! Oh my God, who would do such a thing?"

"I don't know," Lucas said, "but we'll get it figured out. C'mon Carly, we need to let the police take care of their business. I'm sure there'll be time later for you to spend a few more minutes with Trent."

She opened her brown eyes and looked at him. "Promise?" she said it as though she were a small child.

Greg overheard the entire conversation. Lucas looked at Greg, and he nodded.

"Yeah, Mrs. Mahoney, there will be time later. C'mon, we got to get up," he said putting more pressure on her elbow for her to rise. "They've got a job to do."

She stood and wrapped her arms around Lucas's neck, getting bloodstains all over his suit. There were already bloodstains on the suit from before, so he didn't notice. He felt her wet tears on the side of his neck where she had buried her head.

"Thank you, Lucas," she sobbed.

Greg stepped forward. "Mrs. Mahoney, my name is Greg Hanover. I will be investigating your husband's murder. You can rest assured that all the resources of the Concord Police Department are behind this investigation. We will stop at nothing to find the murderer."

Carly stepped away from him, brushed the tears from her eyes, and with years a practice, put on a façade of erudition she used when speaking with anyone in public. The speed in which she did it surprised Lucas. If he were in her shoes, he would be a wreck for days.

She stuck out her hand. "Thank you Mr. Hanover, any help, service, or testimony I can lend is yours. And I'm grateful for anything you could do."

"Thank you Mrs. Mahoney," Greg said.

"No, no," Carly said. "Please, call me Carly. I insist you call me by my first name. I don't like people to call me Mrs. Mahoney, or Mrs. Anything for that matter. If there is anything I can do to help you find whoever did this horrible, despicable thing, let me know."

"Thank you, Carly," Greg said. He handed her the crime-scene log, and she signed it. "Now, if you'll excuse me, I need to go. I will call upon you when we are wrapped up here."

"Thank you," she said. "I will be inside."

Lucas led Carly into the building and deposited her in an office downstairs where she could be to herself while he made a couple of calls. She had resumed crying, so he left her with a fresh box of tissues.

He walked back to the reception desk. From there, he called the guy who was the only security person who worked for the company, Carter Washington, and asked him to come in.

One thing that attracted Mahoney's to Carter when they received his application for the security position was that he lived less than a mile from the office and his training as a Navy Seal.

Carter stormed through the front doors less than five minutes after Lucas called, ripping off a pair of reflective sunglasses. Carter was a beast of a man. He was recruited by many schools to play football at the Division I level after high school if he'd chosen to. The reason he did not was he felt his duty to his country calling, and joined the Marine Corps the day after he graduated from high school. He rose quickly through the ranks because of his physical prowess and keen intelligence, and joined the Seals. While training for his first mission as a Seal, as bad luck would have it, he tore both the ACL and MCL in his left knee. This left him unable to hold up physically to the rigors of being a member of that elite group, or even being in the Marines, period. He took a medical discharge shortly thereafter.

He did not let the injury get him down. Carter Washington was a determined man and used the training he received while in the military. He figured correctly, he would be best suited to the private protection/security field. He stood six-seven and weighed around two-eighty without an ounce of fat on him. He had dark skin, a shaved head, and a menacing goatee. Carter's only flaw was the bad limp when he walked. A leftover from the knee surgery. Lucas had a similar limp from a high-school car accident.

"Okay, what's up?" Carter asked in a deep voice reminiscent of Barry White. He looked at Lucas's bloodied suit. "Man, you need to go change out of those clothes."

Lucas looked down at the bloodstains on his suit and knew it was ruined. He kept a change of clothes up in his office. "Let me go change. I'll be right back."

Lucas went up to his office, changed, and returned to find Carter staring out the window at the crime-scene crawling with techs.

Carter turned from the window to Lucas. "Wow, those boys work fast. What happened?"

"I don't know," he answered. He was technically Carter's boss, but always felt as though he was never in charge when the intimidating man was around. Lucas related the story of how he found Trent Mahoney earlier and followed with his discussion with detective Hanover.

Carter took it in, slowly nodding the entire time. "I know this Greg," he nodded toward the parking lot when he was finished. "He comes off looking and sounding as if he doesn't know what he's talking about, but don't be fooled. He knows what he's doing."

Lucas did not ask how a person relatively new to Concord such as Carter would know a homicide inspector, but whatever. There were items far more important on the agenda to think about.

"How can I help?" Carter asked.

"We need to get copies of the surveillance tapes from last evening and send them over to the Concord PD."

"Sounds about right," Carter murmured. Lucas did not have access to those tapes. The only people who worked for Mahoney's that did were Trent, Quinn, and Carter. They liked to keep the ring of people small so fewer things could get out. "Let's go."

Lucas followed Carter to the elevator, where they descended into the basement. The basement had few furnishings and decorations compared to the rest of the building. The only decorations in the basement were fichus trees scattered up and down the hallways. Carter's security office was located directly across from the elevator. The security monitoring room was to the left.

Carter headed across to his office, unlocked the door, and told Lucas to wait a moment while he got some blank surveillance disks to replace the ones he was about to remove from the mainframe. He returned a few seconds later, discs in hand, and unlocked the door to the monitoring room. Lucas had been in this room only once or twice since they set it up months ago. It was a small room, with two rolling chairs, a desk set along the length of the wall, and a bank of televisions above the desk.

Carter worked seven days a week and rarely took a vacation. He spent much of his time in this room watching live feeds. The job isn't challenging, but he seemed to get some sort of satisfaction out of it. On the weekends, he only came in to swap out the surveillance discs.

Mahoney's used a new state-of-the-art security system incorporating Blu-Ray technology. The system required only three Blu-Ray disks to hold all the information compiled from the dozen cameras scattered about the premises. They kept the discs for three months before reusing them. Carter kept the disks in a huge, locking metal cabinet in his office.

Carter walked over to a large computer along one wall and ejected the three discs contained within it. He then put the three new, blank discs he took from his office into the mainframe and then motioned for Lucas to follow him back to his office. They walked into his sparsely furnished office and Lucas pulled a chair around to Carter's side of the desk so he could see the computer monitor. Lucas didn't know if they should view the disks before forwarding them to the police, but he didn't care, and Carter did not seem to either.

Carter put one disk into his computer under his desk and brought up the Windows Media Player program. "We record these things in ASF format so we can view them on just about any computer if need be, but until now, there has been no need to," he explained. While waiting for the program to load, he said, "Man, I can't believe this is happening. Who would do such a thing?"

"I don't know," Lucas admitted. "Trent never harmed anyone."

"I know. Here we go," he pointed at the screen.

Lucas moved closer for a better view. The feed from this disc showed the views of the four outside cameras, one on each wall. The screen split into four smaller screens, showing each of the views. Each screen had a view from a camera mounted high upon the north, south, east, and west walls.

Carter pointed to the view at the top left portion of the screen. "This is the one we'll be looking at. It shows the camera view from the front of the building, looking out at the parking lot."

Lucas studied the screen. Trent and Lucas arrive before Carter does, so their cars were already in the lot when the tape started. He fast-forwarded through the day, and they saw all the cars enter the park lot, with a few leaving from time to time. The time of day displayed in the upper left corner of the feed. When the time read **17:45:00,** Carter said, "This is about the time I left."

Many of the people who worked the previous day were walking out the front doors towards their respective cars and home for the day.

"There's me," Carter said, pointing at what was obviously his enormous form walking quickly to his Jeep in the now nearly empty parking lot. "In this view, we can see the people walking away after they've left the building."

"Do we have a view from the parking lot showing the front of the building and the people as they walk out the doors?" Lucas asked.

Carter nodded. "Yeah, that's on another disk. I put this one in because this has the closest view of Trent's car, where the murder occurred," he said, pointing at Trent's Lexus in the middle of the screen.

There were a few bushes partially obscuring the view of the car, but only on the passenger side. From the height of the camera perched on the side of the building, the view of Trent's car was almost from directly above.

Lucas's pulse quickened. They had front row seats to a murder.

"What time did you all leave last night?"

"Around seven," Lucas answered.

They watched Carter climb into his Jeep, and suddenly the screen went blank at **17:05:00**.

"Dammit!" Carter said.

Lucas looked at the blank screen in disbelief. "What happened?"

Carter frantically pushed a few keys, trying to get the video back up. "I don't know. It just cut off."

He started the video again, but this time took the slider bar on the timeline all the way to the right side of the screen, to the end of the video. While they watched the video in full-screen mode, the slider bar hid at the bottom of the screen. It does that when no one touches the mouse for a few seconds. They did not notice at first the video was not as long as it should have been. The time display on the bar showed the video was only just over nine hours long, instead of twenty-four hours, as it should have been.

"What about the disk that has the view from the parking lot on it?" Lucas suggested.

Carter ejected the incomplete first disk and put in a second one. "I bet we get the same results."

They waited a moment for the feeds to start. This time, the camera views were from the cameras on top of the light poles in the four corners of the lot. These four cameras looked into the center of the parking lot. Carter fast-forwarded to the end of the new feed with the same result.

Lucas shook his head in frustration. Carter took that disk out and popped the last one in. "This disc holds the feed from the camera in the lobby that looks out the front doors. You can see just the first few parking spots in the parking lot, but maybe there's something here."

Lucas waited a few moments while Carter ran through the same steps with these feeds. When he ran the feed to the end of the line, the feeds on the screen did the same thing as the other discs: it went blank.

"Oh God, this isn't good," Carter said, stating the obvious. "These disks are those new high-capacity disks that can hold a ton of information. We tested these things out and reviewed some tapes from when they first installed this new system. They worked perfectly."

Lucas did not reply. He did not know about these tests, but then again, they would have been of no concern to him. His mind reeled. How could this happen, unless they did it intentionally?

Carter had the same thought. "This *had* to have been done intentionally, but there are only three of us who have access to this room and one of them is dead now. The old man," speaking of the Quinn, "was not here yesterday, and we saw him leave before the tape shut off, and you don't have access to this room," he said, pointing at Lucas.

"That would mean Trent had to be the one to cut off the tapes."

"Yeah," Carter agreed, "But why?"

CHAPTER THREE

Lucas called Greg Hanover to deliver the news. Greg swore so loudly that Lucas had to pull the phone away from his ear during the tirade.

"Okay, okay," Greg said when he finished. "Let me think."

Greg mumbled to himself, while Lucas thought about this turn of events. He could have Carter retrieve the logs of every time the gate opened after the tape shut off. Because everyone has their own individual pass code, they could see if anyone came in after Lucas left, and then see when they left.

That was why there was a security box on the inside of the gate. Lucas thought it was overkill to check on everyone who left the premises. Why not just have the plates in the ground on the inside of the gate that caused the gate to swing open when a car drove across it? But hey, Lucas thought, it wasn't his company. He just worked there. Every company in existence had their own quirks. If one company ran perfectly, then everyone in the world would want to work for that company. But now they could find when the murderer left the parking lot.

A thought made his stomach lurch. He was the last person to leave last night before Trent's murder. The gate logs would show this. Lucas figured Greg considered him a suspect to begin with. If Lucas were the only person to show up on those gate logs, then that would not look good on him in the eyes of the police.

Greg had this thought at the same time as Lucas, because he asked, "When did you say you left the office there last night?"

"I think it was around seven," Lucas replied. "I was the last person to leave before Trent did."

"Mr. Caine, you realize what that would imply to someone such as me?"

Lucas gulped. "Yes, sir." There was silence on the other end for a few seconds. He hoped Greg did not think *he* killed Trent, which a person could get from his previous admission. "One thing I could do," Lucas suggested, "is pull the logs of everyone that punched out through the gate last night. It's possible some-one may have come in after I left."

"How can you tell individual people who come in and out of the gate?"

Lucas explained to him about the unique pass code system for entering and leaving the gate. Greg seemed to think having a security box on either side of the gate was a brilliant idea.

"Carter Washington is your security man, isn't he?" Greg asked. Lucas said Carter was. "Is he there with you?"

"He's standing beside me."

"Good, put him on."

Carter listened silently to the exchange from a chair beside Lucas. He handed Carter the phone. "Hello," he said gruffly into the phone. He nodded a few times as Greg spoke on the other end. "Yeah, that can be done. That's possible."

Lucas wished he could hear both sides of the conversation, because Carter kept casting glances at him while he listened. It unnerved Lucas.

"Okay," Carter said, "see you in a few minutes." He hung up the phone and rubbed his hands over his face. "This was the last thing I expected when I woke up this morning."

"What's going on?" Lucas asked.

"You know what your problem is?" Carter asked ignoring Lucas's question. "Sometimes you're too damn honest and helpful."

"What do you mean?"

"I mean, when something like this goes down, you've got to think about what you say before you say it. I'm not thinking you're a suspect, but you really pointed the finger at yourself by telling Greg you think you were the last person to see Mr. Mahoney alive on a compound that has a good security setup with ways of knowing when people come and go.

"Man," he continued, "I've been around you the whole time I've been here, and you seem like a really bright guy. From watching you, sometimes I think you could run this company better than anyone in the Mahoney family could. But it's just sometimes you come off like a suck-up. Like you and Mr. Mahoney are attached at the hip. I think one reason why I think you could run this company is you were always around when Mr. Mahoney made any type of decision. From what I saw, he always asked your opinion on anything before he made a final decision. I could tell from watching the tapes in this surveillance room."

Lucas raised his eyebrows. He realized he might have under-estimated Carter's intelligence and observational skills. He was more observant than Lucas thought. Perhaps it came from recon training in the military. He wondered what else Carter had learned from watching the surveillance feeds.

"Anyway," Carter said, "when you told Greg about the gate logs, he said he was going to turn around and come right back here. He wanted to get to the tapes before anyone altered them. He wants me to watch you until he gets here."

Lucas took this in stride. That told him Greg considered him a suspect, which was no surprise at this point. When he said he wanted to get at the logs before anyone had a chance to alter them, Lucas wondered, Greg may think Lucas could be a person who could alter the tapes since he was the only person in the building besides Carly and Carter. Maybe Greg thought Carly would do such a thing. When a married person is murdered, one of the first suspects is usually the spouse. Lucas did not know what the percentage of the time a spouse was actually the one that killed the other spouse, but he seemed to remember it was a high number.

He sat down in Carter's chair. Lucas wanted to put his head down on his desk and close his eyes until this day was over, but he had a feeling this could be the longest day of his life.

CHAPTER FOUR

Trent Simon Mahoney (he went by his middle name) was a happy young man. 'Was' being the operative word. Today would be the day Simon's life changed forever.

Simon was the oldest son of the now deceased Trent Mahoney. He attended a private school, and his family was as wealthy as they come. At eighteen, Simon would never have to wonder where the money would come from to pay his mortgage, insurance, or car payments during his lifetime. In fact, he owned his proudest current possession, a shiny, yellow Range Rover free and clear. At sixteen, he went on a trip around the world with his family during the summer between his sophomore and junior years of high school. He has seen the pyramids of Egypt, the Taj Mahal, and the Great Wall of China. He would likely be the member of the family to take over the Mahoney's Diner chain of restaurants when his father retired.

Simon and his younger brother, Brian, were on their way to school. Simon had the radio tuned to the local sports morning show and laughed at some of the over-the-top comments the show's sidekick made. Brian sat in the seat next to Simon, thumbing through his Facebook feed on his phone, ignoring the chatter from the radio.

This was how the two brothers spent many of their mornings on the way to school.

Simon's phone rang from where it sat in the cup holder between the two front seats. "Hello," Simon said, picking up the phone without looking at the caller ID. He knew who it was from the ringtone. The call came from the house. Probably his mother reminding him or his brother forgot something or other at home.

"Simon," his grandfather's voice came over the line.

Surprised, Simon hesitated for a second. It was very unusual for his grandfather to call him so early in the morning. His grandfather, Quinn, retired from the family business nearly five years ago at sixty-three. He came down with cancer, and with his wife's encouragement, stepped down from CEO of the company to let his son run the business so he could concentrate on getting well again. After seeing an oncologist and getting chemotherapy, the cancer went into remission. The chemo left Trent's body drained and weak, although you wouldn't know it by looking at him. Besides his cheeks being more sallow and his body thinner, he still resembled the same man from when he was in his fifties.

Things got better for Quinn. However, his wife, Laura Ann, went through some health problems of her own. She suffered a heart attack just as her husband finished up his chemotherapy treatments. She stayed in the hospital for two weeks before her doctor released her. She was not the same woman coming out of the hospital as she was going in. She became forgetful, neglecting her duties as a wife. She and her husband lived in an enormous mansion just inside the Concord city limits. The family found that with Trent and Laura Ann's health problems; they needed someone to stay with them to help. Instead of hiring a caretaker, they decided to sell their estate and move in with Simon and his family.

"Grandpa," Simon said, "what's up?"

"Where are you right now?"

"We're on our way to school," Simon replied. Something in the way Simon said this caused Brian to put down his game and listen in on Simon's end of the conversation.

"Simon, I'm afraid I've got some bad news."

"Okay, what is it?"

"I'd rather not say over the phone. We'd prefer it if you and Brian would turn around and come home."

"But what about school?"

"Don't worry about it, son. That's not important today. Just, just come home."

"Okay grandpa, we're on our way," Simon said, ending the call. Simon's parents and grandparents instilled the philosophy from day one that school was the most important thing next to church. While Simon did not believe the church would get him anywhere in life, he wholeheartedly believed in the school system. He took his classes seriously, and he expected to graduate near the top of his class in two months. Brian did not excel in school like his brother, but Simon believed it was more that Brian did not take it as seriously. Brian played dumb, but Simon knew otherwise.

"What was that about?" Brian asked.

Simon shook his head. "I don't know, but it sounded serious."

Simon made a U-turn at the next stoplight and returned to the estate, bracing himself for bad news.

Simon did not know what his grandfather had to tell him would be worse than the news he received two nights before. But he did not want to think about that right now.

***

Brian and Simon walked through the door, coming from the garage that led into the east wing of the house. Simon hung his car keys from a hook just inside the door and went in search of his family.

They walked down a long hallway, through a dining room, and into the kitchen. That is where they found their grandparents. Laura Ann clung to her husband, hanging on for dear life. She sobbed into Quinn's plush bathrobe. He had his arms around her, patting her back, murmuring, "There, there."

Quinn and Laura Ann looked up as their grandsons walked into the kitchen. Laura Ann unfolded herself from Quinn and ran across the kitchen to Brian and Simon. She grabbed the two of them and pulled the two teens together in a tight hug.

"You're home. Oh, thank God you're home!" she moaned.

"Grandma, what is it?" Simon asked through clenched teeth. He never knew his grandmother possessed such strength.

Quinn came around and put his hand on Brian's shoulder. "You two should sit down," he said, gesturing at two chairs in the breakfast nook next to the kitchen.

Brian and Simon did as they were told. Laura Ann sat heavily in a chair beside Brian and threw her arms around him. Uncontrollable tears streamed down her face, soaking into Brian's shirt.

"What is it?" Simon asked. "Where's mom?"

"Simon, Brian. I have some horrible, horrible news for you," Quinn said with a slow shake of his head.

Simon had the feeling at this point that someone had died. For a person to have died close enough to the family for his grandparents to react in such a way, Simon had the feeling it was about his dad. He kissed his mother on the cheek goodbye just before he and Brian left for school. She couldn't have died in the fifteen minutes since they left the house. It wasn't possible. There weren't really any relatives they knew well enough to warrant this response.

Quinn looked to his wife, who nodded, and back to the teens. "Your father is dead."

Simon's jaw hung open. Brian immediately threw his arms around his grandmother and joined her with the sobs.

"What? How?" Simon recovered. Simon knew his father did not return home last night. That happened occasionally. His father had a cot at the office for situations like that where he would work so late that he was too tired to drive himself home. It was no surprise when he did not come home last night. What was surprising was he did not call Simon's mother, Carly. On every occasion where this happened, Trent called Carly to alert her.

Quinn took a deep breath before responding. "Someone shot him."

"Someone shot him," Simon repeated in disbelief.

"How did someone shoot dad?" Brian choked out between sobs.

Quinn shook his head. "I don't know. All I know is Lucas came in this morning and found him dead."

"Do they know who did it?" Simon asked.

Another shake of the head. "No, it's still early. The police are looking into it."

"But if someone shot him inside the gate, then it would have to be someone who knew dad," Simon pointed out.

Quinn sighed. "That's what scares me."

Simon knew the pattern with his dad and his assistant, Lucas. They usually arrived at work at around the same time, and they usually departed from the office at the same time. While there, they seemed connected at the hip. Those patterns made Simon think Lucas may have been the last person to see his dad alive. He asked, "Could it have been Lucas?"

"I don't know Simon. Your guess is as good as mine. I don't want to say."

"Yeah," Simon agreed.

"I don't know why in the world Lucas would do such a thing. But I hate to say, it's possible considering the circumstances."

"So, what now?"

"The police are launching an investigation. The police commissioners and the mayors of both Concord and Charlotte have already contacted me to make assurances they will find who did this. Your mother is down there right now."

"I'm going down there too," Simon said.

"Yeah, me too," Brian seconded.

"No, you're not," their grandfather said firmly. "If you go down there now, you'll just get in the way. You don't need to see your father like that."

"But . . ."

Quinn wagged a finger. "We'll have none of that. You're going to stay here. You cannot call anyone to tell them what happened. We want to keep this as quiet as we can for now."

"What about Rachel?" Simon asked, speaking of his girlfriend. He knew she would have a special interest in this.

Quinn knew this too. "Sure, you can call her and have her come over. You're not to tell her what happened until she gets here, in case she tells someone before she arrives."

"Thank you," Simon said and rushed off, already dialing his girlfriend's number before he left the kitchen.

Brian peeled himself away from his grandmother. "I think I need to be alone for a while."

"I understand, dear," Laura Ann said, and kissed Brian on the forehead. He stood and rushed off like a firefighter going to a fire.

Quinn sat down in Brian's vacated chair and put his arms around his wife.

"God be with us all," she whispered into Trent's bathrobe. "Lord be with us."

CHAPTER FIVE

Lucas was not native to the Charlotte metropolitan area. He was originally from the small West Virginia community of Mt. Lookout. If you were to look at the outline of West Virginia, and put your finger in the middle of outline that is the general area of Mt. Lookout. Mt. Lookout had a population of around five hundred, made up mostly of some old farmers and their miscreant offspring. When Lucas lived there, the community was a pleasant place and the people were nice. As he got older, drugs started to come into the small community. When that happened, Mt. Lookout and the people in it went downhill.

When Lucas was in high school, he was in a nasty car accident during the winter of his sophomore year. That one event changed his life completely. He received a severe brain injury, and a broken leg. The broken leg gave him the limp he and Carter have in common. Lucas could not remember any details about the accident. The only reason he knew what happened was that people told him the details.

After the car wreck, the initial diagnosis of his head injury was that it was not severe. Just a concussion. The doctors said after a few months' recovery, he would be back to normal. After his rehabilitation, he began going back to school. He quickly learned he could not handle the routine class schedule of going to school five days a week and he was forgetting many things. That was odd because he *never* used to forget things, having a near photographic memory. When the problems arose with his memory, Lucas went to a neurologist in nearby Beckley and they ran a flurry of tests on him. They found the initial diagnosis after the accident was partially incorrect. The damage to his brain was more severe than originally thought. He sustained some permanent damage to his short-term memory and lost partial control of his motor skills. This meant that his hand-eye coordination would be less than what it was before. They said it would take ten years for his brain to heal fully. That was when they told him about his future working life there would not be much of one. The neurologist said the rigors of holding a full-time job, much less a stressful one, would be too much for his damaged brain to handle.

It's been almost ten years since then, and he could see an improvement in how well he could think and in his motor skills over those years. In the beginning, Lucas was determined to prove the doctors wrong. He was a year away from graduating from school after this diagnosis. He was a typical high school kid at the time who thought he was invincible. Nothing could keep him down. He fought hard and eventually graduated near the top of his high school class. From there, he went on to West Virginia University and graduated with degrees in marketing and economics. Then the Mahoney family hired him.

The car accident proved fatal in many ways. There was another person involved in the accident. His name was Jake Schofield, and he died in the car accident. People told Lucas he and Jake left school that day for unknown reasons, just after it had begun to snow heavily. A large truck going through downtown Summersville sideswiped them.

Lucas forgot meeting Jake. People told him he started going to Lucas's school a few months before the fatal car accident. Because the brain injury Lucas suffered wiped away his short-term memory, he remembered nothing about that school year. Lucas made up for it in home school before he could handle the stresses of going five days a week to high school.

The one good thing that came out of it all was a closer relationship that formed with his close friend, Ashley, over that time. She was there every day for him in the hospital. She would come in some days before school would start, and she would stay some evenings until the nurse woke her up with her head down on the side of his hospital bed, sleeping.

Lucas and Ashley were always good friends before the accident. She told Lucas back then that in the events preceding the accident; she fell in love with him. She said she had liked him for a long time, but she knew he had a crush on her best friend, and she did not want to get in the way. Not that there was ever anything to get in the way of to begin with. Ashley was really the first and only girlfriend Lucas ever had. He dated Ashley's best friend for a couple of months before he got into the car accident, but remembered nothing about the relationship. To him, the relationship with Ashley's best friend did not count. The relationship with Ashley lasted through high school and for much of their college years. They were close. He thought she was his future.

Then, during the summer between their junior and senior years at West Virginia University, Ashley received a fellowship to study abroad in Europe for the summer. That ended up proving to be their downfall, as she met a Frenchman named Francois or something along those lines. Lucas tried not to remember.

When Ashley returned from Europe, Lucas planned to surprise her and meet her at the airport gate. She did not tell Lucas about her new lover before then. He was the one who was surprised when she got off the plane, with her arms around a bearded stranger with scraggly hair. She saw Lucas standing there, flowers in hand, and looking crushed. She apologized profusely and said Frenchy moved her in a way that Lucas never could have. She moved out of their small apartment the same night.

They crossed paths on campus a few times, and she was always arm in arm with what's-his-name. It made Lucas ill. Literally. He got sick to his stomach just thinking about it. During his senior year, he did not go out and party at a school that was one of the top party schools in America. He concentrated on his studies harder than ever, and because of that, he landed the position he has now. Or had, Lucas did not know what would happen to him now following Trent's death.

Lucas did not have many friends in Concord. Most of his immediate family lived a short, two-hour drive down I-85 in Greenville, South Carolina. His dad held a prestigious, managerial job at the BMW plant in Greenville, earning nearly triple the money he earned while working in machine equipment plant near Beckley, West Virginia. His parents bought a much larger house and put all the new furniture in it.

This happened after his brother, Blake, graduated from high school. Blake hated living around dull, slow Summersville, and wanted to move since he was in middle school. When the opportunity arose for their dad down south, Blake went with them, too. Lucas finished his first year at WVU before his parents moved to Greenville. While his parents were looking at homes, Lucas went with them and found he did not care for the area. He did not know if it was because of the congested traffic or the rude people. He went back to Morgantown and finished school.

Lucas never regretted the decision.

Five minutes after Carter hung up the phone from his conversation with Greg, he returned to the office. When Greg reentered the building, he gave Lucas a wary look, and then asked him if he had any success in getting the list of people who left the gate last evening.

"It takes a few minutes to get that," Lucas responded. "Give me and Carter a bit and we'll have it for you."

"Ok," Greg said, "I'll follow you."

Carter had a stony expression on his face. Lucas could tell Carter was in deep thought. He just hoped Carter was not thinking about the probability Lucas's password would be the last entry on the list.

"This way," Carter told Greg in a deep voice.

They followed Carter to the elevator and then down to the basement. When the three disembarked from the elevator, Greg took in the Spartan decorations of the basement. "Nice fichus," he mused, pointing at an expensive-looking plastic tree beside the entrance to Carter's office.

They walked into Carter's office. Carter took a seat in front of the computer. Greg pulled up the only other chair in the room, leaving Lucas standing. He walked around to the other side of the desk to watch what Carter was doing on the computer screen. Carter pulled up the gate security program and leaned forward to watch.

"Everyone here has their own unique pass code," Carter said to Greg. "It's ten digits long, and comprises the last four digits of their Social Security number, and the current day's date. At midnight every night, the date changes. Because of the current date being a part of the pass code, everyone's code has to change. What the computer will show us here in a minute, after it collects its data, and matches up the social security numbers with our employees, is a chronologic listing of everyone that punched in and out of the gate."

"Smart," Greg noted.

After a few seconds, the list popped up on Carter's screen. He scrolled down to the end of the list. Lucas let out a silent breath when he saw his name was not last on the list. In fact, there were two entries after Lucas's entry.

He saw Greg look at him out of the corner of his eye to gauge his reaction. Satisfied Lucas did not have a guilty expression on his face, Greg looked back at the screen and at the last three listings on the page:

"17:03:21- PC: 3696052407, LUCAS CAIN-EXIT"

"17:23:45- PC: UNKNOWN-ENTER"

"18:27:97- PC: UNKNOWN-EXIT"

"What the hell is that?" Greg said, pointing to the two bottom entries.

Carter shook his head. "I don't know. I've never seen that before."

"Lucas, do you have any ideas?" Greg said.

Lucas shrugged. He was clueless, which seemed to be the consensus.

"There's over an hour between this person coming and going," Carter pointed out.

"Enough time to murder someone and cover up a trail," Greg suggested. He asked Lucas, "Did you see anything suspicious when you left here last night?"

"No, when I left the building, I noticed nothing out of the ordinary."

"Is there any way someone can put in a pass code and not have the digits show up on this report? Is there like some sort of administrative pass code used for emergencies and stuff such as that?" Greg asked, gesturing at the screen.

"No, to your first question," Carter replied. "Yes, to the second. There is a pass code we gave out to the Fire Department and the Police Department when we set up this system that would enable you all to get in the gate during an emergency."

"Is that what this is?" Greg pointed at the Unknown name. "An administrative listing?"

"No," Carter answered. "The number would show up, and instead of a person's name being listed as the user, the word 'ADMIN' would show up instead. That is when like an ambulance or fire truck would have to come through. That's how we could tell."

"Could it have been someone who worked here?" Greg asked.

Carter shook his head. "Yeah, that's possible. But with the way this was done, unlikely. I mean, it's feasible someone who worked here could have had the time to sit outside the gate an extra thirty seconds when coming and going to see if they could find out another way in the gate. I don't know why anyone would do that, though. If someone that worked here killed Trent, then it would have been easier to just input their password and come on in."

"True," Greg said, rubbing his chin.

"Besides, no one here knows we have access to this," Carter said, pointing at his computer screen.

Greg rubbed his chin harder and said to himself more than Carter and Lucas, "So, that means I'm going to have to question everyone that works here." He stopped. "Okay, next thing I want from you two is to get me the name and number of the security firm that installed your system. Then I will need a list of all your employees. We're going to have to do a lot of legwork and talk to everyone who has access to your gate."

"Simple," Carter said, and flipped through an old-fashioned Rolodex sitting on his desk. He stopped and pulled out an index card. "Here you go, 'Renegar's Custom Security.'"

Greg looked thoughtful for a moment, and then responded, "I've heard of them. They did some work over at the Bank of America Building in uptown Charlotte. Write down their number. I'll call them."

Carter wrote the information on a sticky note and handed it to Greg. Carter then punched a few more keys, and then the printer started spitting out several pages of names and phone numbers. When the printer stopped whirring, Carter retrieved the pages from it. He handed the printed pages to Greg. "There's the employee directory."

Greg perused through the sheets for a few seconds, then stood from his chair. "Okay, let me think about this for a while. You two stay somewhere where I can reach you if I have any more questions, and if you think of anything else that could be useful, call me immediately."

They nodded, and Greg left the room and affixed the sticky note to the employee directory. Lucas and Carter watched the elevator doors close on Greg.

"Give me that card," Lucas said to Carter as he was putting the card back into the Rolodex. He raised an eyebrow and handed Lucas the card. "Thanks."

"What are you going to do with that?" Carter asked.

"I might call them myself." Lucas put his hands behind his head and let out a deep breath. "What do you think?"

"I don't know, man. This is crazy."

"What are you going to do now?"

"I think I'm going to stay around here and see if I can uncover anything else. You?"

"I don't know. I have to get out of here. Go somewhere and think."

"Yeah, I hear ya. You know, seeing your name was not the last one on that list of people who entered and exited the parking lot did a lot for me. I thought for a few minutes I could be working with a cold-blooded killer. That was absolved in my mind when the mystery entry popped up on that list."

"Thanks for not thinking I was a killer," Lucas said wryly. "But man, I gotta tell you, when I left the parking lot last night, there was no one else here besides Trent. I swear. He said he had few more things to wrap up, and then he would leave shortly after me. It was the end of a normal day."

"You know that's not going to change much in the cops' eyes, don't ya," Carter said.

"What do you mean?"

"You're still the last confirmed person to see him alive in a high security area. You're most likely still a suspect in Greg's eyes. In fact, they may focus much of their attention upon you, trying to punch holes in your story. This is going to be a high-profile case of the highest degree. National, you know? There is going to be a lot of pressure put upon Greg and his boys to find out who did this quickly. That's why he told us to stay close in case he had more to ask about. What I think he meant was to stay close in case he sees the need to bring you in for further questioning."

Lucas's heart plummeted in his chest. He was not out of the woods yet, it seemed. Carter was an intelligent man, and Lucas would do well to listen to him.

Lucas had to clear his head. He told Carter he would be back soon. Carter said he would call if he found out anything. Lucas said he would do the same.

Lucas peeled out of the parking lot with thoughts of his dead employer. Trent Mahoney was a great man and people would surely miss him. Mostly, Lucas wondered how someone got some sort of secret password to get through the gate. The gate was supposed to be foolproof. Could someone just invent a password to get through? Was it that easy? Lucas knew little about the software involved, but that seemed farfetched even to him. The only thing Lucas could think of was this was some sort of backdoor. That backdoor was no accident. Someone designed it that way. Lucas decided he would go to this Renegar's Security place and try to find out.

CHAPTER SIX

When Lucas pulled out onto Copperfield, it was still early. Before ten. He was close to where he usually ate lunch. He wasn't hungry, but needed somewhere to go, grab a cup of coffee, and clear his head.

He was a suspect in a high-profile murder investigation, after all. If the police questioned him further, then he would need to have his story down pat. Lucas never thought in his life he would need to rehearse an alibi.

He went straight through one stoplight where Branchview crossed over Copperfield, then made a right at the next light down the hill, pulling into the Carolina Mall. He drove up a hill to the back of the mall where the food court was, across from a huge hospital complex.

The mall was older, run down. It had a simple, cream-colored cinderblock exterior. On the outside, the food court at least looked impressive. Its façade was entirely glass faced with triangles engraved into the upper two tiers of windows. A nice, inviting look, Lucas thought, but not the reason he came here.

The inside of the food court was a large, open area. He entered through a double set of doors. The few patrons seemed to be older, retired, gray-headed men and women either enjoying a morning coffee, a stroll around the mall, or just enjoying each other's company. There were tropical looking trees lined up inside of the glass-enclosed room. The closely set tables comprised yellow, deep purples. Green Formica tops mixed with each other.

Though the food court itself was large, the food selection was not. There were the normal places you would see in a food court: the pizza place, a Chinese food place, a more formal sit-down café, a chicken place, and a place that specialized in hot dogs.

Lucas's first destination was the small café. He ordered a large cappuccino and a bear claw. He exited the café and found a table near the hot dog place. This was his second and final destination. It was a Wednesday, and he knew she would be working. She worked every Wednesday.

The sign above the hot dog place read: 'Not Just Franks'. Franks had a smaller restaurant front in contrast to some of the other places in the food court. There was a glass partition on the front, left side of the counter showing different specials and advertisements. There was a well-tanned, intelligent looking guy and a tall, attractive girl working behind the counter. They both wore khaki hats embroidered with the 'Not Just Franks' logo and aprons.

The girl captivated Lucas. She had since the first time Lucas set foot in the food court. She was tall and had long, dark hair hidden beneath the hat. She possessed high cheekbones, had bright green eyes underneath long eyelashes. Most notable were her lips. In the age of collagen, this girl had a pair of lips, many women much older than she would pay a lot of money to possess. She looked healthy, and not anorexic, as many of the girls seemed to want to be nowadays. She looked as though she were in her early twenties. Younger than Lucas, but he did not mind.

During the time Lucas had been coming here, he had watched her interact with customers. She seemed to have a golden personality. He watched her banter and flirt with some of the older men that come to her for food. She had a magnificent smile, and when her natural laugh flowed across the dining area, it was music to Lucas's ear. She never seemed to force a smile or a giggle.

Lucas would have to guess because he had never spoken to her. He has been coming here for well over a year, but he has never eaten at Franks. It is not because he does not care for hot dogs, in fact he loved them. It is because he was too shy to talk to her. He knew her name is Kristen. He had gotten close enough to read the nametag on her apron. He checked for a ring, too. There wasn't one, which is why he was hopeful someday he would have the guts to speak to her.

It is just that after what happened with Ashley, he could not speak to another girl in the way he wanted to. He did not want to have to face the heartbreak that would surely happen. He knew someday to conserve his sanity he would eventually have to talk to a girl. Right now, he devoted himself to work. It was all he thought about in his off time. He strived to be the best at his job he could be, and he knew he had an excellent opportunity in working for the Mahoney family. Lucas did not want to screw up. He gave that excuse for not socializing much with the opposite sex. Or anyone, for that matter.

He wallowed in his self-pity for a few minutes before he focused his attention on the more important matter at hand. He looked around at the people milling around his corner of the mall. He wondered if everyone would be as pleasant and smiling if they were to find one leader of the community died violently last evening. Probably not, he figured.

He looked to his left, out the tall windows, and viewed the large, sprawling hospital across the street. The Mahoney family had been a large contributor to the building of the hospital. Trent was a big philanthropist and was a driving force behind how much money the family donated to a cause. Unlike many people who give their money to colleges and hospitals who hope to get their name emblazoned upon whatever building their money helps to erect, the Mahoney's expected nothing in return. There were many places in the area the Mahoney family was wholly or partly responsible for. They asked not to have their name associated with these places because they do not want the spotlight.

Lucas saw a guy wearing baggy jeans, light skin, a brightly colored polo shirt, a white Yankees hat cocked to one side, a big diamond in one ear, and a couple of gold chains dangling around his neck, come around the corner. He looked familiar, but Lucas could not quite place him.

The other guy seemed to recognize Lucas as his face brightened. He walked over to Lucas's table unabashedly. "You're Lucas, right?" he asked.

"Yeah," Lucas answered, still trying to place him. "Who are you?"

The guy's face sagged in disappointment, as though he thought everyone should know him. "Hey, my name is Sully Cavanaugh. I'm friends with Simon Mahoney."

Ah, that name. Now Lucas knew who this was. This kid was bad news. He helped to advertise the fact by the way he dressed.

"Oh right," Lucas said.

"This seat taken?" Sully asked, gesturing at the three empty seats at Lucas's table. Lucas felt as though he were being railroaded.

"No man, have a seat if you want to," Lucas said, but Sully had already sat down.

"I just thought we should meet. I've heard a lot about you."

"Really?" Lucas said. "Like what?"

The question seemed to surprise Sully. Put on the spot, he thought for a second. "Simon seems to like you. He says you're smart."

Lucas wondered if Simon saying Lucas was smart meant he had said a lot about him. Up close, he saw Sully could not seem to sit still. He was fidgety, constantly trying to find something to do with his hands, adjusting the sleeves on his shirt, the bill of his hat, or the diamond encrusted watch on his arm. The questionable exterior belied a set of dark eyes that hinted at great intelligence.

Lucas reflected on what he knew about Sully. It was Lucas's business to know about Trent's children and their close associates. He had seen Sully one or two other times from a distance, but he knew a lot about him through Trent and Carter. They had government-like dossiers on all the friends of the Mahoney kids. They liked to make sure their children were around the right people.

From what Lucas knew of Sully, Sully was the wrong type of association in what Simon's parents wanted. Sully's dad owned one of the largest construction companies in the area, and had had more wives in the past than Larry King. He was married to number five right now. Sully's real mom died of cancer when he was just four. He had no sort of stable childhood. Sully's dad made a name by receiving the contract to build what was the second tallest building in Charlotte and the Coliseum for the Charlotte Hornets. The construction company came into existence in the late eighties. At school, Sully only appeared in class two or three days a week. Lucas heard Sully's dad paid the principal to pass Sully through school. That was the only way he could have possibly passed coming to school as seldom as he did.

As it was a Wednesday morning, and Sully was not in school, Lucas would assume this is one of Sully's self-granted days off.

"You're getting ready to graduate from high school, right?" Lucas asked.

"Yes, sir," Sully said.

"What are you going to do after that?"

He shrugged his shoulders and wiggled the fingers on his right hand. "Don't know man. This and that."

"No plans?"

Sully gave Lucas a hard stare. "I've thought about a few things, but nothing definite. I figure I'll float around for a year before deciding what to do. I'll probably just work for my Pops though."

Knowing what he knew about Sully's 'Pops,' that did not like a bad idea on his part.

There was a moment of silence as Lucas sipped from his cappuccino. Lucas saw a thought flash across Sully's face a few seconds before he spoke again.

"Do you know what Simon is going to be doing later? I know you sometimes know what his family has planned."

If Sully knew anything about Simon and his relationship to Lucas, Sully should know Lucas and Simon rarely did anything together. Lucas simply did not associate with too many people, and that included the Mahoney family. Because he worked closely with Simon's father, he sometimes would know if the family was doing anything. However, what was odd about the question was why would Sully ask him? Lucas thought if Simon and Sully were as tight as Lucas thought they were, then Sully would know about Simon's actions well before Lucas. Because of Trent's death, Lucas had a good idea of what would go on in the Mahoney household today. No one else should know about this yet, so he could not tell this to Sully.

"I don't know man," Lucas answered.

Sully glanced at his watch and frowned. "Look dude, it was nice meeting you, but I got to run."

"Same here."

Sully rose and without another word hurried out the double doors as though he were a firefighter going to a fire. A few moments later Lucas saw Sully get into a tricked out Escalade, peel out of a handicapped space, and speed away from the building.

An odd meeting, Lucas thought, and an odd coincidence. It almost appeared Sully was not completely surprised to find Lucas sitting here. Why? He brushed it from his mind and got back to feeling sorry for himself and for Trent.

He sat there for a while with the mall getting busier, lost in thought, thinking of everything and nothing at the same time. He felt numb, as though there was nothing he could do. He kept seeing Trent's dead eyes pop into his head. That image would remain with Lucas for the rest of his life.

With everything that went on back at the office, Lucas felt as though Carter was correct, and Lucas would seem to be the most likely person the police would focus their investigation upon. If this were something the police and politicians in the area would want to have wrapped up quickly, logic would dictate to find a suspect quickly, make the evidence fit, and make an arrest even quicker. Lucas was sure no high-ranking official would want this murder to hover over the area for any extended period.

Lucas almost felt *he* was the one who needed to dig deeper. Maybe he should go talk with the Mahoney family, and, using his position, ask a few questions. He knew the family faced questioning as well, but with his more intimate knowledge of the family, Lucas could probably come up with better questions in his search than Greg Hanover.

While he was thinking, the girl from Franks came from behind the counter, took a tray with a drink and two hotdogs on it, brought the tray to the table next to Lucas's and sat down. Lucas's heart raced, the previous thoughts that he had vanished.

He knew it sounded stalker-ish, but he had never been this close to Kristen. Literally. He liked to sit at a safe distance from Franks when he was here. He stole glances at her now and then, but not so much he felt like a pervert leering at strange women. He had a schoolboy crush on her, but he has been so afraid that he had not let himself get close enough even to say 'hi' to her.

Out of the corner of his eye, he could see her unwrap a hot dog and take a hungry bite of it. She seemed to savor the flavor for a few seconds before taking another bite.

As he took another sip of his cappuccino, he heard her say, "You look morose today."

It took him a moment to register she was talking to him.

"What?" he looked at her, dazed.

She wiped something from the corner of her mouth. "I said you look glum. You usually look like you're in a better mood when you come in here."

The fact she knew Lucas was in here a lot did not surprise him. When Lucas worked retail for a few months after high school, he got a feel of the people who were regular customers. What surprised him, however, was she knew he was in a different mood than he usually was. Had she watched him too?

"Umm," he said.

"Don't be shocked," she said, "you're in here most every day throughout the week. I know who all the regulars are in this mall. Do you see that couple over there?" she asked, pointing at an old gray-haired couple sitting near the immense windows. The husband relaxed in a chair while reading a newspaper, and the wife sat in a wheelchair, content to watch all the passersby through the windows. "They're here every day."

"Really?"

"Yeah, been coming in here for years. They're a sweet couple."

"Worked here for a while?"

"Yeah, since I was sixteen."

"How old are you now?"

She flashed a set of perfect pearly whites, then said with a southern accent, "My, my, aren't you bold in asking a woman her age at a first meeting?"

Lucas's face flushed.

She giggled. It was as cute as the rest of her. "Just kidding. I'm nineteen. You?"

"Twenty-six."

Her brow furrowed. "So you're not Sully's age?"

Lucas took it she saw him talking with Sully. "No," he answered, "just met him for the first time."

"Really?" she sat back in her seat. She seemed to be relieved of something. "Huh."

"What?"

"It's just I have a restraining order against Sully." Lucas did not know how to respond to that. She continued, "I dated Sully the year before I graduated from high school. He, of course, went to a private school, and I went to a public one, J.M. Robinson High School. We met one evening at a football game. I was just there to get out of the house. Sully was there to develop contacts."

"What do you mean?"

She told Lucas some things he did not know about Sully Cavanaugh. Sully's real mom died of cancer when he was just four. He had no sort of stable childhood. Lucas knew that. In middle school, Sully started getting heavily into drugs. Then, he started selling at school. Those were the only days he showed up at school, when he knew he had a deal going down with some of his classmates or even teachers. Sully's dad had major money and influence on the school board. His dad built the private school Sully attended, and word around town was Sully's dad gave them a sweet deal to do it. So everyone figured the board thought they owed it to Sully's dad to give his son a free pass, to look the other way when rumors of what he was doing surfaced.

Towards the end of Kristen's senior year, Sully's junior year, he stepped up his minor operation. Kristen knew he had to be getting his drugs from somewhere, and she thought he had some connection with a major gang in Charlotte. Those guys were rumored to be rougher than anyone else in town. Drugs, gun running, prostitution, child porn, human trafficking, you name it, and Kristen believed at the end of her run in school, Sully was into all of it.

Before she knew all of this, they dated for a while. They met that night at the football game. He got her number. Sully asked her out a week later, and Kristen accepted. On their date, Sully showed Kristen something she had never experienced before: money. He picked her up in a brand new Mercedes, took her to an expensive restaurant, and played the part of the perfect gentleman. He swept her off her feet.

They began dating, and at some point, all of Sully's secrets came out. When Kristen approached Sully with what she heard, he did not deny any of it. Instead, he asked her if that made her more interested. He wanted to know if she liked that sort of thing. Kristen said she was repulsed and broke up with him on the spot.

Over the next few weeks, Sully would not go away. He shadowed her everywhere she went. He would sit outside of her house at night. He would wait for her in the parking lot when she got out of school. He called her constantly.

Kristen said at first, all of it was a nuisance. Later on, he threatened her. Since she would not answer his phone calls, he dropped an angry letter in her mailbox, asking her why she was treating him this way. He had done nothing wrong. *She* was the one who was crazy. At that point, Sully went from being a nuisance to a concern. When she did not reply in any form to his letter, Sully made a drastic move.

He knocked on their door one night. A night when he knew Kristen's aunt would not be at home, and forced his way inside of Kristen's home. He tackled her and tried to pull her clothes off. She grabbed a lamp off a table and hit him over the head with it, knocking him out. She ran out of the house, went to a neighbor's house, and called 911. By the time the police responded to the call, Sully was long gone.

The next day, Kristen and her aunt went down to the courthouse and requested a restraining order against Sully Cavanaugh. The judge granted the request.

"I had not seen him since that night," Kristen said, "until just now when he was in here talking to you. And I knew from seeing you around here you did not look like the type who would associate with a person like Sully."

"I'm sorry," was all Lucas could think to say.

"No, no, don't be sorry," she said, reaching across, and patting his hand. "I'm just being cautious. I need to know who I know that knows him. You know? For my own safety. Understand?"

Lucas nodded. It was refreshing to get his mind off the events from this morning, at least temporarily. He knew as soon as he left here he would need to go up to the Mahoney Estate and let the family know all of what was happening. He figured after Carly came to her senses, she would return home to be with her family. Lucas did not want to face that yet. Right now, he was doing something he had dreamed of doing for months now, and he did not want it to end yet.

She looked at Lucas to see if he comprehended her situation. Satisfied, she took another bite of her hot dog. He realized he had not eaten since early that morning, but he was not hungry. Seeing a dead body will take your appetite away.

"So, what do you do? Business executive? Young attorney?"

"No," he laughed. "Why do you ask?"

"Well, because you always come in here looking nice. You wear a shirt and tie every day, and sometimes it's an expensive-looking suit."

"Thanks," he said, accepting the compliment. She had noticed him, and she admitted she thought he looked 'nice.' He could settle for 'nice' coming from such a beautiful young woman. "I work for the Mahoney Corporation."

She looked impressed. "What do you do there?"

The question stung. No one knew what happened there last night, and he would not be the first to let anyone outside of the Mahoney family and the police know. With Trent dead, he did not know what his job would be. He answered her with the broadest answer he could think of. "I work there in an advisory position."

"Meaning what?"

"I look at their business plans, give advice on how their plans could be made better, what they should nix, and come up with some things of my own. I help to drive their social media campaigns. I also arrange Mr. Mahoney's days."

"Really? How did you land that?"

He told her about how the Mahoney family hired him right out of college. She was even more impressed. He judged by the look on her face that he was scoring points. She was nearly six years his junior, but he did not care. Points were points.

"Where are you from?" she asked.

"I'm from near a small town in West Virginia named Summersville. You?"

"I've lived in this area my entire life." She stopped and took another bite of her hot dog. "There are many people from West Virginia in this area. I see people with that West Virginia University logo on the bumpers of their cars."

Lucas saw she was nearly finished with her hot dog. He looked at his watch as though he cared what time it was. He could sit there all day if he could and speak with her. He thought this was actually going well. "Look," he said, "I've got to get back to the office. Could we continue this conversation another time?"

She bit her lower lip.

Damn, that was sexy, Lucas thought.

"You know what? Yeah, I'd like that. Here's my number." She took a pen out of her apron, and wrote her number down on a napkin. "Don't lose this," she said, handing it to him.

"Don't worry, I won't." He stuffed the napkin in his shirt pocket. He would transfer the number into his cell phone as soon as she was out of sight. He thought he might frame the small piece of paper.

They stood together. He picked up her empty tray from the table to throw it away, in what, he hoped, she thought a chivalrous gesture.

"Oh, you don't have to do that," she said.

"No, that's fine. I've got to throw away my cup, anyway."

They stood there awkwardly for a few seconds. At last, she thrust out her hand. Lucas took it, and stared levelly into a pair of lovely green eyes. It was rare for him to look a girl directly in the eyes considering his height.

"Nice to meet you," Lucas said.

"You as well," she smiled, and bit her lip again, "I get off around two. Call me later if you'd like to finish this conversation."

I would love to finish this conversation, Lucas wanted to say, but responded with a cooler, "Sure thing."

He gave her one last smile, turned, threw the trash away, and left the mall without looking back at her. He hoped he played it cool, and that she watched his exit. It was all he could do to not turn around and look at her again. Finally, he had spoken to her, and he didn't have to make the first move. Lucas mused about their meeting happening on such a horrible day. He would love nothing more than to call her later, but he knew this day was shaping up to be one of the craziest days of his life, and the chances he could call her were slim.

CHAPTER SEVEN

Lucas walked out of the mall and into the sweltering heat. He climbed in his car, broke out into an instant sweat, and cranked the air-conditioner to full blast.

His love life over the past several years has been nonexistent. After he moved to Concord, he did not have the time to think about going out and meeting people, especially women, and having a relationship. That is what he told the people when asked if he had a girlfriend. In reality, he threw all of his concentration into his job because he did not want to get hurt again. He had his heart ripped up one time, and three years later, he was not ready to go through that again. What happened in the food court with Kristen felt natural somehow. It felt right. He wanted to talk more with her, find out more about her. He felt as though he cleared a big hurdle, and did not stumble or make a big fool of himself.

All of that was for later. In the meantime, he had to focus on something else. He had more immediate concerns.

That mysterious entry into the gate system had him worried. It concerned him because of what it implied. Unless someone hacked into the gate, which would explain the way the entry showed up on the report. If that was not the case, Lucas thought the mysterious entry meant Trent did something he wanted no one else to know about. Lucas knew Trent did not have the tech-savvy expertise to come up with a hack to the gate by himself. He had to have help. The most obvious place the help could have come from was from the people who installed the gate.

He called Carter while still sitting in the parking lot waiting for the temperature in his car to go from 'furnace' to at least 'sauna.' Carter picked up after half a ring.

"Go."

"Have you found anything else out?"

"No," Carter responded, "but Carly finally composed herself enough to drive home. The chief of police was here for a few minutes, as was the mayor of Concord, and the cops came back and dust for prints shortly after Carly left."

"Where all did they dust?"

"They dusted Trent's car, the handles on the front door, and the number pad at the exit gate."

"So they can see if the killer's prints are still fresh," Lucas reasoned.

"Yeah, but they won't find anything," Carter said. "Whoever did this was smooth. They this planned it to a T. For the killer to have a slip-up, such as not wearing gloves or wiping their prints afterwards, sounds farfetched to me."

"I agree." Lucas thought about what they would find. He thought he touched the wheel well on the driver's side when he bent over to check on Trent when he first found him, and he was the only person to have touched the number pad on the exit gate since last night. His pulse quickened when he realized they were going to find his prints all over everything they checked.

He wondered if they would discount his prints because they knew he had touched those things.

He hoped so at least. If he were a strong suspect now, then finding his prints fresh everywhere would only strengthen that.

"Keep thinking about it," Lucas said, "and call me if you think of or find anything."

"I will boss," Carter said, and hung up the phone.

Lucas left the parking lot and pulled back out onto Copperfield, but instead of going straight through the large intersection, he turned right onto Branchview.

Textile mills were once big in Concord and in neighboring Kannapolis. With much of the textile industry shipped overseas, mills started shutting down. A portion of the local population left with the closing of the mills. Now with the new hospital, S&D Coffee, Charlotte Motor Speedway and its neighboring drag strip, the NASCAR teams that come with the speedway, a billion dollar scientific research complex to Kannapolis, and its vicinity to the largest city in the Carolinas, the population in the immediate area grew again. The population of the county more than doubled during the 1990's. Now, Concord is one of the fastest growing cities in the country.

Lucas directed his car down Branchview which traveled along the northern side of Concord across town from Route 29, the other major pipeline in and out of Concord other than Interstate 85. He drove down Branchview for a few miles, and then turned left onto Old Salisbury-Concord road. This road was a busy, curvy, two-lane road. He drove a few miles, out of the town limits, past a large shoulder on the left where people parked their cars so they could carpool, and turned right onto

Neisler Street. There was a sign just before the road pointing towards Concord Middle School. He took Neisler for about half a mile through a densely wooded area, before the trees broke off revealing acres of feeble, withered corn stalks.

He came to the boundary of a large, ten foot tall wrought-iron fence running along the left side of the road for a hundred yards. Ahead on the same side of the road was a large ornamental gate with a big 'M' designed into the wrought iron, separating the driveway from Neisler Street. He pulled to the gate and rolled down the window. There was an intercom built into the gray stonework with a red button sitting in a brushed steel housing on it he pressed. The number pad was similar to the one at the office. Lucas assumed the Mahoney family probably had Renegar's Security do both gates.

After a few seconds, Carly's clear, pleasant, southern accented female voice spoke clearly through the intercom. She seemed much more composed now than when Lucas saw her last. "Welcome to the Mahoney's. May I ask who this is?"

Lucas thought Carly Mahoney sounded chipper now despite her husband dying. He looked above the speaker box and saw the camera lens at the top of the intercom. He leaned out the window, and before he could say anything, Carly recognized him. "Oh, Lucas, you're here. I'll open the gate."

He rolled up the window and the wrought-iron gates spread apart. He drove up a driveway that seemed at least a quarter of a mile long. The morning sun glistened off an expansive, well-kept green lawn dotted with flowerbeds and two huge, yellow birch trees. A large wooden gazebo sat at the center of one of the flower gardens. The red-bricked house itself is one of the nicest homes Lucas had ever seen. A stream of water emanated from the finger of an angel sitting atop a large, marble water fountain in the middle of a circular driveway.

The house was a massive three-storied, twenty-thousand square foot Victorian redbrick mansion with a gabled roof and gray shingles. It had a remarkable fourteen bedrooms. The eyes are first drawn to the large tower jutting from the east side of the house, capped with a pointed roof. An enclosed porch wrapped around two sides of the house with elaborate, hand-carved wooden cornices on the underside of the porch roof. At the bottom of the tower set an immense bay window that wrapped around the curve of the tower. The ornate wooden double doors had gold engraved sidelights, and a transom with a beautiful gold sunburst design. Two fifty-foot yellow birch trees dominated either end of the vast, four-acre front yard slanted down toward Neisler Street with the driveway ending at the gate. Many flowerbeds dotted the front lawn along the driveway with several flowering Bradford Pear trees emanating a strong fishy odor.

Lucas parked before the steps leading to the ornate set of double doors. Usually, a member of the Mahoney family was gracious enough to come out of the front doors to greet any guest who made it through the gate. Today, however, he did not expect that to happen. He expected the entire family to be huddled inside, commiserating the death of Trent.

Quinn and Laura Ann lived in one wing of the house. The two youngest members, Simon and Brian, and their parents, Carly and Trent, lived in the other wing. The house was large enough so, if one wanted to, a person could avoid coming in contact with the other members of the household for days.

Infighting abounded in the Mahoney family, especially between Laura Ann and Carly. They had grudges against each other, dating back twenty years. They were both proud women who refused to back down from their views. They used to be the biggest cause of strife in the household.

That honor now fell upon Simon and Brian. Simon was set to graduate from high school in a few months, and Brian was a year behind. Simon was the family socialite. Lucas hated to admit, but for Simon's age, he was an attractive guy who did not shy away from publicity or anyone else. He let people know who he was, what he was about to become, and how much money he possessed. Many people thought Simon was by far the more intelligent of the two youngest members of the family, and those same people figured Simon would be the one to take over the family empire someday.

Now that day may be sooner rather than later following Trent's murder. Lucas felt that Simon would have to mature a great deal to get there.

Brian was the polar opposite of his brother. A year younger than Simon, Brian was not quite the social butterfly Simon was. Brian was introverted and did not speak to many people outside of the immediate family. Even then, besides his father, Brian did not communicate with the family well. Brian worshipped his father. Brian was the only member of the family, besides Quinn, of course, to make regular appearances at the main office.

While Simon had the potential sex appeal to be on magazine covers, Brian resembled more of the Hunchback of Notre Dame than anything else. He was short, pudgy, and at seventeen, already had a receding hairline. He wore thick, black-framed glasses that made his eyes seem small and beady. He bathed irregularly and was prone to flatulence. No one could figure out why Brian looked the way he did. His father was a handsome man and his mother was a beauty on a high level. His grandparents, even in their advanced age, were a handsome couple. He resembled no one else in the family. He had no health problems. He never got sick.

Lucas climbed from the car and walked up the steps to the front door. The double doors opened before he could raise his hand to knock.

At the door was Laura Ann, the matriarch of the family, the one whom Lucas feared the most out of anyone in the family. As did everyone else. Laura Ann had raven colored hair streaked with gray, pulled into a tight bun. She still looked beautiful, with a regal bearing about her compared to the pictures taken from the fifties and sixties scattered around the house.

What made her so intimidating was the religious condescension she treated everyone with. If a person made one innocent comment, Laura Ann could take that innocent comment, turn it around on the commenter, and make that person feel as though they were going to hell. Soon.

"Hello, Lucas," she said to him with a wan smile. "Come on in."

She stood aside and gestured for Lucas to enter the grand house. He came into a striking, two-story foyer with a monstrous crystal chandelier hanging from the ceiling. He followed Laura Ann through two wide, burgundy painted hallways lined with several, tasteful sculptures sitting atop roman styled pedestals. Two original oil portraits of Laura Ann and Quinn, painted when they were much younger, hung on opposite walls. Several other still-life paintings also decorated the walls. Expensive looking crown moldings lined the corners of the hallways.

They came to an extravagant set of French doors and entered an elegant lengthy dining room with large windows along one wall, a luxurious china cabinet on the other, and a long, black, walnut table sitting in the center of the room. A white laced tablecloth lay across the length of the table. Several empty serving dishes, trays, and bowls sat near the center of the table. At the center sat a tasteful flower arrangement. There were enough place settings to feed twelve people.

Lucas walked around the table into the stainless steel kitchen with a breakfast nook tucked into an area jutting from the back with an enormous bay window overlooking a pond in the backyard. All the appliances were stainless, the countertops granite, a gigantic Viking range, and a tiled backsplash finished a refined kitchen. Lucas imagined that Wolfgang Puck and Emeril Lagasse would be jealous of this kitchen. The smells emanating from the kitchen were blissful. The scents of baked bread, soup, and something sweet wafted throughout the room in a melange that made Lucas's stomach rumble.

Even when having lunch, the Mahoney family went all out.

Lucas noticed Carly changed into a blue fitness outfit with Guess silk-screened in the middle of the hooded shirt. She seemed more composed now. Her eyes did not appear puffy or bloodshot from crying, as Lucas would have expected from someone whose husband had just died. Remarkable.

She looked up as he came in. "Oh, Lucas, we were just getting ready to sit down and have some lunch. There's some extra if you want."

"No thanks," Lucas answered. He wanted to come and catch the family up on what he knew, and leave quickly. He did not want to disturb them unnecessarily on this most horrible of days.

"How about something to drink? A glass of wine or beer?"

As much as Lucas could have enjoyed some sort of alcohol, he declined. "How about some water?"

"Coming right up."

While Lucas and Carly conversed, Laura Ann made the final preparations for their lunch, stirring the pot of soup and pulling a loaf of bread out of the oven. Carly poured him a glass of filtered water from a pitcher she pulled out of the huge refrigerator and handed it to him.

"Thanks," he said, and then got down to business. "We haven't heard anything recently from the cops, but Carter said they came back and dust for prints."

A surprised look crossed Carly's face he could not fathom, but thought nothing more of it.

"Save all the details for a few moments. Quinn and the boys will be right down, and then you can catch everyone up on what's happening," Carly said, touching his hand.

Laura Ann walked to where an intercom sat on a wall by the refrigerator, pressed a button, and said in a soft voice, "Okay, everyone, lunch is ready. Come on in."

Lucas heard her message echo from other intercom speakers near the kitchen. It must be nice to have your own PA system in your home, he thought. Really, in a house this size, you would have to have an intercom built in to announce dinner was served, drinks were beside the pool in the backyard, or the house was on fire. Lucas imagined if one end of the house were to catch fire, then those on the other end would have awhile before they had to get out. He thought it would take that long for the entire house to burn.

A few moments later, Quinn walked into the kitchen. He was a towering older man, with short, gray, balding hair, and a pair of silver glasses perched on his nose, giving him a distinguished look. He had a mellifluous voice that made him sound like a narrator of documentaries on the National Geographic Channel. Quinn did some of the voiceover work on the nationally broad-casted commercials for Mahoney's Diner. Even though Quinn did not come to the office often since he handed the reins over to his son several years ago, he still wore a suit everywhere. Even at home. Today he looked resplendent in a black wool Armani suit, blue Ralph Lauren shirt, Hermes tie, and Gucci cuff links. However, Lucas wondered if the black suit was a symbol of grievance over the death of his only child.

"Hello Lucas," Quinn said in a gravelly voice, extending his hand.

"Good morning, sir. I'm sorry about your son," Lucas said.

Quinn looked miserable for a beat, but recovered quickly. "Yes, this is one of the saddest days of my life. No parent should outlive their child."

Lucas had no comment about that. He was glad when Brian walked into the kitchen. The two Mahoney boys looked similar in the face. However, that is where the similarities ended. Brian was a head shorter than his older brother Simon, but easily weighed fifty more pounds. His black-rimmed glasses were as thick as Plexiglas. His prematurely receding hairline did nothing to help his appearance. Today, he wore a black punk rock t-shirt and a black pair of jeans.

Why Brian looked the way he does was a mystery. The times Lucas had spoken with him, Lucas came away feeling Brian was a darkly depressed young man. Because the Mahoney's religious beliefs ran deep, they did not believe in professional therapy for Brian, but believed that a healthy dose of religion was all the therapy he needed. The proof, Lucas thought, was in the pudding. Brian also gave the impression he was not intelligent. Lucas did not know if Brian acted in this manner on purpose, or if he was actually dumb. Lucas knew Brian had made good grades in school. That could be the benefit of his teachers having jobs because of the Mahoney family.

"Hey Lucas," Brian said, walking by, not attempting to make eye contact or shake hands.

Quinn looked at Brian's back as he walked by, and raised his eyebrows in apology to Lucas, as though to say, 'What can you do?'

"Honey," Laura Ann walked up and caressed Quinn's arm, "Lucas is going to give us an update after we sit down to eat. Come on and get your food."

"Yes dear," he said, smiling at his wife and gave her a peck on the forehead. He walked over to the counter and grabbed a bowl. Lucas could tell that Quinn still loved his wife very much after fifty years of marriage. Lucas did not know if he could stand a woman like Laura Ann after that amount of time, but to each his own.

A few moments later, Simon walked in with a girl attached to his arm Lucas had never seen before.

"Sup, Lucas," Simon said, walking over and giving him a man's hug. Lucas noted an underlying note of cigarette smoke below the heavy dose of cologne on his clothes as they drew close. "How you doing?"

"There have been better days," Lucas said.

"I hear ya'," Simon said somberly before brightening slightly. "Lucas, this is my girlfriend, Rachel. Rachel, this is Lucas. He works with our family down at the office."

"Pleased to meet you," she said, extending her hand as though she wanted him to kiss it in a chivalrous fashion. "Simon has told me about you."

"Oh, that's nice," Lucas said. Rachel had long, dark red, curly hair streaming midway down her back, high cheekbones, large doe-like hazel eyes, and a young, pert body. She was a total knockout, but Lucas would expect nothing less from Simon Mahoney. Kristen was a girl Lucas had his eye on not only because she was beautiful, but Lucas also thought she was in his ballpark. He had to admit the girl standing before him would have been way out of his league had they been the same age.

Simon was nearly six feet tall, had an athletic build, blond frosted tips in his hair, and blue eyes bracketing a well-formed nose. He looked fit for doing ads for J. Crew or Abercrombie & Fitch.

They moved on to the kitchen to get their lunch. Carly, Laura Ann, and Quinn sat at the smaller dinner table in the breakfast nook, waiting for the other children to join them. When they got their plates ready, they sat down, bowed their heads, and Quinn said grace. Lucas stood behind the table and bowed his head respectfully in case Laura Ann looked up to see if he was following suit.

"Amen," they all said in unison. Lucas lagged a split second behind, drawing a glare from Laura Ann. Nothing escaped this woman.

"Carly told us what she knew," Quinn said. "What is the latest?"

Lucas told them about the police coming back and checking for prints, but now they were collecting evidence. It was still too early to know anything for sure.

Simon slurped some of his soup and said to him, "Tell us what you found this morning. We're still in the dark."

Lucas gave the family a detailed description of what he found, though he hated to do it while they were eating. As he stood over the family and watched their expressions from his narrative, he saw five still unbelieving faces. Carly matched their expressions as though she had seen Trent's dead body with her own eyes. Lucas saw tears forming at the corners of Laura Ann's eyes, and likewise, Carly's eyes misted again. Brian seemed utterly destroyed, while Simon took the news stoically. Lucas was still in shock, but this was a member of *their* family. He could not imagine how it affected them.

Quinn laid his spoon down and rubbed his chin in deep thought. "You were the last one there last night?" he asked Lucas.

"I thought I was," Lucas answered. "But when we checked the logs of entry and exits, there was a mysterious entry about twenty minutes after I left of someone coming in and leaving."

"Who was it?" Simon asked.

Lucas shrugged his shoulders. "That's just it. We don't know, and can't figure it out. The pass code the person used just showed up as Unknown. Carter and I can't figure out how that happened."

Lucas saw Trent shoot Laura Ann a questioning look. That struck him as odd. Could they know how someone could get in without leaving a trail? He would not ask now, but filed it away to ask Quinn about it later. After they finished eating. In another room. The other members of the Mahoney family looked baffled, and he detected no hint of anything suspicious.

"Could that have been the killer?" Brian asked.

Lucas shrugged again. "Possibly. Like I said, it's too early to tell." he turned to Carly. "Did you two have any plans last night?"

"No, not that I recall. He called me earlier in the day to tell me he may be late getting home, and not to worry about making him dinner, but as you well know, that's been common of late."

"Yeah," Lucas conceded. He had another thought. "How late has he been getting home in recent weeks?" Lucas asked this question knowing how late he had been staying at the office, and he had a good idea of when Trent should have left those nights as well.

She looked at her two sons. "It usually happened just one or two days out of the week. Tuesdays were when it happened most often. What do you think guys, nine, ten o'clock when he got in late?"

Brian and Simon looked at each other and nodded.

"Yeah, sounds about right," Simon said.

"Then, on other evenings, he made it home by six or so. Why do you ask?" Carly said.

"No reason," Lucas lied. "Just checking."

Lucas's answer placated Carly. Simon gave Lucas a questioning look.

The phone rang in Lucas's pocket. He excused himself, left the kitchen, and walked out into the hall.

He accepted the call and said, "Hello?"

It was Carter. "Hey, get back here."

"Why?"

"I can't say over the phone. Believe me, you just need to get back here." He sounded demanding, as only Carter can.

"Okay, fifteen minutes," Lucas said, closing the phone, and then walked back into the kitchen. "Hey, I've got to run."

"Something up?" Quinn asked.

"I don't know," Lucas said, "But that was Carter, and he sounded insistent I get back there in a hurry. I'll call as soon as I know something."

"You do that," Carly said. "And Lucas?"

"Yes?"

"Thank you for all you're doing. I know all of this wasn't part of your job."

"You're welcome," Lucas said.

Quinn rose from his chair and followed Lucas to the front door.

"Son," the eldest Mahoney said to Lucas, clapping him on the shoulder, "I just want you to know no matter what happens here, you'll still have a job with this company. You're too valuable a man to not find a position for considering what happened."

He seemed to have been reading Lucas's mind, and he breathed a sigh of relief. "Thank you, sir. I've been wondering about that."

"Lucas," Quinn smiled, "you have nothing to be afraid of."

"Thank you," Lucas repeated. "Can I ask you a question real fast before I go?"

"Sure, anything."

"When I mentioned about that weird entry into our gate, you gave your wife a look."

"What sort of look?" Quinn said, probably wondering what Lucas thought before he answered. Quinn knew he gave his wife a look.

"It almost looked as though it were a look of understanding. As though it was something you expected."

"Very astute," Quinn said. "We both, Laura Ann and I just thought something like this was going to happen."

"What do you mean?"

"Well, when Trent came to me and asked about installing that big, elaborate security setup, Laura Ann and I did not like the idea. We are all about keeping it simple, and we do not trust all the technology you have nowadays. But we agreed to it, thinking the whole time something bad could happen with something that complex."

"I see what you're saying," Lucas agreed. "Anything's possible."

"Yeah, we've seen Jurassic Park," Quinn said.

Lucas wanted to laugh, but Quinn seemed serious. In that movie, scientists invent dinosaurs and have an elaborate security system to keep the dinosaurs under control. All it took was Newman from Seinfeld to screw things up and all hell broke loose. Lucas liked the movie, but like many people who reads a book that goes along with the movie, liked Michael Crichton's novelization of the story better.

Lucas saw the correlation in Quinn's thinking, and it was possible something like that could have happened here.

"I see," Lucas said, and did.

CHAPTER EIGHT

On the way back to the office, Lucas thought about how the Mahoney's were holding up. They seemed remarkably composed for a family who lost the cog in the family. Carly seemed to have composed herself. Laura Ann was her same old, dispassionate self. The boys behaved about as he expected. Brian crushed and Simon accepting. Quinn put on the visage of being the pillar of the family, but Lucas could see in the older man's eyes that he would like nothing more to find the killer and destroy him or her.

When he pulled into the parking lot of the Mahoney's headquarters, Carter stood underneath the portico by the front doors.

"What's up?" Lucas said as he climbed from the car.

"Couple of things," Carter said, motioning him to look behind the group of tall bushes that ran alongside the building. There was about a two-foot gap in between the edge of the bushes and the wall.

"What?"

"Look at the ground about five feet down the wall."

Lucas squinted. "I don't see anything."

"Exactly," Carter said. "Climb back in there."

Lucas shot Carter a look, took off his navy sport coat, and handed it to Carter. The classic navy could go with about anything in a pinch. Lucas kept this spare jacket in his office. He did not want to ruin a second one this early in the morning.

He pressed his back against the wall and sucked in his stomach, trying to make himself flatter. He sidled down the wall, using his right hand to keep the foliage out of his face. The flowers in bloom around the bush smelled nice.

"Do you see it?" Carter asked after Lucas was about ten feet down the wall.

Lucas stopped and looked down around him. There, on the ground, the dirt lay freshly disturbed. At first, he thought an animal had gotten in through the fence, but when he looked closer, he saw footprints.

"Don't disturb it," Carter said.

Lucas did not intend to do so.

He took a step back and kneeled for a closer look. The footprints were central to that spot. There were no footprints going in either direction down the wall. Not from where Lucas entered the hedge and not coming from the other direction.

"What the hell?" Lucas said under his breath. He looked at the wall. Solid as a rock. Then looked to the bushes. There was a small gap in between the two bushes in front of the disturbed dirt. He investigated the small gap and saw some branches were broken. Someone had come into the bushes at this point and hid here. He hated to do it, but on a hunch, he bent down and sniffed around the wall beside the disturbed dirt. Smelling nothing, he discarded the theory someone hid here to urinate. Why someone would creep between the bushes here to do that when a bathroom was located just inside the lobby, not twenty feet away, Lucas did not know. It was just a hunch.

He snaked back to where Carter waited and walked down the ten feet to the small gap in the bushes. Lucas looked down at the ground where whoever it was would have emerged from the bushes and looked at the parking lot. Dark mulch covered the ground by this side of the bush. The peat ran to the sidewalk and along its path. He did not see any footprints in the mulch, but that did not mean much. The person who hid in the bushes could have easily stepped over the thin strip of earth between the bushes and the sidewalk.

Lucas looked to where Trent had parked his car yesterday. It was less than ten feet away from the gap in the bush.

"Oh, man," Lucas said. "How did the cops not see this?"

Carter shook his head. "Dunno. I barely caught it myself."

"Can the cops match up the footprints?"

"To what? Those footprints could have been anyone's. They looked like running shoe prints for all that's worth. How many people in this city do you think wear size seven or eight shoes? Twenty thousand?"

"I see your point. Well, we know where the killer hid."

"Maybe," Carter replied. They stood there for a few seconds, letting this new development percolate. "That's not all."

"What else?"

Carter motioned for Lucas to follow him inside. They journeyed down to Carter's office in the basement.

"After you left here," he said, "I went back and checked out the logs to see if there were any other entries like the one we saw from last night."

"And...?"

"And the answer is yes," Carter said, gesturing at the monitor.

Lucas's eyes went wide. "How many?"

"It's not only how many," Carter said, wagging a finger at him, "it's how often."

"What do you mean?"

"Someone was coming in and leaving about once or twice a week that way."

"How did we not see this before?"

"Because we've never had a reason to check it before," Carter said.

"How long has this been going on?"

"I haven't had time to go back a long way, but it's been going on for at least a couple of months."

Lucas let out a low whistle. "What times were these entries being logged?"

"It was about the same as we saw earlier. Your name would pop up as leaving the gate, then that mystery entry would pop in a couple of minutes later."

"Was Trent seeing someone on the side?"

"You tell me, boss. You were closer to him than me."

"He never gave any indication of it. Then again, how would I know?"

"True," Carter said.

"So, the question we have to ask is: are we looking for a woman?"

Carter's expression was all the answer Lucas needed.

CHAPTER NINE

Carter called Greg before Lucas arrived and informed Greg of his discoveries. The forensics people from earlier returned. They crawled through the bushes and used plaster-of-Paris to make molds of the footprints. They left as quickly as they arrived. They had work to do.

Earlier, Lucas gave Greg the ADMIN pass code to come and go through the gate as he pleased. He returned about five minutes after the footprint forensics people left.

Carter and Lucas met Greg at the front door. "C'mon guys, let's go inside. We need to talk."

They ensconced themselves in Lucas's office. Carter gave Lucas and Greg some coffee from a pot he had brewed earlier.

Greg took a sip from his mug and flinched as the hot coffee hit his tongue. "Okay, here's what I think happened. Feel free to jump in if you have any suggestions. Frankly, at this point, there's just not much evidence. We have some preliminary findings, but there's just not much there. My theory is going to have a bunch of holes, so feel free to add your two cents."

Lucas and Carter shared a look and nodded for Greg to continue.

"It's simple. Lucas, about twenty minutes after you left last night, an unknown person passed through the gate to, I assume, meet with Mr. Mahoney. This may have been someone Trent was having a meeting with and someone he did not want anyone to know about. Could have been a shady business associate, or for a tryst with some woman." He shrugged. "I don't know. There was no sign of a struggle on Trent's part. That leads me to believe Mr. Mahoney knew this person well enough to let this person get as close as they were when the shot was fired. We think from the size of the entry wound and the lack of an exit would the shot was fired from within ten feet. The bullet came from a small-caliber handgun, possibly a 9mm. Whoever shot him left no shell casing behind, so we will have to wait for the ballistics to come back before we can tell the type of gun. With me so far?"

They nodded.

Greg continued, "After that, the killer, knowing he or she did not leave any fingerprints or other evidence behind, calmly got into their car and exited the same way they arrived. I say the person calmly exited because there was no sign of tire marks leaving the gate. The person had committed a clean, righteous murder, and they knew it was going to be hard to find out who did it. What do you two think?"

"What about the gap between the times this person came in and left? An hour passed during that time. You make it sound like it was a quick stop-and-pop," Carter said.

Lucas saw the gears turning in Greg's brain. "Don't know. Maybe they argued for a while before the assailant pulled the gun and did the deed."

"Makes sense," Lucas said. "Who do you think could have done this?"

"Like I said," Greg said, "I think it had to have been someone Mr. Mahoney knew well. It had to have been someone with inside knowledge of how your security system works, to block out the security tapes, much less get in and out of the gate the way they did."

A thought struck Lucas. "What about that security tape?"

"What about it?"

"The tape was stopped before this person came in."

Greg looked like someone dropped a bowling ball in his lap. "Dammit, I didn't think about that."

"Me neither," Carter said.

"I'm telling you, as far as I know, Trent was the only person in this building when I left," Lucas said.

"But that means he didn't want anyone knowing whom he was meeting, and he didn't wait long to turn the tapes off after you left," Carter said. "I already checked the gate logs and discovered the mysterious entries occurred fairly often. I need to go pull the security tapes from the other days when this mysterious person came."

"Go ahead and do that," Greg suggested. "We'll wait here."

"Might take a while," Carter warned.

"How long?"

"Ten, fifteen minutes."

"We'll wait."

Carter looked at Greg and shook his head. He stood up and left the room.

"What now?" Lucas asked.

"Do you want the good news or the bad news first?"

"There's good news and bad news?" Lucas said. Greg nodded, and Lucas chose to hear the positive side first.

"The good news is," Greg said, "this effectively lets you off the hook in my eyes. We've shown there's no way you could have been here when those tapes stopped, because the time they were stopped was shortly after you left, and the mystery person came in."

Lucas breathed a sigh of relief. Greg caught it. He probably knew Lucas thought he was a suspect.

"And the bad?" Lucas said.

"The bad news is it really could have been almost anyone if Trent was really being secretive about whom he was meeting after hours."

"Trent's wife told me there were nights where he came home well after office hours, and well after when I left. I did not tell her I knew this when she said that."

"That's probably good for now," Greg agreed. "We don't want to get her going crazy thinking her husband was cheating on her."

"Yeah."

Carter returned a few minutes later, shaking his head.

"What?" Lucas said, knowing the answer.

"It's going to take a lot of time to go through all the tapes, but I selected a few of the most recent occurrences, and all of the other times this person popped through the gate, the tapes were stopped before their entry. I'll go back and review some more tapes, to see if they somehow slipped up and kept the tapes rolling."

Lucas shook his head. Greg did the same. Lucas knew what he was thinking. Greg was thinking the ghost of Trent Mahoney was making it difficult to find his killer. By Trent going down whatever path he went down to get to this point, he had effectively erased much of the evidence they needed to find out who did this.

"Okay, guys," Greg said, putting down the coffee mug on the desk and rising heavily to his feet. "I need to get down to the station and wait for some forensics to come back, so maybe we can get a better picture of the type of person who did this."

"What do you mean?"

Greg shrugged. "When the blood spray pattern comes back, we can determine within a few inches the height of the perp, and exactly where the shooter was standing in relation to Trent's body. I hope we will be able to discern something from the shoe casts we took from behind those bushes, and you never know when the fingerprints will turn up something interesting. I am going to go interview the family, and then I'm going to make some calls to see what else I can dig up. In the meantime, you and Carter keep yourselves available. I may need to call you and pick your brains."

"Yes, sir," Lucas said.

Greg wagged a finger. "What did I tell you about that 'sir' stuff?"

"Yes, Greg."

"Alright, I'm going now."

They shook hands, and Greg left the building.

"What now?" Carter asked as they stood alone in Lucas's office.

Lucas looked at his watch. It was just after two. It seemed as though it should be getting dark soon. "I don't know. I'm going to sit here for a few minutes and see if anything comes to me. You?"

"I think I'm going to go back downstairs and go over some tapes. See if anything turns up."

"Good idea."

"Alright," Carter said, and left the office.

The small space was quiet. The steady drone of the air conditioning unit was the only noise. Outside, Lucas could hear the occasional shout from one of the crime scene techs. He thought about where they were in the investigation. All of this left them at the same place they started. There still were no suspects, no murder weapon, and no clue as to how someone got through the gate. And the biggest piece of the puzzle. Why would someone want to murder Trent Mahoney? The question was not only why someone would want to murder Trent, but why shoot him in the face from up close? That was a cold-blooded way to kill someone, and that was what baffled Lucas. If he could figure out the motive, he could figure out who did this. He hoped.

Where to start looking? Trent did not have many personal dealings with people outside of his family and the office. He made himself available when he went out in public, but never maintained anything more than superficial relationships with people. That was why Trent hired people like Lucas to do his face-to-face work. No, Trent was more of a visionary than anything else, a man who liked to keep his personal life private. It was possible there was something in his life that was too private. It was possible his secret was controversial enough that someone killed him over it.

Who would know if that was the case? If someone killed Trent over something, then there was at least one person who knew. What if this was a business deal gone bad, he had no knowledge about? What if he had an affair? Then there would be the woman he was having an affair with, plus any other person she may have told.

What were Lucas's options? He could closely examine Trent's schedule over the past couple of months to see if any abnormalities popped up, and then see if that led anywhere. He could also question his family. Trent's wife, Carly, already mentioned he had been getting home later in recent months. Had she noticed anything else? Did Trent's father, the founder of the company, know of any business dealings Lucas did not know about? He could see if Trent and his father discussed anything like that. What about the two sons? What was their relationship like with their father? Good, great, or strained? He knew Trent's point of view on that question. However, what would Brian and Simon say? Again, where to start?

After some more deliberation, he examined more closely Trent's schedule over the past several months to see if he missed anything. After ten minutes of pouring over Trent's schedule on Outlook, he saw nothing, and turned off the computer in disgust.

He needed to get out of the office. Clear his head.

He walked out of the building and into the sweltering heat. The crime-scene tape still hung between the light poles. There were two forensic technicians studying the blood spatter on the pavement near where Trent used to be. Lucas excused himself and walked around the techs to his car. He sat in the car with the air conditioner turned up to full blast. He felt helpless and unsure of what to do next. He had few friends outside of the Mahoney family here in Concord and no one to talk to. He did not want to go home. To him that would like saying "I quit."

Looking at the clock on the car's console, he saw it was near the time Kristen said she would be getting off work. The mall was less than five minutes from where he sat. She seemed interested earlier, and he thought maybe, with nothing else to do now he would try to meet her as she was getting off, and offer to take her to a late lunch, an early dinner or a cup of coffee at the Starbuck's next to the mall.

He wanted to get his mind off Trent's murder and try to get Trent's dead eyes out of his head. He just wanted to escape it all for a bit and then travel to Harrisburg to talk to someone at Renegar's Custom Security. Maybe someone there would have answers how someone made it through the gate in the manner they did. Lucas knew Greg said that he would contact them, but like some of the other things in this investigation, Lucas thought he had a unique insight that may field some different answers from what the police found.

He pulled through the gate and out onto Copperfield. The light just before the mall entrance turned red. He rolled to a stop. As he sat at the light behind a few cars, he noticed his hands shaking on the steering wheel and felt the butterflies in his stomach. Had it really been that long since he desired to, and had the chance to flirt with a woman he was interested in?

Lucas resisted the urge to turn left when the light turned green, and drive in the opposite direction of the mall, content to give up before he even tried. Much to his surprise, he went straight, turned right at the next light, and went up the hill to the mall.

He parked his car in a space near the front of the near empty parking lot. He took a deep breath and climbed from his car. He made his way to the sidewalk that ran the length of the parking lot from front to back. A kid hopped out of the passenger's side of an old, black car parked near Lucas's, and cut onto the sidewalk in front of Lucas. The kid was probably in his mid-teens, had on a t-shirt that looked about ten sizes too large for him, and his pants were sagging down to his knees, revealing a dirty-looking pair of gray boxers. Lucas hated seeing kids dressed that way. The person driving the car backed out, pulled away, and disappeared around the side of the mall.

Coming from the entrance of the mall, he saw Kristen throwing her pocketbook over her shoulder, walking through the doors. His heart started to race at the thought of doing what he was planning. At about that time, the kid in front of him looked around, and then turned and gave Lucas an intimidating stare. He almost laughed because he was nearly double this kid's size.

Then the kid did the most inexplicable thing. He broke into a dead run away from Lucas. Towards Kristen.

He then saw the reason why the kid ran away. When he reached her, he stopped and yelled something. She shrunk back in fear. Then his hand darted out, reaching for her pocketbook. He grabbed the black strap and tried to rip the pocketbook off her shoulder. Both of her hands clung to the pocketbook as they struggled for control.

Seeing what was happening, Lucas started running as fast as he could, bad limp and all, to try to help her. When he got to within ten feet of the scuffle, the kid still had not managed to wrestle the pocketbook from her, nor had he heard Lucas's approach.

Kristen looked over the kid's shoulder at Lucas, and her green eyes grew wide. When Lucas was close enough, he leaped. Kristen stepped aside and let go of the pocketbook.

When the kid gained possession of the pocketbook, he thought he had won. In the next moment, the bigger Lucas tackled the kid to the sidewalk. Lucas felt and heard the kid's shoulder snap when they landed on the concrete.

The kid screamed in pain. Lucas turned him over, straddling him. The kid looked at Lucas and tried to give him the same intimidating stare as before, except the punk was in no position to do so.

"Oh, cut the crap," Lucas said to the kid just before he punched him square in the face. Blood spurted out of the youth's nose, and he lay still. Out cold.

Tires squealed on the pavement near Lucas and the kid. The same car the kid got out of moments ago. The car pulled to a stop beside Lucas, the kid, and Kristen. Lucas got a good look at the driver. The thug had a black Mohawk, with piercings and small tattoos scattered over his face. The driver gave him a confused, almost frightened expression. Lucas glared at the kid.

The thug gave up on his partner, put the car in gear, and sped away.

CHAPTER TEN

There was a small police precinct built into the other side of the mall, across from the parking deck, so the police were quick to respond. Four officers in two police cruisers came to investigate. One officer waved smelling salts underneath the thug's bloody nose, and he awoke with a start from the slumber that Lucas knocked into him. The thug snorted out more blood before they put him into a police cruiser and drove to downtown Concord, to the main jail. They asked Kristen and Lucas to climb into the other cruiser and drove around the mall up to the entrance of the small precinct.

A station nurse checked Kristen's condition to make sure she was unhurt. She told the police Lucas was the one who came to her aid. They let her go but held Lucas until they got his side of the story. He explained his role in the incident. That corroborated with the story Kristen told them, and for the second time this day, the police told Lucas to stay available for any further questioning.

After a few minutes of waiting in a small room, they said he could leave.

Lucas walked out the tinted door and down the concrete steps of the small precinct and into the glaring early-afternoon sunlight. He shaded his eyes with his hand and looked to see if Kristen was waiting for him. Seeing she was not, he entered the mall from a side entrance nearby. He figured she would go to the food court, and that was where he found her. Just like earlier, there was the scattering of older people and women with baby strollers sitting around, conversing. There were some teenagers starting to filter into the crowd now that some of the local schools were letting out. Sitting at a table near the large windows, Lucas saw Kristen at one table with her head down.

He walked to where she sat, but she did not notice his arrival. She was weeping into her arms with her head down on the surface of the teal table. He sat down in the seat beside her, and still she did not stir.

He reached out tentatively and placed a hand on her shoulder. "Kristen?" She sniffled, and a soft 'yes' came from her bowed head. "I was just checking to see if you were okay."

She looked up, and Lucas withdrew his hand. She sniffled and wiped her nose. Makeup ran down her face and her eyes were a bloodshot red. Without a word, she rose out of her chair and enveloped him in a hug that, while not firm, had an intimacy he had not experienced in a long time.

His heart raced. With all that happened this morning, he could not help but think about how lonely he was for the past couple of years since Ashley broke it off with him, and how sad it was that in this time and place, that he was happy to be getting a hug.

"Oh, thank you so much," she whispered in his ear. He could feel her warm tears on his face. "I was afraid he was going to kill me."

She broke the hug. He could see her arms had scratches from the struggle.

"Are you okay?" he asked again.

"Yes, thanks to you." She smiled. "I don't know what would have happened had you not been there."

He did not know what to say to that. He did not want to think about what could have happened. "It was the only thing I could do. I couldn't stand by and watch someone get robbed or anything, knowing I could do something to stop it."

"I still can't believe a person that I've known for all of five minutes would come to my rescue that way," she said.

There was an awkward silence as they stood there looking at each other. He was again amazed at how beautiful she was. For the first time, the thought flickered through his head about how dangerous it was for him to attempt to break up the attempted mugging.

"Do you want to talk about it?" he asked.

She shook her head and ignored his suggestion. She sat down and motioned Lucas to a chair beside her. "Tell me about Summersville. Where is it?"

She wanted to distance herself from Concord for the moment, mentally, to escape to somewhere else.

Lucas sat down. "If you were to look at a map of West Virginia and put your finger right smack dab in the middle of the state, that's where Summersville is."

"Really? Sounds like it's out in the middle of nowhere."

"No, not really. It's a common belief that there is nothing in West Virginia except for deer, cows, and hillbillies." She laughed. "Summersville is a nice little town, where there's not much crime and everyone is friendly to each other. The schools are small. There were less than seven hundred people in my high school."

"It sounds nice," she said, with a faraway look in her eyes. He could tell she wanted to escape. "There were a couple thousand kids in the school I went to. It was stifling."

Lucas did not know what to do at this point. He did not know much about her, or if she had a boyfriend, she could call to tell what happened. He could tell she was unengaged. Her ring finger was bare. But he'd known that factoid for weeks.

As much as he wanted to speak with her for a long, long time, Lucas realized his goal in getting out of the office and his mind off of Trent's murder had been met. The altercation with the kid, and the subsequent visit to the police precinct, got his mind off matters entirely. Now torn, Lucas needed to decide between getting back to work, or to continue to keep his mind off Trent's death.

Kristen had a solution to Lucas's dilemma. "Do you want to get out of here and get a bite to eat or something? Anything."

Lucas smiled. "Yeah, we can do that. I can drive if you want."

Kristen returned the smile. "That'd be nice."

She grabbed her pocketbook off the back of the chair, and they left the mall. The police had the area where the attempted mugging occurred cordoned off. The sidewalks were busier now, with people getting out of school or off work. There were several people wearing hospital scrubs from the large hospital across the parking lot. Kristen could not take her eyes off the place on the sidewalk where the attempted mugging occurred.

There was dried blood all over where Lucas broke the guy's nose.

Lucas reached over and grabbed her wrist, trying to get her to look away from that spot. "Try not to think about it. It's over. The kid is in jail and you're going to be fine."

She threaded her fingers through his. Her hand was warm and sent a shiver down his spine. It felt awkward to him to hold a girl's hand for the first time in so long. Somehow, it felt right.

"Where do you want to go?" he asked when they reached his car.

She ignored the question. She was looking around his Scion. "I've never been in one of these. This is cool."

"Thanks." Lucas wondered why Kristen had made no move to contact a friend or family member. He imagined if what happened to Kristen had happened to him, he would call a friend or someone from his family to come help. He did not know enough about her at this point to know if she had any friends or family. He thought back to the article he read in the paper this morning and wondered if what almost happened to Kristen had anything to do with the crime wave in the article.

The last time Lucas could recall being this nervous was his first day working for the Mahoney family. Crazy things happened over the past couple of hours, with all the events from this morning. None of which he was able to assess yet. Somehow, he now had a very beautiful, young woman sitting in the seat next to him who smelled wonderful. He noticed that now they were in close quarters together for the first time. Her hair smelled the way Ashley's hair used to. The smell of Ashley's hair used to drive him crazy.

Crazy in a good way.

The whole situation had his heart racing. All of what happened this morning occurred so quickly, it almost felt normal for him to have Kristen sitting in the passenger seat of his car. He felt that what had happened had formed a sort of invisible bond between them. He asked, "Okay, so what do you want to do?"

Kristen put her seatbelt on while looking out of the front of the windshield at the clear blue sky. "It's nice out. Want to go for a walk? I know just the spot."

"Sure," he smiled. "Where do you want to go?"

"Frank Liske Park," she replied. "Do you know where that is?"

He thought about it, he heard of it, but after a slight hesitation, he said, "Not really."

"That's okay," she said. "I can show you the way."

She pointed for him to get out on 29 and head south towards Charlotte. They drove down 29 for a few miles, crested a ridge, and came to a stoplight, where Kristen directed him to get into the turn lane to go left.

The enormous structure of Charlotte Motor Speedway loomed in the near distance. The huge stadium is the home of NASCAR races and car shows. Holding over one hundred-sixty thousand people when full, the Concord becomes the third largest city in the state next to the capital city of Raleigh, and nearby Charlotte.

The light turned green, and they turned down Pitts School Road. The Speedway faded behind the trees and hills to their right. Kristen directed him to go down a couple of different roads to Stough, leading to Frank Liske Park. They made a left off Stough Rd., through the entrance of the park. Shortly, they came to a railroad crossing. The sign said the tracks were for a private railroad. The crossing had none of the crossing arms that come down when a train approaches, just a stop sign saying to look both ways before crossing.

After crossing the tracks and through a copse of trees on either side of the road, the view of the park opened up. There were broad, empty fields expanding off in all directions. Two large, wooden signs pointed the ways to the many attractions of the park including a soccer field, paddleboats, putt-putt golf and baseball fields among many other attractions. Kristen directed him to veer left when the road forked in the direction of a walking path. They drove by a beach volleyball court and a covered picnic area. Around the parking lot were young trees that swayed gently in the warm, soft breeze.

Before he shut off the car, he looked at Kristen. She was staring out the windshield of the car without blinking. She still looked shaken, not that he could blame her. He would probably be doing the same thing himself if he were in her shoes. He pictured himself in a fetal position.

He realized if he ever had a chance at having a relationship with Kristen, this was an excellent opportunity to show her what sort of person he was.

They sat there for a few moments, and she still had not attempted to exit the car. He reached over and laid his hand on her arm.

"Hey, are you okay?"

She broke out of her trance and gave him a halfhearted smile. "I'll be fine," she said. "Thanks for asking."

"C'mon, let's go take your mind off things."

She nodded. They got out of the car and started down a gravel path that went between a brown wooden restroom and a small, outdoor amphitheater. There were some long-haired teenagers riding skateboards and doing tricks on the amphitheater stage.

As they walked down the path, they avoided any mention of what had happened earlier. Kristen did not talk about herself much, but instead asked Lucas many questions. He painted a depressing story. He did not mean for it to come out that way. As he talked, he painted that picture. He told her about the car accident. He explained about how he thought his life ended at the age of seventeen. It was a lengthy telling, and he assumed she was still so shaken she may have just wanted to listen to someone else talk.

She seemed to have sympathy for him, at least he thought so, because she would rub his arm when something was particularly depressing. As they walked, they no longer held hands. The euphoric rush from the botched robbery attempt started to wear off and the displays of affection from her seemed to be over. It left Lucas disappointed.

A dense, verdant canopy hung over their heads, obscuring the bright sun in the cloudless sky. Birds chattered and sang. The insects droned. The gravel on the path ended and was replaced by densely packed dirt that was dry and cracked from the lack of rain. Soon after the trail changed, they crossed over a small wooden bridge going over a shallow creek. There was a horse-riding trail on the other side of the creek, where a small child rode a small, noisy gasoline dirt bike. Lucas thought it was one of the oddest things he had ever seen and was wholly unexpected in what had, thus far, been a quiet, peaceful walk.

They crossed another larger bridge that passed near a small cascading waterfall. They stopped at the center of the bridge and regarded the flowing water in silence. The ebb of the conversation slowed to the speed of the slowly babbling brook in front of them. Lucas ran out of things to say due in large part to Kristen not asking any more questions. She seemed to have her mind on other things now and seemed to be content, enjoying the walk on the trail.

After a few minutes spent taking in the gurgling sounds coming from the waterfall, they continued the stroll. They soon came upon a large open area where there was a large pond that had five flowing fountains spraying multiple soft streams of water. The path circled along the shore of the pond. It was a beautiful area. Near where the trail came out into the open, there was an old, wooden park bench. Lucas followed Kristen's lead by joining her on the bench.

There was a soft breeze blowing just enough so they could feel the cool spray of water coming from the fountains. On a blazing hot day like today, it felt positively wonderful. The sky was a light blue, with a few wispy cirrus clouds scattered across it high in the atmosphere. Geese basked and honked in the sun on a small, isolated island at the far end of the pond. A train whistle blew somewhere in the distance.

A group of middle-aged women sat by the water in the grass. Some people had lawn chairs and had a lazy fishing line cast in the water. A group of three small children played tag along the trail that skirted the edge of the pond. A large group of people gathered around another picnic area off in the distance. Many happy, content people gathered around two decidedly unhappy and discontent people.

Lucas decided since he had done all the talking, he would try to get Kristen to talk. "So, tell me about yourself."

She stirred. "Like what?"

"Well, like how old are you? Are you from here, etc.? You know, like the questions that you have been asking of me."

"Oh, I'm sorry," she giggled sadly and patted his hand, sending another shiver up his spine, "I didn't realize you had been doing all the talking. How selfish of me."

"No, it's alright. You've been through a lot today. I could understand if you're still shocked."

She bit her lower lip before speaking in the same sexy gesture from earlier. "Well, I'm originally from Charlotte. I was only a couple of years old when I moved in with my aunt here in Concord."

"Your aunt?"

"Yeah, my mom died when I was two."

"How did that happen, if you don't mind my asking?"

"No, no, it's okay. She died of AIDS. This was back in the early to mid-eighties when AIDS first became widespread. She was actually one of the first to die from it in Charlotte." She did not sound proud of it. It was just a statement.

"What about your dad?"

She shrugged her shoulders. "I have no idea who my father is. My mom was an exotic dancer at a club in Charlotte, and she turned tricks on the side to make more money. So, when she got pregnant, and this is all what my aunt told me, when she got pregnant. She had no idea who the father was since she slept with a different guy almost every night. This was back during a time when using a condom was almost unheard of."

"Did she have AIDS while she was pregnant with you?"

"I don't know. I can only assume so. HIV at least. I'm not sure when AIDS went full blown. Anyway, it didn't transmit through the womb. I got lucky… I guess."

Lucas took it from that depressing sounding statement and the droop of her shoulders that Kristen might not be the happiest girl in the world. He cautiously draped his arm over her shoulders. She seemed to welcome the comfort as she leaned into him. She felt soft, but soft in a good way.

He thought he would try a different tack and get her talking about something that would not make her depressed. "How old are you?"

"Twenty," she answered. "I'm trying to make my way through nursing school, but it's been a struggle."

"Oh, that's nice," he said. He knew nursing was a rapidly growing field in the area, and it seemed as though every girl he came across around here was trying to get into the nursing field. "You said you lived with your aunt. What does she do for a living?"

"Not much. She's never been able to keep a job. When she does have a job, she blows all of her money on liquor and cigarettes. She's never been married. She's repulsive to tell the truth," she said. "I can't see how any man would ever want to go on a date with her, much less marry her."

It looked as though he picked another bad subject to talk about. She painted a dreary picture of her background.

"But she seems to be okay with that," she continued. "As long as I'm making enough money to support her, she's not inclined to do anything with her miserable life."

She started to sob. Lucas did not know if it was because of her life with her aunt, the attempted robbery from earlier, or a mixture of both. He tried to soothe her as best he could. Lucas was uncomfortable around women who cried. It was something Ashley never did. He needed to try to forget any comparisons with Ashley. She was in the past.

He tightened his arm around her. She cried into his shoulder for a few minutes before she lifted her head and wiped her nose with the back of her hand. The cloth of his dress shirt felt damp because of it. He left his jacket in the car.

"Every day it's a struggle for us," she said. "But we do it one day at a time. We get by. I don't know what the future holds. I don't know if I'll ever be able to leave my aunt, but I know that with the way she is now, if I leave, she'll be homeless within three months."

"Does she have a job right now?"

"Yeah, she's a server at Troutman's Barbeque right now. She just got this job a couple of weeks ago. I know she is at work right now. Wednesday is one of her big days at Troutman's, and I didn't really want to go home to an empty, smelly, smoky house and be by myself this afternoon. Thank you for hanging out with me."

"You're welcome," he said, and they lapsed into a thoughtful silence.

He looked at her to see that she was looking out over the pond with a faraway look in her green eyes. She has had at least one bad relationship with a guy, and not a great life up to this point. He wondered where her mind was. Was she dwelling upon what happened earlier? Was she thinking of her aunt? Was she thinking about some distant land from which she could escape? Something else entirely, or all of the above?

Lucas's cell phone rang. He looked at Kristen in apology, she nodded that it was okay, and he snapped open the phone. It was Carter. "What's up?"

"Where are you, man?" he asked. Lucas told Carter he was at the park with Kristen. He believed he mentioned Kristen a time or two to Carter. Carter knew why Lucas got his lunch at the mall almost every day. "Aww, you dog. Listen, I called the security firm that installed the gate, asked a few questions, and found out who the tech was that actually installed the software for the codes."

"Oh really? What did he say?"

"I didn't get to talk to him, but I was told he was out on a service call, and that he'd be back around three."

Lucas looked at his watch. It was approaching that time. "Look, I'm near there," he said. "I could go over there and see if I can talk to him."

"I hoped you'd say that. To them, I'm just some dude who claims to work for Mr. Mahoney, but I'm sure they know exactly who you are. You could probably learn more than I could."

"Okay, I'll run over there in a minute," Lucas said. He thanked Carter for the information and hung up the phone.

Kristen had separated herself from him while he spoke on the phone and had heard his end of the conversation. "Work?"

"Yeah, would you mind riding along while I go talk to a guy in Harrisburg?"

Her face brightened. "After all you've done for me today, it's the least that I could do."

"Thanks. Look, if you're going to go along with me on this, there's something you need to know."

"What is it?"

"Do you remember earlier when you asked me why I looked so down?"

"Yeah."

"And I didn't really give you a straight answer?"

"Umm, yeah."

"The reason being is, well, Trent Mahoney was murdered last night."

Her jaw dropped. "You've got to be kidding."

He shook his head.

She covered her mouth with her hand. "Oh, my God. I can't believe it. How?"

He explained to her about finding Trent's body that morning. His dead eyes stared at Lucas. He shook his head to clear that vision out of his head.

"Oh, my God," she repeated. "That must have been horrible." He had no response for that. She gave him a quick hug. "I'm sorry. I did not know. Do they know who did it?"

"No, they don't even have a suspect at this point beyond me."

"Why you?"

"Because I was the last person known to have seen him alive, but because of some other things, I've been cleared. It's because of those 'other things' that I need to go talk to this guy in

Harrisburg." He explained to her about the mysterious entries at the gate. "This guy in Harrisburg may be able to explain that."

She sprang from the bench. He looked up at her. "C'mon," she said, "let's go to Harrisburg."

"Yes ma'am," he smiled.

They left the bench and completed a leisurely circuit of the pond. She held his hand while they walked. The grip was loose, almost casual. Like two old friends who had not seen each other in a long time and were again reacquainted. She seemed content for him to lead the way in silence.

Perhaps he had let her exorcise a few of her demons. It sounded to him as though Kristen was lonely and rarely had the opportunity to tell or vent her frustrations concerning her life. She seemed like one of those intelligent people who somehow slipped through the cracks and had not been afforded the chance to make something out of their lives.

Lucas was a good friend with a guy like that in high school. He was, and still is, one of the brightest persons Lucas ever met. The guy made A's on nearly every test and was able to answer any question a teacher ever put to him without hesitation. Lucas heard he took an IQ test and scored close to genius. However, he did not study or do homework, and his grades suffered because of it. He did not take school seriously. He came from a background where his family could not afford to send him off to college, and he never thought about his future after high school. He graduated near the middle of their senior class and did not receive any type of scholarship offer that those that graduated in the top twenty of the small class received. After high school, he went to work for the local big-box retail store in Summersville.

He excelled there. Had certain things went the right way for this guy, Lucas was confident he could have done anything he put his mind to.

Kristen seemed like that sort; an intelligent person who had some bad breaks in her life.

CHAPTER ELEVEN

They made it to the parking lot, got in the car, and drove out of the park, turning left onto Stough. They followed it for about a mile until hitting the four-lane highway of Route 49. They turned right. Railroad tracks ran alongside the highway on their left. They drove through rural terrain and a few scattered billboards for the three miles into the town limits of Harrisburg.

The first building that came into view after they passed the last group of trees was a mostly gray, one-story building that had two bright blue entrances shaped like the face of a cartoonish house. It had windows with bright orange borders. Lucas knew this was the first of the two daycare centers owned by two former Carolina Panthers players. Past that was a string of drive-thru restaurants. Behind the string of restaurants was a large three-story apartment complex and the large, grand Harrisburg Town Hall marked by four impressive white stone columns.

He turned on the next road on the right, Roberta. He took the second right into a two-story, brick shopping area. The address he took from the Rolodex brought him to a parking lot around the back of the small area. He parked in a small lot that had a Bank of the Carolinas, Rocky River Coffee Co., and a pub called Three Monkeys enclosed in a two-story brick building with blue shutters. He parked next to an expensive Mercedes-Benz with a vanity plate that read *RENEGRRS*. The security place was directly above Three Monkeys. A small sign in the corner of one of the second story windows advertised Renegar's Custom Security.

They climbed from the car and walked over to a set of stairs situated in the corner of the building. They climbed the stairs, down a short walkway, and to the main entrance for Renegar's. They entered a small reception area with an attractive, blond secretary sitting behind a computer desk on the far side of the room. The walls were oak paneled, and there were a few lithographs of paintings by Mort Kunstler depicting the Civil War scattered on the walls. On the left wall looked to be some sort of dump bin for discarded electronic devices with circuit boards and wires hanging from the bin.

The bored looking secretary looked up from whatever she was looking at on the internet and greeted us with a smile. "Welcome to Renegar's," she said, with a strong southern accent. "How can I help you?"

"I need to see Mr. Renegar please," Lucas said. "It's a matter of urgent business."

She studied him with a judgmental eye before responding, "I'm sorry, Mr. Renegar is on vacation in Aruba at the moment. He should be back next week sometime."

Lucas wished Carter had told him the name of the person he spoke to at this office. Calling her bluff, he asked, "Does Mr. Renegar drive a Mercedes?"

She sat back in her chair. "Yes, he does."

"Then what is it doing in the parking lot if he's in Aruba?"

She fumbled for words for a moment. Apparently, she had no practiced response to that question. He thought this secretary's job was to divert traffic from Mr. Renegar and to answer the phones. He hated to do the name-dropping bit, but he decided he would not see Mr. Renegar unless he told this girl who he was.

Before she could answer, Lucas said, "Look, my name is Lucas Caine, and I work directly for Trent Mahoney. Your company installed our security system, and they have sent here me with a few questions from the family."

Everyone in the area knew who Trent Mahoney was.

She sat up in her chair. The girl realized she needed to take Lucas seriously. He thought it amazing what name-dropping in this town accomplished when people realized who he was and who he worked for.

She smiled nervously and waived towards a couple of chairs. "Have a seat," she said, "I'll let Mr. Renegar know you're here."

"Thank you," he said, "but we would prefer to stand. Tell Mr. Renegar we are in a bit of a hurry and won't take much of his time."

"Y-yes sir," she stuttered. "Just a sec." She picked up the phone from the desk, whispered a few quick words into the phone, and put it back in its cradle. "He'll be right out."

Almost immediately, the door behind her opened and a large, bulky man appeared. He had on a blue polo shirt with Renegar's logo on it and was in the process of tucking it into his khaki pants as he opened the door. The man stuck out a hand, and almost out of breath said, "Hi, I'm Edgar Renegar."

Lucas grabbed his hand. "My name is Lucas Caine, and this is my associate, Kristen…"

"Rose," Kristen said, and shook his hand. It was the first time Lucas heard her last name. "It's a pleasure to meet you."

Edgar gave her a quick once over, and in predictable fashion said, "No, pleasure's all mine."

It took an effort for Edgar to peel his eyes off Kristen and look back to Lucas. "What can I do for you Mr. Caine? And how is Mr. Mahoney?"

Lucas hesitated a moment before answering. "Mr. Mahoney was murdered last night."

Shock registered on Edgar's face. "Oh my God. I hadn't heard."

"No one has heard yet. We've managed to keep it quiet for now. Can we go to your office? I have something I need to discuss with you."

"Yes, sure, anything," Edgar said. "Do you need anything to drink?"

Lucas declined the offer, but Kristen said she could use some water. Edgar told his secretary to grab a bottle of water from the fridge and bring it to Kristen.

They followed Edgar through the door from which he had come and followed him down a short hallway into a cluttered office with more Kunstler lithographs. Almost before they sat down, the secretary brought Kristen a bottle of water. Lucas wondered what it was about some Southerners, who more than a century and a half later, could not let the Civil War go.

"Thanks," Kristen murmured, unscrewing the lid on the bottle.

The secretary left the room and closed the door behind her.

Edgar put his elbows up on the desk and formed a steeple with his fingers. "Now, Mr. Caine, what can I do for you?" he asked, exuding confidence.

Lucas was sure what he had to say would melt away some of that confidence. Lucas explained the events of Trent's murder. When he told Edgar about the mysterious gate entrances and exits, Edgar looked horrified. Lucas could see the word 'lawsuit' dancing behind his eyes. There went the confidence.

"Well, well, Mr. Caine," Edgar blubbered when Lucas finished, "I don't know how such a thing could happen."

"What do you mean you don't know how such a thing could happen? We're talking about your gate and security system. There was a backdoor no one knew about except for Mr. Mahoney. I find it hard to believe that he could have done that by himself. Don't you know how your products work? Another associate of mine informed me you had another guy that was out on a call earlier and he should be back in. Whoever my associate spoke to, said this tech was the one who helped install the system."

Lucas's barrage of accusatory questions set Edgar back in his plush office chair. "Now, Mr. Caine," he placated, holding up his hands, "hold on here. Let me think about what you're saying." He scratched his chin and appeared to study a crack in his ceiling. "It sounds like a software issue to me. I design the hardware, and make sure that what we do is as indestructible as possible. Hold on," he raised a finger. He looked at his closed office door, and shouted, "Cody!"

"Yeah?" They heard a muffled reply come through the door.

"Get in here!"

"Yes, sir!"

"Cody is my software expert," Edgar explained to us, "He is probably the one your associate heard about earlier. He's the one who wrote the software for the Mahoney's security system. If anyone could explain what happened, it's him. He's a regular genius with this stuff. That's why I hired him."

It seemed to Lucas that Edgar Renegar was exactly what he appeared. A pompous windbag who could not take responsibility for his products, looking to place blame on someone else for a fatal screw-up. He did not seem like the type who could provide answers to much of anything.

A moment later, a young, tall, painfully thin, blond-headed kid came through the door.

"You wanted to see me Mr. Renegar?" the kid asked with a trembling voice.

"Yes, Cody, come in and shut the door," Edgar ordered.

Cody closed the door softly. He looked like he was trying not to break it.

Lucas rose from his chair and extended his hand. "Hi, my name is Lucas Caine. I work for Trent Mahoney, and this is my associate Kristen Rose."

Cody gulped and then looked at Lucas's hand as though it were going to bite him. He shook it with a feeble grip and then shook Kristen's proffered hand. "N-nice to meet you," he said with a half-smile.

"Mr. Caine here," Edgar gestured at Lucas, speaking to Cody, "has a few questions about the security software you installed up at their office."

"O-okay, like what?"

Lucas could tell quickly that Cody was a shy young man. He was cautious, almost afraid, in the way he approached his boss and then Lucas. He had short hair on the sides, but his bangs were long enough that they covered his eyes making it so he had to look through the blond locks of hair to see anything.

Lucas gave Cody the gist of what happened. He looked frightened, but Lucas could not tell if that was his natural reaction to anything or what. Lucas could have told him they were going around giving away free puppies and Cody may have tensed up. Who knew?

"Do you know how someone could get in the gate the way this person did?" Lucas asked.

Cody looked at his boss, almost seeking permission to answer. Edgar stared back with a vacant look. Lucas thought that everyone in the room knew Edgar had no answers, even having just met him.

Cody took his eyes off his boss and stared down at his fingers. "It was a back door," he said as quiet as a mouse.

"What was that?" Lucas asked Cody to repeat himself.

Cody cleared his throat. "It was a backdoor," he said with more confidence.

Edgar had a priceless look on his face when Cody said this. From Edgar's reaction, Lucas assumed he knew nothing about what Cody said.

"Did you put that in the system?" Edgar asked.

"Y-yes sir."

"Was that your idea?"

"N-no sir."

That there was a backdoor designed into the system did not surprise Lucas at this point. It was that or somehow a hacker had figured out a way to do that to the security system. Lucas could not see someone wanting to do that at the Mahoney Corporation offices.

"Whose idea was it?" Lucas asked.

Cody gulped again and looked from Lucas to Kristen to his boss nervously. Cody obviously was uncomfortable in talking about this. He knew something. Though he said nothing to Mr. Renegar, Lucas had a good idea Trent was the one behind the backdoor. It would be difficult to explain it any other way. Unless Cody planned to sneak through the gate, and murder Trent months in advance. Lucas could not see this kid doing anything like that.

After a moment, Cody made up his mind. "It was Mr., um, Mr. Mahoney's idea."

"Explain," Lucas said.

Cody cleared his throat. "Mr. Mahoney came to me during the installation and asked if I could do him a favor. He asked me if I could design a way for him to let people in and out of the gate with no record of who the entrant was. I could not figure out a way to get someone in with no trace. But figuring out a way to disguise entry into the parking lot was easy. I just made a set password and blanked out the digits put in the number pad. The entrant's name would show up as 'UNKNOWN.' Your codes change from day to day, but this one remains the same. If you were to get a listing of every password, the gate system recognizes, I made it to where this code will not show up on any list."

"What was it? The code?"

"Simple, just seven ones followed by nine."

Lucas stared at Cody blankly. Edgar seemed on the verge of having a blood vessel burst in his forehead. Kristen stared in awe.

"That's it? Seven ones and a nine?" Lucas asked, amazed. Cody nodded. "Damn, it's a wonder we never got broken into."

"Well, think about it," Cody said. "Say you're a hacker trying to get into the gate. You know that if you are trying to break into Mahoney Incorporated, you are going to have to get in and out of there fast. A guy, or girl, would have had to have done a lot of planning to do something like that."

"I follow."

"Okay," Cody continued. He seemed to gain more poise now that he was in his realm of knowledge. "If you're a gatecrasher, you know there's a security system there, and the easiest way into the facility would be just to put in a number. So, you go home, get on Google or whatever, and research the hell out of the Mahoney family. You look at the family members' birthdays, anniversaries, or other important dates. It would be something everyone in the company would know. At least, this is what a would-be thief might think.

"The hardest possible thing for a gatecrasher to do would be to break a pass code that changes every day and differs from employee to employee. Like it does in this case. Someone could sell their code or have it coerced from them. We considered that possibility. Can't do anything about that. Mr. Mahoney wanted it that way, and it was a safe way to keep people out.

"What it all boiled down to," Cody finished, "was we figured any person would have at the most five minutes to figure out the pass code. Think of the odds of some random person coming in and punching in seven ones and one nine."

They nodded simultaneously. Lucas saw the simple logic in what Cody did.

"Did Mr. Mahoney pay you to do this?" Lucas asked.

Cody looked hesitantly at his boss before answering. He knew this could get him in trouble. "Um, yes."

"How much?" Edgar demanded vehemently.

Lucas held up a hand to Edgar. "You two can talk about this later. For now, I have a few more questions, and then we'll leave." Edgar gave Cody an angry look. Lucas pressed on. "Cody, did Mr. Mahoney tell you *why* he wanted this done?"

"No, not really," Cody answered. "But he seemed nervous the entire time. He said he didn't want anyone else to know about it."

"Did you tell anyone else?"

"Just you," Cody hesitated a moment. "He also asked me to show him how to shut down the camera system."

Lucas forgot about that detail. His focus was upon how someone got in the gate. He forgot Trent had to know how to shut down the facility's camera system. A small piece of the puzzle fell into place.

"Something else," Lucas said. "I noticed the way the gate set up at the office and at the Mahoney Estate are similar. Did your company do the home setup as well?"

"Yeah," Edgar responded. "We set up all the security for both Quinn and Trent's estates three or four years ago. We used the same hardware during both setups, if that's what you're asking about."

Lucas nodded. "At Trent's home gate, they have the added feature of the camera. Why didn't they do that at the office?"

Edgar shifted in his chair. "I think their whole intent at the office was to keep it simple. If we set up a camera feed at the gate, then there would have to be somebody standing by checking everyone that passed through that gate. They don't have nearly as much traffic at home as they do the office, so it wasn't that big of an inconvenience to have that set up at both estates."

That made sense, Lucas thought. "Was there the same sort of backdoor built in to the home gate as there was the office gate?"

Edgar shook his head. "Not that I know of. We were a fledgling company at the time we did the home setup, and the person we had at the time that set up the security stuff wasn't as good as what Cody here is." Cody smiled at the compliment. "That's why I let the old guy go and hired Cody. The guy didn't have a clue what he was doing."

Lucas considered asking if Edgar could get him in touch with his old software guy. It seemed unlikely Trent would set up something like what he did at the office at his home; too much risk involved. Lucas asked Edgar for the old tech's contact information in case it seemed pertinent down the line.

"Thanks Cody and Mr. Renegar for your time," Lucas said as he stood up and motioned for Kristen to do the same. "We'll be in contact if we have any more questions, and you could probably figure the police will be here to ask questions."

When Lucas mentioned the police could come here, Edgar waxed pale, and broke out in flop sweat. Hmm.

They made their goodbyes and left Renegar's.

CHAPTER TWELVE

Back in the car, Lucas called Carter.

"Did you find out anything?" Carter asked as soon as he answered his phone.

"Yeah," Lucas said, "I talked to the programmer who installed the software for the gate. He told me Trent came to him in private and asked him to put a backdoor into the gate that would disguise whoever the entrant was."

"Did the kid say why Trent wanted that?"

"Nope, but he said Trent was nervous the whole time, and wanted to keep it all hush-hush."

"That doesn't make sense. Why would Trent want to do such a thing?"

"I don't know. I'm thinking I didn't know Trent nearly as well as I thought I did. Maybe he was seeing some girl in his office after hours, or he was doing some business dealings he didn't want anyone else to know about. That's the only thing I could see."

"Yeah, but that's not what Trent was about," Carter pointed out. "He was the most honest person I ever knew."

"Yeah, I agree. But he was doing something he didn't want anyone else to see, and he went to great lengths to make that happen. Maybe he was leading a double life."

"Is there any way to figure out what he was doing?"

"I don't know. I'm going to go talk with the family after we get a bite to eat."

"Alright," he said, "Keep in touch."

Kristen directed Lucas to a nearby Mexican restaurant named 'Casa Grande,' in a sprawling Super Wal-Mart shopping center. They walked through the front entrance and into a small waiting area with a cash register taking up most of it. The restaurant bustled with business. Festive Spanish music played in the overhead speakers. A wood-paneled bar stood off to one side where light from a neon beer sign lit most of the area. The smell of cigarette smoke came from that area. A server promptly seated Lucas and Kristen in the main dining room, away from the bar. Tasteful murals adorned the walls, depicting the old Spanish way of life from a bygone era. Whatever that was.

A server set some chips and salsa on the table, took their drink orders, and scurried away. They perused their menus in silence. It was not until the efficient server took their orders and scurried away to one of the dark corners of the restaurant that they spoke again to each other.

Although Lucas and Kristen spent an eventful afternoon together, sharing an experience neither was likely to forget, then getting to know each other while sharing a mid-afternoon walk, he still barely knew her. As they went from the comfortable, somewhat private setting of the park to a more public, one-on-one setting of a booth in a dimly lit restaurant, a sense of unease fell over Lucas.

He found himself in a situation he did not expect to be in when he woke up this morning. He would not have had the courage or wherewithal to ever speak to Kristen in such a way that would lead them to this point were it not for the tragic events of this morning. Now that reality had set in, he realized he was the same bumbling idiot he was when he went to bed last night. He was in his mid-twenties, and only had one other real girlfriend in his life, and she ended up running off with another man. That certainly did not help his confidence any with the opposite sex.

Every table in the dining area was full, and most people were attentive to the people they were with. There were a few families, a few couples, and some people dining alone.

There was an elderly couple sitting in one corner of the dining room. The woman had a good view of everyone in the restaurant. She was short, had thick curly hair, and was grossly overweight. Her husband struck quite a contrast with her. He was tall, bald on top, but had curly clown-like hair going around his scalp. He had on a sweater that comprised bright reds and yellows over a black background in a pattern. To Lucas, the guy's sweater looked like a lava lamp gone out of control and way out of place on his muggy day. The restaurant was busy, and there was a long wait for the food. However, this woman was impatient and loud. After a while, she took to yelling out at any of the passing wait staff over the status of their order. Her husband would try to get her to shush, but she would give him a cross look, and he would put his head down. Lucas felt sorry for the old man.

What Lucas found unbelievable about this woman was that while all of this was going on, the old woman had the forethought to bring a book with her to read while they waited. Lucas wondered what the old woman's hurry was if she brought along her own reading materials.

"Wow, I still can't believe Mr. Mahoney is dead," Kristen said, if for no other reason than to start a conversation.

For that, Lucas was relieved. "Did you ever meet Trent, er...? Mr. Mahoney?"

Trent Mahoney made it a point during his life to get out, mingle, and meet as many people as he could. To show he did not feel he was better than everyone else. When Concord held a festival on Union Street in the downtown area, Trent, the multi-millionaire, would show up like anyone else and take part in the festivities. The Mahoney family held season tickets to the Carolina Panthers and for the Charlotte Hornets' basketball teams. But unlike most of the rich corporate executives in the area who purchased the fancy luxury boxes to reward employees or to entertain potential clients, the Mahoney's made it a point to get their seats right in the middle of a lower-level section at both venues so they could sit and watch the games with everyone else. Even though Trent liked to make public appearances, he was extremely private. He rarely took Simon or Brian to these events, largely to protect them from public scrutiny.

It would not surprise Lucas if Trent and Kristen crossed paths at some point.

"Yeah, I knew him," she said matter-of-factly.

How she said that startled Lucas. "Really?"

"Yeah," she sighed, "Sully was friends with Simon Mahoney when I dated Sully."

"They must go back farther than I thought. I knew that Simon and Sully had some sort of relationship. I really don't know who the Mahoney boys hang around. I don't know if Brian hangs out with anybody, really."

"Yeah," she agreed. "As far as I know, Brian's a loner. But when I got to know Sully more, he would talk about hanging out with Simon Mahoney. I thought Sully ran in high circles. Here I was, brought up in a poor background and suddenly, here I am running around with the richest of the rich. It was overwhelming."

"I was about the same growing up, but I'm still getting used to the amount of money I deal with on a day-to-day basis."

"I can only imagine. Working for Frank's is small peanuts compared to what you deal with."

Lucas did not voice a response. He felt his response would put down her current life's work.

"You told me this morning," Lucas said, as something in her previous statement about Sully and Simon hit on something in the back of his mind, "one of the big reasons you broke it off with Sully was because of some of the stuff he was into such as the drug dealing and the guns. Do you know if he was into that sort of stuff before he knew Simon or after?" She stared at Lucas blankly for a moment. "What I am trying to get at," he explained, "is I'm trying to figure out where Simon went bad, and if Sully had anything to do with it. I recently moved here, so

I'm not familiar with the whole timeline in the decline of Simon Mahoney."

She bit her lip again as she thought about how to word her response. Lucas wondered if she knew how sexy she looked when she bit her lip like that. It was the third time today she had done that, and Lucas's heart sped up all three times.

"As far as I knew by reputation, Simon Mahoney was flawless," Kristen said. "Not a bad mark to his name. Say you have two clotheslines strung up side-by-side, and you hang two white linen sheets on either of the lines. One is a freshly washed sheet, not a spot on it. The sheet on the other line is a muddy sheet. Are you with me so far?" Lucas nodded. She continued. "Now let's say a breeze blows, causing the two sheets to brush together. Do you think the clean sheet is going to rub off on the dirty sheet and make it cleaner?"

"No," he answered. "The clean sheet is going to get filthy."

"Exactly," she said. "And that is how it was with Simon and Sully. Simon had the clean rep, and Sully had the bad one. Simon wasn't going to get Sully to behave the right way suddenly. It was the other way around. The clean sheet will never make the dirty sheet clean."

"So, what made Simon want to hang out with someone like that?"

"Your guess is as good as mine. I think they were friends long before I came along. They went to the same private school, I think."

"That's probably it," he said. "Do you know what all Sully got Simon into?"

She shook her head. "Everyone knows about Simon's DUI, but other than that, I don't know."

Lucas looked out the window. Did this have anything to do with Trent's death? He hoped not, but he locked that little tidbit of information somewhere in the deep recesses of his mind. More than likely, Simon was just another misguided youth gone astray.

The short Spanish server arrived with the food and set it down. Satisfied that what they ordered was what was in front of them, the server said a quick, "Gracias," and scurried away as quickly as he came.

They dug into their food, which was quite good. Lucas had a California Quesadilla. It was a large flour tortilla folded over with shrimp, scrambled eggs, refried beans, and, of course, cheese. He had had nothing like it before, but it was good. There were few culturally diverse restaurants around where he grew up in West Virginia.

They ate in silence, and it gave him a few moments to reflect more upon the murder of Trent Mahoney. After Lucas left work yesterday, Trent stayed behind, ostensibly to wait on someone. But who? How often did Trent do such a thing? Trent could have been up to no good every day, and Lucas would have never known. Trent was always the last person to leave the building every day. Apparently, from Lucas's conversation with Cody, this was something Trent planned. Otherwise, why the subterfuge? Was it something he was doing before, and was looking for a way to cover his tracks? Or was it something he wanted to put in place in case he ever fooled around on Carly or start engaging in some shady business dealings?

Lucas tried to reconstruct what happened last evening. Lucas left the building, and before he could even get out of the parking lot, Trent disabled the cameras. Was a meeting prearranged, or did he call someone after Lucas left to give them permission to proceed? Lucas made a mental note to suggest to Greg to pull the phone records from that day, both Trent's cell phone and his desk phone, to see if he made any abnormal calls. Especially calls made shortly after Lucas left. Greg had probably already done that, but Lucas wanted to check just in case. Then shortly after Trent disabled the cameras, the mystery person, or persons, entered the gate with a password that, to Lucas's knowledge, only two people in the world knew, Trent and Cody. Trent came out, met and possibly argued with this person, although there were no indications of a struggle.

Then Trent got a bullet in the brain.

The killer did not attempt to conceal the body. Just left Trent lying there to show the world what happened. It was the perfect murder. No prints, no murder weapon, no witnesses, and a secret code.

The question Lucas asked himself before he let the police into the parking lot that morning rushed back to his head: Who would do such a thing? Trent had no enemies Lucas knew of and was a social butterfly. Trent had many business contacts and met literally thousands of people around the area. That narrowed the suspect list to the several million people inhabiting the Charlotte metro area.

Where to begin? Lucas thought some more extensive conversation with the Mahoney family could be fruitful. He knew the police were going to spend a good deal of time speaking with the Mahoney's, but also they were going to concentrate on many of Trent's business associates to see if there was anything there. Lucas thought his unique insight into their family could yield some different answers. Lucas thought he was already up to his neck in the investigation of Trent's murder enough that he needed to do this. Not only for the family, but for himself as well. Lucas considered Trent to be a good friend, though they were years apart in age. They spent many late evenings together where they got to know each other. Lucas thought he knew many of the intimate details of Trent's life. Apparently, not all of them. He knew Trent better than most, and Lucas could not sit there and do nothing if he could help find Trent's killer. He already used his pull to get some answers from Renegar's Security that the police may not have been able to find out.

First, however, he wanted to go back to the office and get the latest news.

"After we leave here," Lucas said, "I'm going to back to the office and get with Carter to see what is going on. After that, I'll probably go over to the Mahoney Estate and catch them up on what is happening. Maybe ask them a few questions. Do you want me to take you home, or do you want to come with me?"

Her large eyes studied Lucas for a few beats. She reached out and put her hand on his. It was no casual gesture.

"Are you trying to get rid of me?" she asked playfully.

Lucas thought Kristen knew he would take her home with him if she wanted to go.

"No, no," Lucas answered, sweating, "I just meant I didn't know if you'd be comfortable going along with me back to the office, and then over to their estate."

"Actually, I've been thinking about that while we've been eating."

"What's that?"

"It occurred to me, even though you've been working with the Mahoney's for a while, I may know some stuff about Brian and Simon you don't. And if this has anything to do with the two of them, I could help you out."

Kristen seemed excited as she said this. It excited her to be a part of something big and important.

"That's probably true," Lucas conceded. "I worked every day with Trent, tossed around many ideas with his dad, and had a decent working relationship with Carly and Laura Ann. But they keep the two boys shielded from me and from everyone else. I have only seen Simon in the office once or twice. Brian comes several times a week, but then only to check in. He spends a lot of time at the diner level. He finds the day-to-day operations of the diner fascinating. I feel in the future, Simon will be the one that handles the corporate side of the business, and Brian will be the one who handles the diner operations." He stopped. "I've only spoken to Brian one or two times at their estate."

This surprised her. "Really? I would think if those two were going to eventually run the company that they would be around the office more."

"That's what I would think as well, but maybe for now, their parents want for them to concentrate on their schooling."

She squeezed his hand, and smiled, "Well, let's go do whatever it is you need to do, and then go talk to them."

CHAPTER THIRTEEN

Lucas paid the check, and they walked into the smoldering heat in the parking lot. As he reached for the door handle of his car, the cell phone rang in his pocket. He did not recognize the number on the caller ID, but he could tell it was a local number. "Hello," he answered.

"Hey," said a vaguely familiar voice, which seemed surprised to be talking. "Is this Lucas?"

"Yeah."

"H-hey man... It's Brian." He almost sounded excited.

"How are you doing?" Lucas asked. He opened the door and climbed into the driver's seat, but did not start the car.

"I'm okay, I guess, all things considered. Look, where are you right now?" Lucas told Brian his whereabouts. "I'm near there. Wait a few minutes. I want to talk to you."

"Why aren't you at home?"

"I-I just had to get out of there. It's unreal what's going on there."

"Why? What's going on there?"

There was silence on the other end of the line. Lucas almost repeated his question when Brian said, "It's kind of weird. Mom has been in the kitchen baking stuff all day, not even crying.

She's doing it all with a straight face, and Grandma has been helping her. They've been doing it in peace too. That's what surprises me. They're not fighting or anything."

"Sometimes people use something mindless, or something they know how to do by heart, and they go at it as a way of grieving. I can picture your mother and grandmother baking together as their way of dealing with your father's death. What about your grandfather? Where is he in all of this?"

"Oh, well, he's eating. He's sitting there in his suit, eating muffins and cookies. Someone's got to be a taste tester in all of this."

Lucas thought if this were any other day, he would love to be that taste tester. "And your brother? Is he still there with his girlfriend?"

"They've been in the downstairs living room on the couch together. Just sitting there. I haven't heard them talking, but they may just shut up when I come into the room."

"How have you been holding up during all of this?" Lucas asked.

"Honestly, sitting in my room bawling my eyes out for much of the time."

"Hey, we all deal with loss in our own ways. My grandmother died about two months before I graduated from college. She was the first person I knew close to die. So, when it happened, I thought I would take it like a man and try to hold in the tears to show that I was a man. I went through the wake without shedding a tear as people came in to view the body the day before the funeral. I stood ten feet from her coffin for two hours, shaking people's hands I had never met, as they consoled me about the death of my grandmother, but I held it in. I didn't shed a tear. The next day at the funeral, I sat in the front row between my sobbing brother and sister. Still, I didn't shed a tear."

"Wow," Brian said, impressed.

"I'm not finished," Lucas said. "So then we left the funeral home and proceeded to the cemetery near where I grew up. We get there, and the preacher says a few last words before they lowered the body into the ground. That's when I lost it."

"Really?"

"I don't know what it was. During the whole thing, I was composed and stoic. Then, as they had the coffin above the grave, I lost it. I knew I lost someone I was close to growing up, and I would never see her again. That's when that part hit me."

"Wow," Brian repeated.

"I can't think of a time I cried harder in my entire life, Brian." Lucas stopped to compose himself. The memories were overwhelming. "Look, we all deal with death in our own way, and we all have our beliefs about what happens after a person dies. I have mine. You have yours."

"What's yours?"

Kristen watched Lucas from the passenger seat, listening quietly to his side of the conversation.

He shrugged, even though he knew Brian could not see the gesture. "Not right now. You don't want to know."

"Why not?"

"Well, because your father just died, and my view isn't the happiest, most consoling view. Let's figure all of this out, and then maybe we'll talk about it."

"Okay, look, I'm pulling into the parking lot now. I'll see ya' in a second."

Lucas looked up and saw an expensive BMW M5 pulling into the lot. He got out of his car to meet Brian. Kristen did the same and came around to stand beside Lucas. It made Lucas ill to think a sixteen-year-old kid could have an eighty-thousand-dollar car such as that. It was Brian's sixteenth birthday present.

Brian spotted Lucas's car, and a few seconds later, parked a few spots from Lucas. Brian still wore the rock T-shirt and the black jeans he had on earlier in the day. Those in combination with his black-framed glasses made him totally look emo.

Brian walked over, and this time shook Lucas's hand in stark contrast to this morning when he walked by Lucas, barely acknowledging him. Brian's eyes were red and puffy, the remnants of a good cry. "Hey Lucas. Thanks for waiting for me." He looked over at Kristen and his eyes lingered for a few seconds before returning to Lucas. "Who's that? She looks kind of familiar."

Lucas gave the short story of who Kristen was and how she came to be in his company. "You can trust her. So, what's up?"

"You're looking into what happened to my dad, right?" Lucas nodded. "I just wanted to know if you've found anything out since this morning."

Lucas looked at Brian for a beat. Why did he come seek him out for this? He should know Lucas would keep his family apprised of everything he found out. Was there something he wanted Lucas to know that he did not want his family to hear? Before answering the question, Lucas asked, "How did you get out of your house? I would figure you'd be on a tight leash on a day like today."

Brian shrugged. "Like I said, mom and grandma are preoccupied. It gave me a chance to sneak out. It wouldn't surprise me any if she called here in the next few minutes."

Lucas mulled this over. It made sense. He told Brian he found out how someone could get into and out of the gate. He left out the part where Brian's dad was behind the entire scheme. He would let Brian draw that conclusion himself. No sense in changing Brian's view of his father at this point by telling him his father may have been up to any good.

Brian did some mulling of his own. He seemed satisfied. Lucas did not know if Brian was bright enough to figure out about his dad being behind the whole gate thing.

"Ok, come on Brian," Lucas said. "Why did you really seek me out? There's got to be some reason to sneak out of the house for this."

He let out his breath, glancing at Kristen. "Okay, when that detective was over at the house earlier, asking my family questions, they weren't exactly truthful."

"What do you mean?"

"Well, it's just that, when the detective..."

"Greg Hanover," Lucas filled in the blank.

"Yeah, him. Anyway, when he asked if dad had been having any problems with anyone. Mom, grandpa, and grandma all said 'no.'"

"Yeah, so?"

"That's not entirely true."

"What do you mean?" Lucas crossed his arms and took a step back. It occurred to him his posture might seem threatening to young Brian. He reached forward and clasped Brian on the shoulder. "It's okay, you can tell me."

Lucas tried to make himself look more casual by putting his hands in his pockets.

Brian looked more at ease. "Dad and Simon have been having a lot of fights lately."

"What have they been fighting about?"

"I don't know," Brian answered. "But there were some heated arguments."

"How long has this been going on?"

"A couple of months."

"And you have no idea what they were fighting about? You never heard anything specifically? They never said any names, or places, or anything about school during these arguments?"

Brian stopped to think, which Lucas could tell took some considerable effort. "It couldn't have been about school. Simon just got into Duke. That's where he's wanted to go for his entire life, and that's where dad wanted him to go."

"Could it have been about his girlfriend?" Lucas asked, thinking about the beauty Simon was with this morning.

Brian paused. "Could have been," he admitted.

"Could have been?" Lucas repeated, prompting Brian to explain his statement.

"Rachel is the preacher's daughter."

"Really?" *That* was surprising. He had limited contact with Simon's girlfriend this morning when they met for the first time. That could be a reason. Now he could see where there could be trouble.

"Yeah, they're relatively new to the area. Our old pastor retired about six months ago, and Rachel's family moved down here from Greensboro for her dad to take over. She and Simon met, and it turned out Rachel had a bit of a rebellious side to her."

She would have to, to be hanging around with Simon Mahoney, Lucas thought. "Were they fighting about Simon steering her wrong or something?"

Brian shrugged. "I don't know. What I really thought was maybe you could talk to Simon or something." Brian cast the bait, knowing Lucas would take it. Brian may be smarter than Lucas thought. "It may be," Brian continued, "this has nothing to do with what happened to dad. But if it did, and I learned this from my criminal justice class last year, which if my family held back that dad and Simon were arguing, and it was the reason dad was killed, then that is a felony. And I don't want my entire family to go to jail."

What Brian implied hit hard. "Do you think your brother could have done this? Was he that mad at your father?"

"I don't know. But it's something at least, and the police don't have any idea who did this. I just want to make sure for my own mental well-being that Simon had nothing to do with this."

"Okay Brian. I don't see where it could hurt. I'll talk to Simon."

Brian's eyes pleaded with him. "Just please, don't let Simon or anyone know I talked to you about this."

"Why?"

"I think Simon would hurt me if he found out I talked to you about this," Brian said, and from the tone in his voice, Lucas believed him.

"Alright, I'll go talk to Simon for you, but you have to let me do it on my own time." Brian seemed disappointed, as though it could be on the other end of forever before Lucas spoke to Simon again. "Don't worry, it'll be soon though," Lucas said.

"Thanks, Lucas. You may want to get him out of the house when you talk to him. He wouldn't want mom to know you were talking to him about this. She'd get real mad."

And we didn't want that to happen, Lucas thought. "Okay Brian, I'll think of something."

"Thanks again, Lucas. Just please, do me a favor, don't tell the cops about what I told you. I don't want anyone to get into trouble. I know mom just didn't want anyone to know our family is still having problems with Simon."

Without another word, Brian climbed back into his car and departed just as quickly as he came.

Lucas looked at Kristen with raised eyebrows. She had the same expression etched upon her face.

"Let's go," he said.

She agreed and got into the car.

"That was interesting," Kristen said, after she strapped herself in.

"I'll agree."

"I don't think you know what I found interesting about that entire exchange."

"What's that?"

"Brian doesn't do stuff like what he just did."

"What do you mean?"

"What I mean is, Brian doesn't voluntarily do stuff like that. I know he and his brother don't have a lot in common, but through all the stuff Simon has gotten into, Simon and Brian have been best friends through it all. Simon is about the only friend Brian really has. For Brian to point at Simon tells me there's something going on serious enough for him to think his brother may have had something to do with this. However, Brian is not going to tell us what it is exactly he thinks or knows."

"For Brian to do that, he would be looking at some major trouble from his family." Kristen nodded in agreement. "What you have to keep in mind, Kristen, is image is absolutely every-thing to this family. They would stop at no costs to keep their family's name out of the papers, off the news, and especially out of the tabloids. And most especially if that news was bad enough to cast them in a negative light. That is part of my job, to make sure that doesn't happen."

"This is going to go well against that, isn't it?"

"Oh yeah," Lucas agreed. "When it comes to the point the police have to file their report of whatever that will be, it will then become public record. Then, there will be no privacy for this family. It'll be one of those things where reporters will camp outside of their gates at home and at the office, hoping to get an interview with someone who knows something."

"You'll be one of those people they'll be looking for, won't you?"

Lucas gulped. He had not thought about that. "Yeah, I guess I will. But I'll deal with that when the time comes. Right now, I need to concern myself with finding out who did this as quickly as I can before the public finds out about Trent's death. Once they do, I'm sure I'll be inundated with a media blitz large enough I will have to stay focused on them instead of finding who did this."

She nodded. "Alright, how can I help?"

He set the gears in his head in motion. If he wanted to find out what the friction was between Simon and Trent without arousing the family's suspicion, how would he do that? First, Lucas needed to find out more about Simon before he spoke to him so Lucas would know what he was talking about. He needed an edge on Simon. If Lucas went and asked some hard-hitting questions to Simon about his relationship with his father, then Simon could make up anything, and Lucas would have no idea that Simon was lying. That is why he told Brian he would do it on his own time. Lucas needed to have some idea what to go at Simon with. Brian said he had no idea what Simon and his father were fighting about. Lucas thought Kristen told him everything she knew about Simon. He could ask some of the kids Simon goes to school with. The problem is Lucas did not know any of them.

A thought struck. He knew someone that knew someone. That person sat in his midst.

"Kristen, I know one way you could help, but you're not going to like it."

She regarded him with skepticism. Perhaps she wanted to take back her last statement about helping him. "How's that?"

"You could get me in touch with Sully."

Horror shone in her eyes. The mere thought repulsed her. "No, no, absolutely not. I can't stand to be around him."

"Okay," he paused, "Do you know anyone else Simon hangs around? Someone who would know what he is into?"

She thought about it briefly. "No," she conceded.

"Well, if we're to find anything out about Simon, we need to talk to someone who knows him. That would be Sully."

"What makes you think he's going to talk to you, of all people?"

"I'll let him know it's in his best interests to talk to me."

"How, blackmail?"

"That's what I was thinking."

"What are you going to blackmail him with?"

"Leave that up to me."

She looked at him doubtfully. She looked down, huffed, and said, "Only if you don't let him touch me."

Lucas suppressed a smile. "How do I get in touch with him?"

She held out her hand. "Here, let me see your phone."

CHAPTER FOURTEEN

It turned out it was not that hard for Kristen to set up a meeting with Sully. All it took was a two-minute phone call, and her saying she had come to her senses, and she would like to see him so that they could talk it out. She said she wanted to meet him in a public place, and after some urging Sully agreed to meet her at a Starbucks in the Target off George W Liles Parkway.

She closed the phone and handed it back to Lucas. She exhaled. "Whew, I didn't realize I was holding that in."

He reached for the phone and wrapped his hand around hers. "Are you okay?"

She took a few deep breaths and looked down. "Yeah," she said after a few seconds. "He said he was 'running around.' Whatever that means, and he'd meet us there in about twenty minutes."

"Are you sure that you want to do this? We can just not show up if you want to. I don't want to make you do something you don't want to."

"No, no. This is important. It's something that needs doing. Let's go do it before I have time to think about it."

"You're sure?"

"Yes," she said with finality. "Let's go."

"Thank you," he said, pulled her hand to him, kissed it delicately, and then let it go.

She smiled and blushed at the same time.

Lucas kissed her hand without even thinking about it. It seemed like the right thing to do. They talked about Brian doing something way out of character for him. Kristen did not know it, but Lucas did not do stuff like that.

Maybe, amid all the tragedy today, he was learning things about himself he never thought he would, or could.

Such as independently investigating a high-profile murder.

***

They turned left back onto Route 29 and went up a hill. They turned left at the next light and passed by the great smelling S&D Coffee plant on the corner.

As they drove down Weddington Road, Kristen asked, "So, what's the plan?"

"Have you ever been to this Target?" Target was a large department store chain, largely thought to be more upscale than a Wal-Mart or a K-Mart, with a brighter atmosphere and slightly more upscale products. Lucas liked to go to this particular store to do some grocery shopping and get a caramel macchiato from Starbucks.

"Oh, yeah. I buy, like, all of my clothes there."

"Do you think Sully will beat us there?"

She hesitated. "No, I think we'll beat him there. He was up in China Grove doing something. I don't know what he was doing. Nor do I want to know. He's at least twenty minutes away."

China Grove was a small town between Concord and Salisbury to the north. Lucas's thoughts of it are what he saw when he saw something reported from China Grove on the news: a less wealthy town that seemed to have crime and drug problems. Lucas had an assumption what a person like Sully was doing in that area.

"Alright, well, you go on into Starbucks, and get yourself something to drink. I will wait somewhere in the store, but outside of where you will be, in a position to see Sully come in. Then, as soon as he walks into the place, I'll come in behind him."

"Then what?"

"After he gets over his initial anger at being set up, we'll see if he'll talk to us."

"And how are you going to do that? With your blackmail?"

Lucas nodded. "Yeah, with my 'blackmail."

"And what exactly is that?"

He smiled. "I'll figure that out between here and there. Just let me handle it. Who knows, he may just talk to us without needing motivation."

"We'll see," she said.

They turned right at the next light, onto Kannapolis Parkway, and soon crossed over I-85, where that road turned into George W Liles Parkway. They made an immediate left into the expansive Afton Ridge shopping center. He slowly pulled into the Target parking lot, keeping his eyes peeled for any sign of Sully's Escalade. It would not look good if Sully saw Kristen getting out of Lucas's car. Satisfied Sully had not arrived yet,

Lucas pulled down to the second entrance to the brown and tan bricked Super Target.

They got a spot near the front. Lucas got out of the car and looked around. They beat Sully. A few puffy clouds moved across the sky overhead. It was still boiling hot, and the sunlight made Lucas squint as they walked up the parking lot. They went through the front entrance, and walked in to a clean looking produce department of a grocery store, with a deli/bakery counter wrapped around the front wall. The smell of chicken and fresh produce clung to the air. The small Starbucks was just inside the entrance on the left.

Kristen had a hold of his hand. "You're not going to let him do anything to me, are you?"

He squeezed her hand. "Kristen, I'm going to do everything in my power to make sure you leave here in the same condition you are now. I promise you that." He tried to ooze confidence.

This seemed to ease her somewhat. "Okay," she said. "Wish me luck."

He smiled, and then she squeezed his hand before parting. Lucas watched her walk into the darker area of Starbucks and up to the counter where a young barista took her order.

He turned and walked a short distance across the brightly lit store towards the pharmacy area. It was the middle of a Wednesday afternoon, and the store was not busy. That would make it harder to blend in with the crowd since there was not one. He hoped Sully would do exactly as they did and come in and go directly into Starbucks. That would reduce the chance of Sully seeing him. If Sully saw Lucas, he did not think he would be too suspicious. After all, Sully had no reason to think Lucas had anything to do with Kristen. If he did see Lucas, then hopefully Sully would chalk that up to nothing more than coincidence.

Lucas stood behind the second row of greeting cards, in between funny birthday cards and religious sympathy cards. Great marketing, he thought, as he looked out between the aisles. From there, he had a good view of the main entrance, and a superb view into Starbucks.

He saw two or three employees over in the produce area putting out various fruits and vegetables. There was a tall, skinny, young employee putting out lettuce, and another shorter, stockier employee with a goatee appearing to play with the oranges. The other, slightly older gentleman seemed to be the one in charge. He stood with a military bearing, with his back turned to the other two employees working with pre-cut bags of lettuce. He had no clue the stocky employee was juggling three oranges ten feet away from him.

Lucas almost laughed but did not want to draw attention. He wondered what they could learn from this meeting. He figured Sully would refuse to talk about Simon. If Sully did talk, he would tell them nothing new. Lucas hoped they would learn something to alleviate the thought that Simon had anything to do with his father's death. That should be enough to console Brian. What if Sully said something incriminating? What then? Of course, Lucas would tell Greg Hanover what he found.

He made a mental note to call Greg after leaving here no matter what they found. If Sully could not help with Simon, Lucas would next go talk to the family and ask them what they were doing last night while Trent was at work.

For that matter, going back to the family, what would Carly have to gain from Trent's sudden demise? To this point, Lucas did not consider her to have anything to do with her husband's death. He did not know how happy their marriage was. He knew Trent was often frustrated with Carly because of her shopping sprees and travels around the world. Trent was thrifty, and even though he was rich beyond imagination, he knew the value of a dollar. He saved where he could. Lucas regularly saw Trent on Monday mornings sitting in his office clipping coupons from the previous days Charlotte Observer. Millionaire many times over, Trent Mahoney clipping coupons! Lucas wanted to laugh when he saw Trent doing that, but it made Lucas respect him, and learn that Trent knew money would not rule his life much the way it ruled Carly.

During this line of thought, Sully walked through the main entrance as Lucas hoped. He strutted, because there was no other word for it, straight into Starbucks. Lucas would wait about two minutes before he made his appearance. That way, as discussed in the car, Kristen could reel Sully in, and make him think everything between them could be okay.

As Lucas poked his head around the corner, one of the red and khaki clad male employees came and stood beside him. The employee said nothing at first, nor was Lucas inclined to say anything. The employee seemed interested in what interested Lucas. The employee looked in the same direction as Lucas.

Lucas felt the employee look from him to Starbucks and back again. "Can I help you find something?" The employee said in a voice that made him sound as though he had a permanent cold. "Or have you already found it?" he gestured towards where Kristen sat.

"No, I'm good," Lucas smiled.

"Okay. Sure," the employee said, "it's just we have a lot of talent that comes in here, and sometimes guys like to follow the talent around."

"Talent?"

"Yeah, talent, the girls that come in here. Some days, this place is loaded with talent."

"Oh, I get it." This was something Lucas noticed when he first moved here from West Virginia. In West Virginia, you occasionally saw a beautiful girl stand out in the crowd. Around here, it was commonplace. Lucas's brother said it best when he said he thought that there was something in the water, down in the south, making the girls so attractive.

Lucas glanced at the guy next to him. He was about average height, had short hair, a compact muscularity, light colored beard, and he clearly seemed like an unhappy employee.

The employee proved Lucas's hunch as he turned and walked away muttering, shaking his head, "This place sucks the life out of me."

Interesting guy, Lucas thought.

He figured by now Sully had had enough time to be sitting down across from Kristen and should be so deep into their conversation Lucas's entrance would go unnoticed. He hoped Kristen had seated herself facing the entrance, so if Sully sat across from her, he would have his back to Lucas as he entered the coffee shop.

Lucas walked across fifty feet, dodging a few of the customers along the way to the Starbucks entrance. When Lucas could see inside, he was relieved to see Sully had his back to him, hunched over the table, engrossed in whatever line of B.S. Kristen fed him.

Lucas walked in and took a seat beside Kristen. The primary sources of lighting were from two globe lights hanging low from the ceiling over the coffee machine, and there were recessed lights in the ceiling adding some light to the fake gloom. The ceiling was black to give off the effect of the area being darker than it was. A large, brightly colored painting covered the wall to the left of the counter that looked much like a Pollock painting. The painting had the only bright colors in the cozy room. Round wooden tables with wooden chairs made up the sitting arrangement. There was a singular rectangular wooden table set up in the corner meant for the handicapped. Square, light brown ceramic tiles covered the floor. On the far wall, a large, round window looked out into the parking lot. Overhead, a jazzy tune from the Dave Matthews Band played. A chalkboard hung on the wall behind the counter that said, "Daily Offerings: Try a Cinnamon Dolce Latte. Be sure to ask your barista about our Low-Fat options."

Lucas went to the counter and asked for a venti version of the special offering of the day. He watched Sully and Kristen converse. Sully took no notice of Lucas. Kristen seemed confident now, and Lucas got the impression she was in charge. Sully had no choice. Otherwise, he could scare Kristen away.

Lucas got his latte and sat down next to Kristen. Sully drew away from Kristen and retreated to his side of the table. He was obviously surprised to see Lucas there.

"What's up, Sully?" Lucas said, drawing his chair close.

Sully blinked a few times before answering rudely. Not at all in the civil way in which they conversed earlier. "Just talking to my friend here."

"I know."

"How do you know?"

"Because I'm the one who told her to call you to meet us here."

"Lucas figured I could get you to meet me somewhere at the drop of a hat," Kristen said.

Sully fidgeted. Lucas thought for a moment that Sully was going to get up and leave. That Kristen tricked Sully into showing up obviously made him angry and it disappointed him the reason he showed was a sham. With Sully being the young urban entrepreneur he was, Lucas hoped Sully would draw the quick conclusion he could still gain something from this after all.

Lucas had nothing for Sully to gain.

"So why am I here?" Sully said.

"I needed to ask you a few questions," Lucas responded.

"You tricked me into coming here. What you have to ask cannot be good," Sully said, but still made no move to leave.

"It has nothing to do with you. I just need to know a few things about Simon."

This made him more uncomfortable. "What are you and Kristen doing here together, tag-teaming me on this? I didn't even know you two knew each other."

Lucas realized Sully was trying to change the subject before it got started. Lucas needed to humor Sully and let him feel as though this was going to be a two-way conversation, and Sully would not be doing all the talking.

"Have you seen the papers recently?" Lucas asked. Sully shook his head. When Lucas was his age, the only time he ever paid attention to the news or read the paper was for the latest sports scores and comics. "There's been a rash of robberies in the area going on in the area for a few months. Someone tried to rob Kristen earlier, and I stopped it."

Sully blinked twice. "You stopped it?"

"Yeah," Lucas said, and related the story of how Lucas followed the guy after he got out of a car, how the guy tried to accost Kristen, and then how Lucas subsequently stopped him. The story made Kristen uneasy, and she grabbed Lucas's arm as she remembered the events. He did not want to return the affectation. The last thing Lucas needed was a jealous Sully.

Sully gulped and asked, "Had you ever seen this guy before?"

"No, never," Lucas answered. Sully's mood brightened to a small degree at Lucas's answer. Hmm. Sully *did* know something, Lucas thought. "How closely are you associated with Simon?" he asked, already knowing at least part of the answer. Sully did not know Lucas knew. He wanted to see how truthful Sully was going to be.

"We're pals," Sully answered. "We hang out sometimes. Do a little partying."

That much was true, at least. "What kind of partying?"

He wagged his finger. "No, no, I'm not going into those kinds of details."

Lucas nodded his head. He could accept this. He already had some idea of what they did, so it was not important to get Sully to admit it here and now.

"Okay, you're right," Lucas conceded. "I'm not going to pry into what you two do."

"Alright," Sully said, getting impatient, "What am I here for?"

"I just wanted to know what you knew about Simon and his dad. You know, like their relationship."

"Why ask me?" he said gruffly.

Lucas breathed in before answering. "Someone murdered Trent Mahoney last night."

Sully looked at Lucas in disbelief. Lucas stared back, unblinking. Sully looked at Kristen for confirmation.

"It's true," she whispered.

Sully sat back and put a hand over his mouth. "Oh, man. How did this happen?"

After getting Sully to swear he would tell no one, Lucas related the details of Trent's murder. After Lucas finished, Sully said, "So someone got inside the gate and popped Trent?"

"That's how it happened."

"Wow. I can't believe it." Sully sat back and stared out the large, round window into the parking lot. He tried to process what he had just heard.

Lucas could tell from Sully's reaction that this was the first time he heard about it. Either that or he was a talented actor. That, at least, told Lucas he had not been in contact with Simon so far today.

Sully snapped back to attention as it hit him with what Lucas could want from him. "Whoa, whoa, you don't think I had anything to do with this, do you?"

"No, not at all Sully. I could not imagine why in a million years why you would kill Simon's father. That, and honestly, I can't see you taking the time to figure out how to break in the gate the way the killer did."

"How did whoever did this get in?"

Lucas shook his head. "I'm not going to talk about that. Right now, I don't want Simon to know I'm asking about him."

"Why are you asking me about Simon? Do you think *he* had something to do with this?" Lucas did not immediately answer. It was all the answer Sully needed. "How do you know I won't call him when I leave here and warn him you're up to something?"

"Because it's not in your best interests," Lucas said.

Sully stared at Lucas from across the table. He then looked at Kristen, gauging whether she had told Lucas anything incriminating about him.

He remained silent, so Lucas tried to persuade him to come out of his shell. "Do you remember when Simon got that DWI?" Lucas asked.

He smiled. "Yeah, he was going home from my house that night. He was plowed. I told him not to go, but the idiot wouldn't listen. Simon's about the smartest guy I've ever met, but he sure doesn't have any common sense sometimes."

Lucas made no comment about the admission. Simon refused to tell his parents exactly where he was coming from when the

DWI happened. Simon just said he was coming home from a party and had had too much to drink.

"Well, after that happened," Lucas said, "The family started keeping someone on Simon when he went out to see what he was up to. Simon never knew, of course, and he's not going to know, right?"

Sully shrugged his shoulders. "Again, how do you know I'm not going to go tell him about this conversation when I leave here?"

For a teenager, it was easy for Lucas to tell Sully thought highly of himself. Even in the face of Lucas's implied threat, Sully still tried to control the conversation. He thought Lucas had nothing on him. That was true to a degree, but Sully did not have to know that. Lucas just had to give the impression he had something on Sully to keep Sully quiet, and to get him to tell Lucas what he wanted.

"Well, when we saw how much time Simon spent in your company, we checked you out, too. You know, to see if you were the type of person Simon should spend his time with."

"Then you found nothing," Sully said, as if he had won. "Simon and I still spend as much time together as we did before. If your investigator monkey had found out anything solid on me, then Simon's parents wouldn't let him come out of the house."

"How do you know Trent had not waited a bit to lower the boom on Simon? Like maybe wait until he graduates to let him know he wasn't going to be getting that trust fund."

Something flashed behind Sully's eyes. Lucas knew he hit upon something. He could tell by Sully's reaction he knew about the trust fund. They set the trust fund up without it being public knowledge. Only friends of the family knew anything about it.

"Then you know," Lucas continued, "That if it comes down Simon has been up to no good, he doesn't get anything." Sully nodded again. "C'mon Sully, you know what Simon has been into. And through that, we know you've been up to no good yourself."

Sully looked around the small café uncomfortably. He did not ask for any details, but he knew it was possible that he was busted. Lucas wondered if Sully ever thought he could get in trouble for the deeds he did, or if Sully thought because of his money, he could not get into any trouble.

Lucas decided to take a leap. "How did you talk your cronies into snatching purses from old ladies?"

He thought Sully was going to jump across the table at him. Sully's face turned red, and he broke out in a sweat. He did not answer. He did not even deny it. Maybe Sully was not as bright as Lucas thought. "How did you know?" Sully said, his voice full of malice.

Lucas nodded at Kristen, and then told a small fib, "Kristen said the guy who tried to rob her was one of your pals. She recognized him from one of your little outings before you two broke up, and said she thought she also recognized the guy driving the getaway car. Then, the way your guy tried to rob her fit the M.O. of the other reported robberies."

"So what makes you think I'm the mastermind behind the entire operation?"

"Call it an educated guess," Lucas said. "All I have to do is call my pal, Greg Hanover, over at the Concord P.D. I'll let him know what I think and present him with what I already know. Then, even if you have nothing to do with it, they will still investigate you. They would watch you, watch what you do, who you associate with, and where you take that big, pimped out Escalade that looks like, to others, it was paid for with dirty money."

"What do you want?" Sully caved. He knew he did not want that to happen, and he was smart enough to know what Lucas was saying was true.

"All I want," Lucas held up his hands, "is to know what you know about Simon's relationship with his father. It's simple, man. Let me know what you know, and I'll forget about every-thing."

"How do I know you won't go tell, anyway?" Sully was ready to play ball.

"All you have is my word. Sully, I'm an honest guy. If I tell you I'm going to do something, then I come through."

Sully weighed his options. He would not call Lucas's bluff. He asked, "Okay, what do you want to know?"

"I've heard Simon and his father have been having problems lately . . .," Lucas said, leading him.

Sully looked puzzled. "I hope you aren't thinking Simon somehow did this."

"All I'm doing," Lucas said, "is trying to do as much as I can for the police to narrow their suspect list."

"Why bother? Why not let them do all the work?"

"Because I was the last known person to see Trent alive."

Sully understood the significance of that statement. "You're trying to prove you're not the one who pulled the trigger?"

"Bingo."

"So, you think I'm going to help you by asking me if I thought Simon could do it."

"That's the gist of it." Lucas let his earlier threat dangle unspoken.

"Did they have problems?" Sully asked rhetorically. "Yes, they had their problems. Do I think Simon could have done such a thing?" He paused and considered it. "No."

"Why do you say that?"

Sully shrugged. "Well, it's just not in his personality. The guy wouldn't harm a fly."

"You never know what a person could do if they get backed into a corner. People are capable of horrible, grotesque things if the circumstances are right. Or wrong, I should say. The Donner Party, for example."

A grimace. Sully may not spend much time in school, but he knew what the Donner party was. "Yeah."

"So, what was it with his dad that had them at such odds with each other? Simon obviously was doing well in school, getting into Duke and all. And it appears he was staying out of trouble."

Another grimace. "You're right on the school part. The guy's a freakin' nerd. We hang out, and he would bring his books over in case he got to study. Though I tried not to let him. Really, he had been trying to stay away from the drinking and the drugs and stuff."

Lucas' eyes widened. The admission of drugs was news to him. Simon may be the richest teenager Lucas ever met, but Simon was a teenager, nonetheless. Boys will be boys. Kristen stayed still and silent beside him, content to let him ask the questions while she waited for the end of the conversation. She wanted to get as far away from Sully as soon as possible.

Sully continued. "I think most of their problems lay in Simon's girlfriend, Rachel."

"How so?"

"She's a preacher's kid. If Simon behaved the way his parents and grandparents wanted him to, then it wouldn't be a problem."

Sully seemed more comfortable now that the conversation was not about him. He took a leisurely sip of his drink while looking around the coffee bar. He seemed more like the way Lucas remembered him from earlier in the day.

"How's that?" Lucas enjoyed playing the part of the prosecutor, asking leading questions to keep him talking.

"You know. They would like him to be like any other preacher's kid. Tie his shoes a certain way. Put his pants on one particular pant leg at a time and keep his nose clean."

Sully was mixing his metaphors now, but Lucas understood what he was saying. "In other words," Lucas said, "They want him to be a good kid."

Sully gestured emphatically. "Exactly! That's good for your simple-minded zombie-like people that will accept anything they're told. Man, everybody needs to cut loose and sow some oats when they're young. That's how you find out what sort of person who you are going to be when you actually grow up. Right now," he pointed at his chest, "right now, dude, I'm just living and having fun. But I know in a few years, I'm going to have to stop doing all the stuff I do now, grow up, and be a man."

Lucas went to school with this guy. That is, guys like him. Screw-ups, drug-addicts, and all the other hyphenated adjectives you could think of to describe a guy like Sully. A guy such as Sully was probably ten or eleven years old when he had his first puff of a cigarette. He probably made good grades before then, but once those kids get a taste of cigarettes or alcohol, it all changes. They dress differently, talk differently and behave differently.

"But grow up I will," he continued. "I know all the stuff I do is temporary, but I know I will eventually have to man up and run my father's business. I'll have to leave the stuff I do behind. But you know what? I'll do it in a heartbeat. That's where my life and my money are going to be."

Lucas made a face but did not reply. Sully made his point. He portrayed himself as a tough guy, a screw-up, but he seemed to have his ducks in a row. Since he dropped the tough guy façade, he also lost the urban accent he used to make himself sound like a tough guy. He was a smart kid, with a good vocabulary. Not what you would expect from someone who portrayed himself as a thug.

They were silent for a moment as everyone thought about living in a family whose standards were so strict.

Lucas took a sip of his latte. "Tell me more about Rachel," he said.

Sully looked at the dark ceiling. "I really don't know much about her. All I know is that Simon doesn't bring her around me too often. He's been spending less time with me since he's been dating her, but if I had a girlfriend that looked like her, you wouldn't see me much either."

Lucas conceded the point. He thought the girl sitting beside him fit that description. Maybe not to the level of someone like Rachel, but close.

When Lucas met Rachel this morning, he thought she was one of those trophy girls you saw the good-looking rich guys with. It is a common belief those girls are not much more than great looks and shallow giggles. One could say the same thing about Kristen just by looking at her, but now that he was around her, he could see that she was a deeper young woman than what met the eye. She had a fire that shined in her eyes that spoke of a quick wit and sharp intelligence. Not like something you see in a typical trophy wife. Before, when Lucas did not have the courage to talk to Kristen, just be a voyeur, she intrigued him with her beauty. Now that he glimpsed what lay in her personality, he found himself more intrigued by her than he had been by a woman in a long, long time.

"You think she's the reason behind the problems with Simon and his dad?" Lucas asked.

Without hesitation, Sully replied, "Oh yeah, without a doubt. I think Trent was mainly the mouthpiece for the rest of the family in arguing with Simon. He expressed views to Simon that were contrary to what he wanted to hear."

"What views were those?"

"That they were spending too much time together, and they were spending too much time alone. More than what a preacher's daughter should be doing. That they should try to spend more time at home so the family could keep an eye on them, and make sure they weren't screwing around."

"Where were Rachel's parents in all of this? Her dad is part of the clergy. Shouldn't they have been doing their part to keep their precious daughter under control?"

He shrugged. "Yeah, that bothered me, too. All the other preacher's kids I have been around are usually under the tight control of their parents, but this Rachel girl doesn't seem to be that way. I don't know if she lies to her parents when she goes out, or if she sneaks out of the house. I'm sure that because of the Mahoney's standing in the church, both sets of parents communicate with each other about their children. They know their kids are dating. There's no way they don't. But why Rachel's parents continue to let them spend as much time together as they do, I don't know. I figure Simon's parents would think Rachel was a good influence on Simon."

"What if it were reversed?" Lucas asked, thinking aloud.

"What do you mean?" Kristen asked. It was only the second time she had spoken since Lucas sat down.

"What if Rachel was a bad influence on Simon?" Sully and Kristen stared at Lucas with glazed eyes. "I knew kids growing up in West Virginia whose parents were zealously religious and forced them to practice whatever religion they were a part of. Some of these kids did not like having their beliefs forced upon them and rebelled. Sometimes they did not like their parents limiting their social lives, and the second they had the chance, they went out and did their own thing. What if Rachel is one of those kids? What if Rachel is acting out against her parents, and she and Simon got caught doing something they weren't supposed to be doing, and that's where the problems started?"

Sully rubbed his chin, sat back, and said, "If they were screwing around, then Simon would have told me about it."

"You sure? You said Simon did not bring her around you much. What if he was doing that because he did not want you to know the details of his relationship with her?"

"I don't know," he conceded.

Lucas concluded he had reached a dead end in this conversation. He tried to blackmail Sully. He knew he could mess up Sully's life, and the best thing Lucas could come up with was that Simon and Trent were disagreeing over Simon's girlfriend. Brian told Lucas they were having problems, but he did not tell Lucas why. Sully, on the other hand, knew little about why they were having disagreements. He thought it was because Simon and Rachel were spending the wrong kind of time together. That was the best Lucas could do. It gave him something to look at, but he had hoped for more from Sully. He hoped for something that would either tell him whether or not Simon killed his father. A smoking gun or a solid alibi would have been nice.

Speaking of which, he did not ask Sully if he knew of Simon's whereabouts for the previous evening. Therefore, he asked him now.

He was prepared with an answer. He must have seen the question coming. "I don't know, man," he answered. "I saw him at school yesterday, and I asked him if he wanted to do something afterwards. He said thanks, but no thanks. Said he had something to do."

That was interesting. Simon gave Sully a vague response by not telling Sully where he would be or where he was going. That left the door open.

Speaking of school. "Sully, today's a school day, right?"

"I just had other things to do," was all he said.

Lucas was not a truant officer. He did not concern himself with how this misguided youth spent his time. "Sully, I'm sorry if we had to trick you into coming in and talk to me, but I did not want you to know you were going to be coming in and talking about Trent and Simon Mahoney. I did not know before I walked in here if you had heard about what happened to Trent. If you knew, and I called and wanted to speak with you out of the blue, then I feared you would not see me because you would think I thought you or Simon had something to do with Trent's murder."

He gave Lucas a cross look. During the conversation, Sully forgot the circumstances why he was here to begin with. Until Lucas reminded him.

"Are we done here?" Sully asked.

Lucas nodded, and with one lingering gaze at Kristen, Sully got up and tramped away. Kristen shivered as he left, then put her face in her hands and cried softly. Lucas put his arm around her to comfort her.

"Hey," Lucas said, "I'm sorry I had to put you through that."

She sniffled and looked up at him with red eyes. "I did this for you. I figured after you saved my life, it was the least I could do." She rubbed her nose. "That was so hard. I sat here, seething with anger. I just wanted to throw myself across the table and slap the crap out of him."

Lucas could not think of a time when someone went out of their way and made a departure from what was comfortable for them to do something like this for him. He remembered Ashley helped speed him back to recovery after his car accident so many years ago. But that was a natural thing for her to do. They were lifelong friends until then, and because of what happened, they became more than that. What Kristen had just done was something on a much different level. She got herself into a potentially dangerous situation with an ex-boyfriend whom she had a restraining order against to help Lucas in his investigation of a person's death she had only met on a few occasions. However, Lucas did not want her to think she had to do stuff to show her gratitude.

He expressed this much to her. "Look, Kristen, what I did for you earlier is something any man should do when they see something like that happening. I did not even have time to think I was putting myself in danger. I saw what I thought was happening and reacted to it. I would have done the same for you, or any other person the guy may have potentially robbed. You do not need to show your appreciation for what I did."

She reached down and pulled both of his hands into her lap. "Lucas, I don't care what you say. That was the bravest thing I have ever seen, not to mention the nicest thing anyone has ever done for me. Put yourself in my shoes, if the situation had been reversed, and I was the one who saved your life, wouldn't you express your feelings to me for what I did?"

Lucas did not even have to think about it. "You're right."

They stared at each other for what seemed like an eternity. Here were two people that, until today, were complete strangers. Now, they shared something together that, thankfully, most people never have to experience. Some sort of intangible bond formed between them. Lucas felt it, and he thought he could see it in her eyes as well. She admitted she had walls she put up around herself to guard her from getting hurt again. For a young woman her age, that was a shame. Somewhere in the past hour or so, he saw those walls crumble around her. When she looked to him for guidance, he saw trust. This came from a woman who, as much as stated she did not trust men whatsoever.

Lucas too, erected walls around himself since Ashley left him over a year ago. He, too, did not want to go through the pain and betrayal again that marked his prior relationship. Many people, when they go through a bad relationship with a bad outcome, base many of their thoughts and feelings about having future relationships on the bad one. They get afraid the same thing could happen repeatedly with person after person. So, when someone comes around that may be interested, and that person takes an interest in the person coming around, they take a guarded approach. Instead of letting it happen, they put the person through a gauntlet of tests to make sure the bad things would not happen again. Then, if they passed those tests, they were still scrutinized during the entire course of the relationship.

Lucas did not want to live in that kind of world. He felt Kristen was different. He hoped she felt the same towards him.

"Okay," she said, thankfully changing the subject, "what now?"

"First, I'm going to call Greg Hanover, and see if I can't get an update on what's going on. Then second, I'm going to go over to the Mahoney's place and catch them up and possibly talk to Simon."

"And you still want for me to come with you, right?"

He nodded. "I don't want you to think I'm using you, but thus far you've been helpful in getting me in a position to talk to Sully, and I think you could be even more helpful when I go talk to Simon. Like you said, I may not be familiar with the timelines of the rise and fall of Simon Mahoney, and you could point me in the right direction to ask the right questions."

Relief flooded her face. Lucas thought she was afraid she had used up her usefulness or that he would not want her to go through anything else emotional and take her home. He wanted her around for a variety of reasons.

He pulled out his cell and called Greg. He answered after only half of a ring.

"Greg Hanover," he said in a hurried voice.

"Hey Greg, it's Lucas Caine."

"Lucas, how are you holding up?" he asked, slowing down.

"Me? I'm doing fine. Do you have any updates?"

"As you could guess, the M.E. labeled the official cause of death as a fatal gunshot wound. The lividity of the skin shows that Trent was killed sometime between five and eight o'clock yesterday evening. The initial forensics is back, and from the angle of the bullet hole, and from the blood spray pattern, it appears our suspect is about average height. And from the plaster casings of the footprints that you found, the suspect wears about a size seven shoe, and it could be a man or a woman's shoe. The pattern looks like a generic tennis shoe that could be found at just about any bargain shoe or department store."

Lucas mulled this over for a moment. "So it could be anyone."

"Yeah, it looks that way. We have eliminated dwarfs and giants, but that's about it."

"And I would guess any shoes or clothing the killer was wearing would be long gone by now."

"From the intelligent way it looks like this was planned, I would have to agree with you. For someone to get past that gate, to leave no other clues that someone was even there, and to have such a lapse in judgment as to have bloody clothes, shoes, and the murder weapon lying around somewhere would be a major gaff. I don't see this killer doing that."

"I agree. All of that is long gone by now."

"At this point, unless someone actually admits to it, and unless we find the murder weapon in someone's possession, we would have to build an extremely solid case based upon circumstantial evidence, and we know how often that works in a court of law."

"O.J. Simpson," Lucas said.

"Exactly. I have my men out, canvassing the local businesses there along Copperfield, seeing if anyone saw anything or heard gunshots. My guess is we're going to come up empty."

"Yeah, back to square one."

"Tell me what you've found out."

Lucas related what happened earlier with stopping the robbery attempt on Kristen. Greg mumbled something about hearing about a botched robbery attempt. When Lucas told Greg what he found out about the gate, the pass codes, and how Trent arranged for that from the beginning, he perked up.

"The person would have had to have known Trent."

"Very well, I would say. That was something I'm not sure anyone in the Mahoney family had any knowledge about, besides Trent."

"Have you spoken to them since you found out about the gate?"

Lucas told a small fib, leaving out the part about getting together with Brian and him relaying his suspicions of his brother. "No, I was actually getting ready to go over there and catch them up on what I've found out."

"I have spoken to members of the family several times this afternoon," Greg said, "keeping them apprised of the situation. I interviewed all of them earlier, and they couldn't tell me anything."

"Possibly my unique insights into the family could yield some different answers."

Greg gnawed on that suggestion for a second. Lucas was going to talk to them no matter what Greg said next anyway, but it would be nice to have an official blessing beforehand. That way, they could not accuse Lucas down the line of interfering with a police investigation.

"I don't think it could hurt, but like I said, I couldn't get anything out of them. I'm going to look into some of Trent's business dealings and see if there's anything there."

"Okay."

"You mentioned that yesterday you all set a deal with a distributor for them to give you a substantial discount?"

"Yeah, from Long's Foodservice Distributing. They are our main distributor here in the southeast. They are up in Thomasville up I-85. That's where their main offices are. You should have their contact information in the files I sent over to you earlier."

"Is there anyone else you've made bend over backwards to stay associated with you?"

Lucas laughed. "Yeah, there's a few." he named a few others Greg could look into, but Lucas didn't think it would lead anywhere.

"Look, Lucas, thanks for the lead, and keep me up to date with what you find out. It looks as though you are handling your own private investigation, and that is fine. I will not tell you to stop what you are doing because you have already provided us with some key information and some nice leads. Just don't get in our way, is all I ask."

"Don't worry," Lucas said. "If I feel like I'm getting in over my head, I'll back off and let your people handle it. It's just I was the last person to see Trent alive, and I feel as though I owe it to the family to find his killer."

A pause. "I understand, son. Good luck. Don't bite off more than you can chew."

With that, the connection was broken, and the call was gone. Lucas exhaled slowly.

"What's up?" Kristen asked.

"They just confirmed Trent was killed sometime within twelve hours of me finding him in the parking lot, and it was by someone who was of average height with size seven shoes."

"So it could still be about anyone?"

He shrugged. "That's about it. They're canvassing the area now, to see if anyone heard or saw anything, but I suspect that with the location of the building, and as loud as Copperfield Boulevard can be, they'll come up with nothing."

"So what now?"

"Greg is going to look into the lead I gave him on the distributing company we screwed over yesterday and see if there's anything there. I doubt it. That tells me they have no actual suspects in this case. They've already talked to the family and eliminated them from their suspect list."

"So why are you looking into them if the police already discounted them?"

"I guess because that's about all I can do. I did not know Trent on a personal level well enough to know the people he associated with outside of the office. I don't think he had many friends, though. I just have this nagging suspicion there is something there. Brian proved that. He thinks there is something there as well. This family is so exclusive they do not even let me know much about their personal day-to-day dealings. I guess it's really for my piece of mind, and possibly to prove to them their company still needs me, even though the person I was a personal assistant to is dead."

"So, you're trying to protect your job, too?"

He nodded. "Yeah, and I feel like I should be doing *something*. I did not think I should just go home and do nothing today. I wouldn't have felt right."

She regarded him warily. "Okay. What now?"

"Let's go over to the Mahoney place."

CHAPTER FIFTEEN

Twenty minutes later, they pulled up to the gate at the foot of the estate. Lucas did not have the code for this gate, and again, he had to wait for someone inside to respond to the signal that there was someone at the gate.

In the places where the trees did not obscure the horizon, Lucas saw tall, dark clouds gathering. He wondered if that was a harbinger of things to come.

After a few seconds, Laura Ann's crackly voice came over the speaker. "Who is it?"

"It's me, Lucas," he called into the speaker.

"Oh, okay," she said. Without another word, the gate opened.

The atmosphere inside the mansion was much the same as it was earlier. Simon and Rachel, who he now looked at in a different light, still sat together on a loveseat in a den off from the main entrance. Simon spoke quietly to someone on his cell phone. Carly and Laura Ann were, for whatever reason, still cooking food. There were platters and trays covering the large, ovular dining room table. It was as though they were going to feed the entire town. There was almost enough food here to do that. Lucas thought it a shame to think most of the food was probably going to go to waste. It was the Mahoney women's way of dealing with Trent's death, and Quinn was making no move to stop them. It appeared as though his way of dealing with his only son's death was eating.

Brian was somewhere else in the house's labyrinth. Lucas asked Carly where Brian was, and she said she assumed he was in his room and then asked what the latest news was.

Lucas did not want to tell Carly too much yet. Nothing he told her at this point was concrete. He did not want her more stressed than she already was. He would tell her later about the gate and about Trent setting up the secret pass code. He told her he was going to try to speak with Simon. She nodded skeptically, then turned around and resumed chopping on some walnuts.

Lucas led Kristen back to the den, where Simon and Rachel sat in silence. Simon had ended his call during the time Lucas was in the kitchen. There was something eerie about the whole setup. The blinds on the large windows were drawn, leaving the room dark. The only light came from a lamp sitting on an end table beside their loveseat. They were not speaking. Rachel stroked his hair, and Simon had a blank expression on his face. Lucas had seen that look before, one of total shock.

Lucas and Kristen sat down on a couch across from them. Simon squinted at Kristen for a second before asking, "Don't I know you?"

She cleared her throat. "Yeah, my name is Kristen. Sully and I used to date. We've met once or twice."

Recognition dawned on Simon's face. If he knew Sully as well as Sully claimed, then Simon would know all about Sully and Kristen's relationship. "Ohhh," he drew out, "what are you doing here?"

She related the events from earlier, casting Lucas in a knight in shining armor manor. Lucas's cheeks flushed. Simon looked at him as she told her story, respect etched on his face.

"Lucas here is a good man," Simon commented to Kristen after she finished. Then, almost embarrassed, he said, gesturing at his girlfriend, "Oh, let me introduce you two to Rachel. Rachel, this is Lucas Caine. He worked for my father, and this is Kristen. I believe she went to J.M. Robinson and was a couple of years ahead of us."

"Nice to meet you," Rachel said with a lilting voice, making Lucas think this was what a fairy would sound like.

Simon and Rachel leaned back on the loveseat. It surprised Simon at first to find the ex-girlfriend of one of his best friends seated across from him, but he recovered quickly.

"Simon, do you mind if I ask you a few questions?" Lucas said.

"About what?"

"About you and your father."

Simon squirmed. Lucas had the feeling Simon did not want to get into it. Especially if he went over this line of questioning earlier with Greg Hanover.

Simon took a deep breath, exhaled, and said, "What do you want to know?"

"Well, I wanted to ask about your relationship with you father and see what you were doing last night."

Simon immediately went on the defensive, putting his hands up. "Whoa, I hope you're not suggesting I had anything to do with this."

"No, no, not at all. The police want my help in this investigation, and they thought my unique insight into your family could help bring out more than what they could. That's all. They just want to see if I can uncover any leads they could not."

"But I've already talked to Greg What's-His-Face. He knows I had nothing to do with this."

"Hey, calm down. I'm not saying that. All I'm doing is eliminating suspects for the police. They figure that once we can cross your family off the list, they can focus their attention outwards. A member of the immediate family commits most murders like this. I'm going to talk to everyone in this house, and you're just the first on the list."

He seemed placated by this. "Okay, go ahead."

"I guess the best place to start would be where you were last evening?"

"I was here," he responded without hesitation.

"What were you doing?"

"Studying."

Lucas took that in. He did not know how true that was, but he would not dig and have Simon close up on him. Lucas needed Simon to be with him for this next line of questions. "I've been told from a couple of different sources your relationship with your father was strained. How so?"

Simon put his face in his hands, then looked at the ceiling, and said as though he were wondering aloud, "I knew as soon as I heard the news this morning this was going to come up." He looked down from the ceiling into Lucas's eyes. "It mostly has to do with Rachel, but there's more than that."

"How did it start?"

Simon paused and took a drink of water from the end table beside him before continuing, "My parents force me to go to church every Sunday morning. I have never liked it. When I go, I act as if I am interested. But really, the only thing I think about while I am there is what I will do when church is finally over. Then, about a year and a half ago, the pastor of the church retired, and the church committee elected Rachel's father from another church to be the new pastor instead of promoting one deacon. Rachel's dad is a lot better than that boring Harris guy that used to be pastor. Rachel's dad was funny in his sermons. Her dad was the first pastor I can remember looking forward to hearing on Sunday's no matter what he was discussing. It was the first time in my life I ever looked forward to going to church. Not for the message, but for the entertainment factor."

He paused. Rachel frowned at Simon's characterization of her father being a funny holy man.

Simon continued, "When they first came to the church, grandma invited their family over for a welcome dinner. That was the first time I met Rachel. I had been out with many girls in school and around the area, but I met no one quite like Rachel." Rachel said nothing beside him, but she was visibly blushing. He continued to extol her virtues. "She was so different from the type of girl I was used to. Most girls back then just wanted to be with me because of my money. I never had to do too much to get girls to go out on dates with me. But when I met Rachel, she was not impressed with who I was."

"So, what was it about her you went for?" Kristen asked, speaking for the first time in a while. Rachel looked at her sharply, as though another girl asking about her personal life offended her. Lucas did not think bringing them together would create some sort of territorial dispute amongst the two beautiful women. He hoped the two girls' modest upbringing would keep that from happening.

"That was it," Simon continued. "That she was just so different. She played hard to get. I don't know if that's just the way she was, or if that was really what she was doing. She was shy that night at dinner. I tried to talk to her. I engaged her in small talk, but she did not say much. Up to that point, I've never had a girl be like that to me. I liked it.

"After that evening, I didn't think much about her." This drew a frown from Rachel. "She was just another girl. Then I started seeing her at church on Sundays. I thought there was something beyond outward appearances that attracted me to her. I don't know if it was her shyness or the way she acted towards me."

Lucas had the impression from the few brief minutes he had been around Rachel that she was indeed a closed person. He found it odd for a girl with her looks. Most women are reticent to one point or another. Some were open and forthcoming at one end of the spectrum, but Rachel seemed to be at the extreme opposite end of that spectrum. Just by looking at her, Lucas would have thought that, even if she were bashful, she would at least talk *some*. He did not have the impression she was by any means stuck-up. And Simon saying that he did not know if he liked her because of the way she looked was underplaying it a bit. Lucas did not think that Simon was lying. He thought Simon saying he 'thought' he liked her because of her looks would be like a man picking a Corvette over a beat-up old clunker because it looked like the better car.

"What changed?" Lucas asked.

Simon looked at the ceiling and collected his thoughts. He laughed to himself, and a mischievous grin appeared on his face. Rachel seemed to sense what he was going to say next and covered her mouth.

"Okay," Simon said, "few know this. Well, they know this, but they do not know what really happened."

"What do you mean?"

"Were you around when I had my tailbone broken?" Simon asked.

Lucas thought back. "No, but it seems like someone mentioned you had just recently done that when I moved here."

"Okay, a while before you came here, I broke my tailbone," he said and grimaced. "The story we came up with was I was helping grandmother put up some draperies at her home and I fell off of a ladder."

Kristen perked up. "I remember that. It made you look like a good grandson."

"But that's not what happened?" Lucas asked.

"Not even close," he responded. Rachel still had her hand over her mouth to keep Kristen and Lucas from seeing her laugh. Whatever Simon was going to say, Lucas had the impression it was going to be embarrassing, as he so often found the case when people break their tailbones. Those were usually some interesting stories.

He would not be disappointed here.

"One night, shortly after Rachel and I started seeing each other, Sully and I went down to the University area." The University area he spoke of was the campus for the University of North Carolina at Charlotte, or UNC Charlotte for short, in northeast Charlotte near the edge of Concord. "We were invited down there by some guys for a frat party. It was rainy, sopping wet, and it was late when this happened. I had been drinking almost nonstop the entire evening when we went home. As drunk as I was, I still don't know to this day why I did what I did."

"What did you do?"

Simon had put the perfect recipe in place for what was coming: college campus, frat house, young men, wet weather, and alcohol.

"It was the middle of the summer, and the dorm was not heavily housed. There were some guys living there, taking summer classes, but the fall semester was still a month from starting, so there was a large, wooden 'For Rent' sign posted by the sidewalk, near the main road. I told Sully I was going to take it down."

"You were going to 'take it down?" Lucas said, repeating Simon's phrasing. "Take it down how?"

Rachel could hardly control herself from laughing at this point.

Simon breathed in, "If I remember correctly, and that's a big 'if', when I made that statement to Sully I did not know how I was going to do it, but it seemed like it needed to be done."

"So that's how you broke your tailbone," Lucas surmised.

"Yes," Simon said, "I took off running down the wet sidewalk at full speed. I decided I was just going to tackle the damn thing. I made it about halfway there when I slipped, both feet came up off the ground, and I landed square on my ass."

Lucas pictured the entire scene in his head and decided that could have been the funniest thing he had ever seen in his life had he been there. Lucas saw some guys do some stupid things in his four years at WVU, but this was the stupidest thing he had ever heard.

"Honestly," Simon laughed, "I didn't feel any pain. It just felt funny. I didn't think anything of it. We somehow made it home, and I got in bed. The next morning, I could not get out of it. I woke up, writhing in pain, and I had to call for help to get up. Mom was nearby and heard my cries for help. She got me out of bed, and never asked me how I did it. She just ran me to the hospital."

"So you all concocted the 'helping to hang drapes' story to explain it away. And by so doing, made you look like a nice young man by helping his dear old grandmother do something domestic," Kristen said in disbelief.

"Bingo," he pointed a finger at her.

"Did this happen before the DUI?" Lucas asked.

That put a damper on his mood. The smile left Simon's face. "Yes," he answered.

"Did your mom and dad ever ask how you broke it?"

"No, never. Until the DUI, they let me do whatever I wanted to. With this, mom came up with the cover story as we were on our way to the hospital. No one would ever know what happened. There was no one else outside of the dorm that late on that stormy, mid-summer night to see what happened. But when the DUI happened, there was no way to cover that up. It was a matter of public record. Everyone in the town knew about it before the ink on my fingerprints was dry." He pointed at Lucas. "Your predecessor quit, literally, the next day. She was lazy and horrible at her job, anyway. She needed to go. At that point, my folks came down hard on my lifestyle, and the problems developed between me and dad. I was at the age where it was time to think about where I was going to go to college. I was trying hard to get into Duke which is where dad wanted me to go."

Simon described how Rachel became the person she was now. Rachel's father wanted her to go to the Piedmont Baptist College up in Winston-Salem. She, however, did not want to go there. She wanted to go to UNC Charlotte to be a nurse. Her father does not approve. He practically ordered her to fill out all the entrance forms for the Baptist college, and that was the only one she has been allowed to petition for admission. He apparently had some pull on the school board there, and it would have been a cinch to get Rachel admitted.

Then Rachel did what any other teenage girl does when she is mad at her parents: she rebelled and did so by pretending to be interested in the church's rebel, Simon. It was not so much the drinking that got it all started between Simon and his father. It was the going after the new pastor's daughter that upset his parents.

"Oh," Kristen and Lucas said in unison when Simon finished.

"*That* was the trigger," Lucas said.

"Exactly," Simon said, slamming his hand in frustration on the arm of the couch. "It all seems so frivolous and stupid now he's gone."

Simon put a hand over his eyes. A few tears streamed from between his fingers. Lucas waited, not rushing Simon. Rachel wrapped her arms around him.

After a bit, Simon picked up where he left off, telling about his relationships with his dad and Rachel. "An interesting thing happened along the way. She started talking to me, knowing I had an interest in her. She did this to get back at her dad. I don't think she ever planned to fall in love with me. I had never been in love until then, either."

Rachel concurred. "I'm not going to say much about my father, but it's just so oppressive at home that I couldn't take it anymore."

"Why did your father let you hang out with Simon to begin with?"

She blinked and then started to come out of her shell. "At first, he didn't. I lied to him. I told him I was going over to a new friend's house. That wasn't a lie. All my friends around here were new. But I misled him by leaving out. I was going over to Simon Mahoney's house."

"And going over to a guy's house was a no-no, right?" Lucas said.

She shook her head. "If he would have known, Armageddon may have come."

"Did he not question who you were hanging out with? I would figure an overprotective set of parents would do a background check on their golden child's prospective friends."

"I told him he was hanging out with a couple of new girls I met at school. My father is not as overprotective as you might think. He and my mom give me some leeway."

"So you all have been dating for a while, and he doesn't know about it yet?"

"Oh yeah, he knows all right. He found out a couple of months ago, and I thought he was going to kill me. He grounded me and almost refused to let me out of the house, even to go to school. The only times I could see Simon were when I was at school. Then one day, my parents sat down with me and said it was okay to see Simon."

"Like that?"

"Just like that."

"And you didn't question why?"

She stuck out her lower lip. "Nope. Never look a gift horse in the mouth."

Words of wisdom, Lucas thought, and then asked Simon, "Did you know anything about this?"

He shook his head. "It came as a total shock to me. I was depressed for a couple of weeks after they banned me from seeing her. Then suddenly, the world got better." Simon smiled for the first time since we sat down and squeezed Rachel's hand.

"How long ago was this?"

"A couple of weeks ago," Simon answered.

"Hmm. So, what were the problems with your dad? Were those problems ongoing?"

"My parents knew I was seeing Rachel for a while before her parents found out. I think they wanted to break us up before her parents found out. I think that was why dad was coming down so hard on me, and the rest of the family felt the same way. Dad was just their mouthpiece. So when Rachel's parents found out, and they kept her from seeing me, things got better between me and dad to a small degree. But, already, the pattern was in place where we fought over just about everything. Things I was doing in my life, school, etc. But really, since I could start seeing Rachel, with her parents' blessing, things really cooled off between the two of us. Dad and me, that is."

"I know you just recently got accepted into Duke University," Lucas said, not a question.

Simon smiled. "Yeah, he was really proud of that." He stopped, considered for a moment, then continued, "Now that I think about it, that was really the turning point between me and dad. He was so proud of me. The other things seemed trivial, and it was shortly after that happened Rachel's parents gave her permission to see me. Though they limited the number of times a week, we could do stuff together. I didn't care. They granted me permission to see her without having to sneak around. When the acceptance letter came in the mail, my grandparents took me and the rest of the family out to celebrate. It was one of the happiest days of my life."

"I remember that night," Lucas said, thinking back. "Your dad got a call. He gave me the news and left work early. I remember that because it was the only day since I started working for him, he left the building before me."

"He did?" Simon asked, surprised.

"Yeah, I assumed he was going to meet you all to celebrate."

This upset Simon. "I don't know what you're talking about. Dad was the only member of the family that didn't show up that night for our celebratory dinner. He said he had to stay late at the office that evening. He made it home before we did, but ultimately, he missed it. I was mad over that for a few days. I was mad until I got the news from Rachel. That happened shortly afterwards."

Rachel shifted uncomfortably beside Simon. When he asked her what was wrong, she hurriedly said, "Nothing. Got an itch."

Lucas wondered why Trent lied to everyone that evening. What was he hiding? Perhaps he was going to meet whoever it was he met last night. Whatever he did must not have taken too long. Simon said Trent was home by the time the family returned. Trent lied to Lucas and told him he was going to do one thing, then turned around and used work as an alibi to do something else. Interesting.

Lucas would call Greg and tell him this little tidbit of information. Then, maybe they could check his cell phone records and bank accounts to see if anything popped up from that evening. That could possibly tell who Trent was meeting if they found something in the phone records, and if something in the bank accounts showed up, then that would at least tell where he went that evening.

An uneasy silence settled over the room. Simon and Lucas were doing the same thing. Pondering why Simon's father lied. Lucas decided he had gotten all he needed from Simon for the time being, and he would leave him and Rachel alone.

"Simon, thanks for talking to me." Simon looked up and nodded silently. Lucas reached over and patted his knee. "Don't worry. We'll find out who did this to your father."

Simon closed his eyes as he shed tears again. "Thank you," he said through clenched teeth.

Lucas said nothing more and motioned for Kristen to get up. Rachel gazed at Lucas in a certain way he could not fathom. He gave her a concerned look, nodded, and led Kristen from the room. As Lucas left the room, he felt that Simon's tears were not forced. Even though they had their differences, Lucas could tell that Simon loved his father very much.

"What now?" Kristen asked in a low voice as Lucas led her through the massive house.

"We'll go find Brian and let him know I don't think his brother had anything to do with it."

"Are you going to tell him what his dad was doing?"

Lucas shook his head. "No, not for now, at least. Right now, Brian has this image of his father he is holding onto, and I don't want to do anything to spoil it."

"How do you know what he thinks of his father?"

Lucas stopped short. "I don't really know," he confessed. "I assume from the way he followed his dad's work that he loved him."

"What if that's not how he thinks?"

"What do you mean?" Lucas asked, stopping at the base of the staircase.

"Well, we all have this one image of Trent, the savvy restauranteur, philanthropist, churchgoer, pillar of the community, and all-around good guy. What if that is not the way he was to his kids? Or at least that's not how they think of him? What if he was hard on them, trying to get them to behave and at least act like good kids?"

"I can't imagine Trent treating them that way. At least, not without urging from the rest of the family."

"Look at the way Simon is rebelling at his age. Drinking and driving, and who knows what else. Why would a normal balanced teenager do that sort of thing?"

Lucas considered what she said. He looked at Kristen in a different light. He hoped she could help him, but this girl was a sharp as and insightful in raising points of view he had not thought about. Lucas guessed because he tried to portray this family in a certain way to the world and the community, he believed the myth they tried to fabricate. Lucas believed wholeheartedly what he shoveled to the media about the behind-the-scenes of one of the richest families in the state. Maybe that was why he was good at it, and they liked his work.

"All I'm saying," she continued, "is that Brian is not as emotionally stable as his brother. He has problems his family does not want you to know about."

"What do you mean?"

She took a deep breath. "Look, when I dated Sully, and he hung out with Simon, they would talk about Brian, and some things he does, or did."

"Like what?"

She cast her eyes about the foyer they were standing in. Simon and Rachel were in the room we just left off to our right, while Carly, Laura Ann, and Quinn were in the dining hall down a hallway to the left.

"I don't want to talk about it here. I don't want these people to know what I've at least heard about Brian."

Lucas saw the earnestness in her eyes. She knew something.

"Okay, later. Let's go talk to Brian."

Lucas wondered what she knew he did not. To tell the truth, he knew less about Brian than any other member of the Mahoney family. When he came on board, he came to know Trent, Quinn, Carly, and Laura Ann. They wanted to keep the children sheltered. However, they called Lucas in to resolve a volatile situation involving Simon getting the DUI at sixteen. Therefore, Lucas had to get to know Simon. However, they kept Brian away from Lucas. Lucas assumed it was because they did not want people prying into Brian's life like they will do to Simon after the DUI. Perhaps there was more to Brian than what anyone let on.

When Lucas woke up this morning, he thought of the Mahoney's as being about as perfect a family as one could imagine coming from the background from which they hailed. In a ten-hour stretch now, he learned Simon was into more stuff than Lucas would have imagined, and Simon's father was doing something he wanted no one to know about, and now Lucas found out Brian might be potentially crazy. It made Lucas wonder what other surprises he might find before the day was out.

He led Kristen up the spiral staircase to the upper level and walked down the long hallway to Brian's bedroom. He rapped on the door and heard a faint, "Come in."

Lucas opened the door to a darkened bedroom. The smell of incense wafted around the room. Brian sat on the floor playing a violent video game.

He turned, "Oh, hey Lucas. I thought it was going to be mom or grandma coming to offer me another muffin or something."

Lucas sat on the bed behind Brian. Kristen remained standing in one corner of the room, content to let Lucas talk with Brian by himself. Maybe she thought just one person was enough for now to speak with Brian in his state of mind. As though she did not want Brian to think he they were ganging up on him. The last thing they needed was for Brian to shut himself off.

Lucas also considered the possibility. In light of what Kristen said at the bottom of the stairs, she could be afraid of Brian.

He continued to play the video game, not even stopping to pause it. Monsters exploded in bloody puffs left and right.

Lucas put his hand on Brian's shoulder. "Brian, I just talked with your brother. I don't think he had anything to do with your dad's death."

Brian paused the game and clinched his eyes shut. "Thanks, Lucas. I knew you could help."

"Can I ask you a few questions?"

Brian thrust his bottom lip out. "Yeah, if you think it will help."

Lucas almost said there was no way of knowing that until the conversation ended. "That is, if you think you're up to it."

"Yeah, let's get this over with."

That was an odd thing to say, Lucas thought. Get *what* over with? "Do you remember when your brother got that acceptance letter to Duke?"

"Yeah."

"Do you remember your family going out that night to celebrate?"

"Yeah, some celebration that was. We celebrated Simon's ability to crash through life doing whatever the hell he wants to, and great things still happen to him. Yeah, I remember that night. I so did not want to be there for that."

"Well, your dad wasn't there . . ."

"Yeah, I know. That wasn't surprising, though. He often worked late, coming home some nights just in time to say 'goodnight.'"

"How often did he come home that late?"

Brian thought for a second. "One or two nights a week."

Somewhere another puzzle piece locked in Lucas's mind. Yes, they worked long hours at the office, but rarely *that* late. Whatever Trent was doing, he was doing it more often than Lucas thought.

"Do you know where he was that night?"

"What do you mean? I thought he was supposed to be at the office."

"No, he actually left early that evening, I thought, to go out with you all."

This troubled Brian. He dropped the video game controller and rubbed his temples with both hands. "It was after that," Brian said. "Dad started to stay at work later than he used to."

"How long did that last?"

"For the three months between then and now."

"And you said he did this a couple of times a week?"

"Yeah," he said.

Hmm, so whatever Trent was doing started at least three months ago. Lucas wondered if he could track back and figure out what Trent was up to, or at least point the police in that direction. Then by doing so, getting out of this matter before he found out more than what he wanted to about the Mahoney family.

This was happening anyway.

"I did not know your dad was doing that. Do you have any idea who he was seeing or what he was doing?"

Brian shut his eyes and shook his head. "Seeing someone? I have no idea."

Lucas's phone vibrated silently in his pocket. He took it out, glanced at the caller ID.

"Excuse me," Lucas said, "It's Carter. I need to take this."

Brian nodded like a king granting his blessing.

He flipped open the phone. "What's up Carter?"

"Man, I think you need to get over here," Carter said.

"Why?"

"The cat's out of the bag. The news media just pulled up in droves. There's two or three news vans parked out front, and some other reporters shaking the gate, wanting to talk to someone."

"Dammit. Who told them?" Kristen and Brian looked at Lucas expectantly. He held the phone to his chest. "The media just showed up at the office. I'm sure that they'll be here next."

Brian moaned and rubbed his hand across his face. "And so it starts."

Lucas stood up with Kristen close behind. "Look, Brian, I appreciate you taking the time to answer my questions. I know this is a rough day for everyone, but it's something that has to be done if we're to find out who killed your dad."

Brian nodded. "I understand. Thank you for all you're doing to help. Am I good?"

"Yeah, I don't think you had anything to do with this. I need to get over to the office and do my job. First, I am going to tell your mom and grandparents what to expect. Thanks again for the time."

They left Brian's room quietly. Monsters were exploding on the screen again before they even closed the door. They walked to the top of the stairway, and Lucas stopped Kristen before descending the staircase.

She looked at him in surprise. "What is it?"

Lucas sighed. "You know, I think I've found out all I can about Trent from the boys. I uncovered Trent's secret life. I think it's time I dropped the matter, give the police all I know, and go and take care of the job I was hired for, which was the media relations part."

Lucas had hit a wall. He sifted through the dirt enough to find out how the killer got into and out the gate. He found out where the killer hid while he or she lied in wait. He knew it sounded cold, but that is more than the Mahoney family hired him to do. Murder investigation, though he may have read and seen a lot on how to do it was not his specialty. For this matter, he needed to step back and let the proper authorities handle the rest. He could speak more with the rest of the family. Carly, Laura Ann, and Quinn, but he did not know if that would be beneficial for anyone.

They stared at each other. They both knew this was the point they needed to separate. She was a godsend and an immense help. He did not want to take her home. The light was dim where they stood. Kristen's hair hung over her eyes. She reached up and tucked the loose strands behind her ear.

She let out a deep breath and said coyly, "Okay, only if you promise to see me again."

Lucas smiled from ear to ear. "I think that can be arranged."

She returned the smile, leaned forward, and briefly touched her lips to his. Lucas felt a sensation run down his spine that he had not felt in a long time. Then, as suddenly as it started, she leaned away from him, closed her eyes, and licked her lips.

He stood speechless, unable to recover from the jolt to his spine.

She grabbed his hand. "Come on, you need to go do your job."

They held hands as they slowly descended the circular staircase. Lucas felt as though he were escorting some beautiful princess down a grand staircase on her way to a glamorous ball.

They made it to the bottom and went into the dark dining room, where Carly, Laura Ann, and Quinn were sitting at the table. Food was piled around them. They sipped from steaming mugs of coffee. It seemed as though the only light on in the entire mansion was from the lamp beside Simon and Rachel. With clouds covering the sky outside the windows, the natural light in the house grew dimmer. It seemed to Lucas as though the Mahoney's were choosing to add to the depressive state of the day by keeping all the rooms dark. He could not do that and not blow his own head off.

They directed wan smiles at Kristen and Lucas. Thankfully, they did not ask any questions about the held hands. Without preamble, Lucas explained the situation with the media to them.

"They're at the office now," he explained. "If they don't get some answers soon, then I'm sure this will be their next stop. I'm surprised they're not here already."

Laura Ann put a hand to her mouth. "I wonder who let it leak."

Lucas shook his head. "I don't know. I don't think that's important right now. What is important is we control this mess and try to keep them out of our hair for a few hours or days while the police have time to figure this out. This is a time for you to mourn and not be bothered by those people. That's one thing you hired me to do."

"I agree Lucas," Quinn said, then added, "You go do what you need to do at the office, and if they come here, I'll handle them."

"Yes, sir."

Kristen and Lucas made their goodbyes and left the mansion.

CHAPTER SIXTEEN

When they returned to the car, Kristen asked, "What do you think that was about with Trent lying to everybody?"

"I assume he was meeting whoever it was that night and did not want anyone to know. When we're done dealing with the media, I'll have Carter go through the videotapes of the day Simon talked about. Look at days other than those where the mystery entries appeared at the gate and see if Trent screwed up somewhere down the line."

"Is there anything I can do to help?" she asked. Her eyes shined with an earnestness so intense that he hated to tell her the next thing.

"Kristen, this situation is about to heat up, and I don't think you need to be around while all of this is happening. I think it's time to take you home."

She nodded. "I was afraid you were going to say that. What about us?"

He thought about their kiss from a few minutes ago, and he wished there would be more of them. He did not know if it happened because she genuinely liked him, or if the emotions of the day caused her to kiss him. He hoped it was the former rather than the latter.

"I don't know," he told her.

"Lucas, I would really like to see you again," she said, reaching for his hand. "You're so different from all the men I've been around. There's something about you I really like I can't put my finger on."

Lucas smiled and squeezed her hand. "And I would definitely love to see you again. But right now, I need to take you home."

She squeezed it back. "I know."

She gave him the directions to her home. She did not live far from Lucas. In fact, she lived in the same neighborhood where he lived.

Thank God for small favors.

He pulled through the gate, got back on Neisler. The puffy clouds Lucas spied earlier were now darkening and creeping overhead. Lucas smelled the fresh scent of rain.

They drove back down Neisler Street towards Old Salisbury-Concord Road. Lucas turned his headlights on because the ambient light was not good enough for him to see where he was going.

Kristen and Lucas were quiet as they proceeded at a slow pace. He was not driving fast. He was in no hurry to meet the media circus that surely waited at the office, and he was certainly in no hurry to take Kristen home. Without a word, she reached over and grabbed his right hand. Their eyes met, and they smiled at each other. They were content to stay lost in their thoughts.

Lucas knew he had to set aside his junior investigation. Maybe tomorrow, if he could get the media aspect under control, he would resume what he was doing. He did not know now what his next step would be, but he figured he had the rest of this evening and the night to figure out what that step may be. He could give Kristen a call to see if she wanted to continue to help. Unless she had to go back to work tomorrow if she felt up to it.

Lucas crossed his fingers she would.

He reached the end of Neisler, and turned left onto the Old Salisbury-Concord Road, headed back towards Concord. The road was empty of other motorists. They quickly came to the small area on their right where cars parked so people could car-pool to and from work. There was only one car parked there. They passed by and saw it was a black sedan. In fact, Lucas thought it looked like the getaway car from this afternoon's attempted mugging. The interior of the car was dark, but he could discern two people sitting in the front seat as they passed. Kristen gave the car no notice.

Almost as soon as they drove by, the dark car's headlights came on and pulled onto the road behind Lucas's car.

Lucas rounded a couple of twists and turns going down a small slope, before the road leveled off into a small straightaway. The black car gained on them around those curves, and now it was less than twenty feet from his rear bumper.

A sense of dread crept through Lucas.

Lucas turned to ask Kristen if she recognized the car behind them when, from behind, he heard a loud pop followed instantaneously by the passenger-side mirror being blown away from the side of his car.

Lucas let out a curse. Kristen looked at him in fear and then turned to look through the rear glass. Lucas punched the gas to gain some distance between them and the tailing car. He was thankful his TC had some power under the hood. He looked in the rearview mirror to see someone wearing dark clothes hanging out of the passenger-side window in the dark sedan, aiming at the back of Lucas's car with a gun in his hand.

"Get down and hold on!" he yelled at Kristen as he reached over and shoved the back of her head towards her lap.

Another explosion boomed from behind, followed immediately by the car's rear glass shattering.

A direct hit!

Kristen screamed.

The impact made him take his foot off the gas, enough so that the driver of the other car could not slow down in time to keep from crashing into Lucas's rear end. Kristen yelled again. The rear two wheels of Lucas's car came off the ground briefly before disengaging from the front bumper of the other car and landing on the pavement with a loud WHAM!

The dark car dropped back a dozen feet as Lucas fought to regain control. He stepped on the gas as they reached the end of the straight stretch and came to an incline curving slightly up to the left. Lucas hoped this would give him a few seconds to put some distance between him and the maniac behind them. Going around the turn would make it hard for the gunman behind to get an accurate aim, and if they tried to rear end Lucas and Kristen, they could go off the road and into one of the trees lining the road ten feet from its edge.

They passed a sign warning that the speed limit dropped to thirty-five miles per hour. They entered Concord's city limits.

Lucas risked another look in the rearview mirror. The kid with the gun leaned out of the window again, ready to take another shot. When he got a better look at him, he knew exactly who it was. It was the kid with the black Mohawk who drove the getaway car from earlier in the day. Only this time, he was the passenger. It did not surprise Lucas to see Sully was the person behind the wheel of the chasing vehicle.

This confirmed Lucas's suspicions about Sully and his crime ring.

Why were these guys shooting at them? Lucas would think about it later. Now, the only thing on Lucas's mind was getting away from the pursuing car. Lucas knew that up ahead, there was a stoplight where Old Salisbury-Concord crossed over busy Branchview. Before that, on the right at the top of the hill, was Burrage road on the right. Lucas wondered whether he should turn onto Burrage, turn onto Branchview at the light, or speed through the stoplight, and go straight into downtown Concord. Turning onto Burrage would take them into a residential area, and he did not want stray gunfire possibly going through the nicer homes down that street. If he turned onto Branchview, it was likely that he could be caught in traffic during this time of day, and then it would be over.

The decision was made for Lucas when he crested the hill and saw the stoplight at Branchview turned green, inviting Lucas to head downtown. There was no one between him and the light, and he was already going well over seventy before coming down the hill. Sully's car lost some distance as they went up the hill and around its subtle curves to where they were now.

"Hold on!" Lucas warned Kristen and put the gas pedal to the floor, accelerating towards the intersection. He desperately hoped the light would stay green until he crossed through.

Even with the back glass shattered, and who knew what type of damage was done to his rear end, the car responded beautifully. Lucas accelerated, getting close to one hundred miles per hour as he neared the intersection.

He knew he was taking a colossal risk. If the light turned red, and the traffic flowed through the intersection going in both directions, they would be dead for sure going at this speed. If he had to stop, they would be dead anyway. Lucas knew these guys would not think twice about shooting at them while they sat an intersection.

He gripped both hands tightly around the steering wheel as they barreled towards the intersection with the chasing car closing the gap. Apparently, Sully made some modifications under the hood. They had no trouble closing the gap, even though Lucas was now traveling over a hundred miles an hour.

They were fifty feet from the intersection when the light turned yellow. Kristen could not take her eyes off the intersection. Lucas could see her life passing before her eyes. His life passed in front of his eyes as well. He knew they'd be cutting it close.

The intersection was still clear as they reached it. They sped through the light, as it turned red at about the white line where they were normally supposed to stop. They yelled as they crossed safely through the intersection in the blink of an eye onto the small bridge on the other side. When the light turned green, the cars that were stopped crept forward in an attempt to cross the intersection. They were a good twenty feet in front of Sully's car as it barreled through the intersection.

A small Toyota came from the right, trying to turn to go downtown. Lucas missed it, but Sully was not so fortunate. The black car crashed into the Toyota's front end, sending it spinning round and round over the embankment, into the small stream below. The black car inexplicably seemed almost unharmed. After pausing for a second, Sully continued after Lucas.

Lucas knew it would be suicide to continue at their current speed, headed towards downtown. He let off the gas, relieved the car behind had its forward motion halted long enough for them to gain an appreciable lead, allowing Lucas to shed some speed safely.

"Are you alright?" he asked his passenger.

"I think I broke my wrist on the door when they rear-ended us," she said through gritted teeth.

Lucas looked over to see her wrist hanging at an odd angle as she grasped it to her body. He felt so guilty for getting her into this mess.

"I'm sorry," he said.

They went through one stoplight where the light stayed green and came to the stoplight where Church Street crossed over Cabarrus Avenue. The light was red. Lucas had to make another choice. Did he take the chance of running the light, hoping no one was coming, or make a right turn?

Lucas glanced to his left, looking down at the upcoming street. There was, in fact, no one coming. He heard another shot ring out from behind as he screeched his tires rounding the curve. Thankfully, the shooter fired an errant shot, blasting into a brick wall across the street. Lucas was discouraged to see

Sully and the shooter had regained their wits enough to keep shooting.

Lucas accelerated on Church Street, going well over the speed limit. He knew they were near the police station, but the turn he made took them farther away from it. The police patrolled this area well, and Lucas hoped one of them would see what was happening. He also hoped someone from the Branchview intersection had the frame of mind to call 911 and tell them about a high-speed chase entering downtown.

Lucas could not count on the police to save the day. He had to figure a way out of this. He knew he would probably have to sacrifice his beloved car in the process. But these guys would not stop until he and Kristen were dead. Lucas knew it, they knew it, and he could see Kristen knew it as well, as she braced herself against the dashboard with her good hand.

Church Street led them through a commercial part of town. There were two and three-story office buildings lining both sides of the street and a few scattered one story, run-down mini malls in between. The black car closed the gap tremendously. The gunman leaned out the window again.

Apparently, they wanted Lucas and Kristen so badly they did not care about anyone else. They were close enough now to where the gunman would have no problem shooting out more windows, or worse yet, their tires. If that happened, they would have been dead for sure.

Lucas knew it was now or never.

"Get your head down!" he yelled. Without protest, she put her head in her lap.

Traveling at high speed, he simultaneously slammed on the brakes and pulled up on his parking brake, causing the engine and tires to squeal in protest. Not having time to react, Sully's car slammed into Lucas's rear end. The guy that was leaning out of the passenger side of the car did not have time to brace himself and was ejected and thrown face-first at high-speed into the wall of a bricked building, killing him instantly as he splattered like a bug against a windshield.

This time, instead of lifting the rear tires off the ground when Sully's car hit, the car hit Lucas's rear end side at an odd angle. Lucas's car spun around to where, after a brief separation of the two cars, Sully's car slammed again into the driver's side of Lucas's car, pushing his car with sparks flying at still a high speed up the road.

Life moved in slow motion. In the streetlight, Lucas got an excellent view of Sully in the other car. Lucas saw a mixture of surprise and anger reflected in Sully's face.

Lucas knew that if he did not do something soon, Sully's momentum would cause Lucas's car to flip over and probably kill both of them.

Lucas was determined not to let that happen. He winked at Sully through the cracked glass, and a puzzled expression crossed the younger man's face.

Lucas released the brake pedal and parking brake at the same time as he slammed on the gas. Lucas's car shot forward, away from the grip of Sully's car. It spun around at a one-hundred-and-eighty-degree angle as Sully's car flew clear.

As soon as Lucas was out of the other car's grip, he hit his brakes again.

With Sully's car no longer having to push Lucas's, Lucas watched as Sully's car went out of control at the sudden disappearance of the weight of Lucas's car. The dark car careened through the parking lot of a small shopping center, barely missing a black post holding a lighted sign for a furniture store.

Hitting that sign may have been the better move for Sully in trying to save his own life. His car then hit a long cement block directly in front of the building, giving the car some air underneath it as it crashed headlong through the plate-glass window of the furniture store, and went into and destroyed the inside of the store before the car came to rest.

Lucas heard sirens in the distance. Help would come soon.

Lucas took inventory of any injuries he had. He felt blood seeping down his scalp from where he cut it somewhere. Other than that, he felt no damage.

Kristen did not fare so well. Her right arm clutched her chest, her good arm held onto her leg. Lucas could see blood coming through her right pants leg, and there was a gash on the right side of her head where, he assumed, she hit her head against the window as Sully crashed into their side.

He checked quickly to see if she would be okay for a few moments. She nodded her head.

He tried to open the door on his side, where Sully had crashed into it. At first, it did not budge, but Lucas figured the car was totaled anyway and kicked the door open. The door came off its hinges and fell with a crash to the pavement.

Lucas's car came to a rest in the middle of Church Street. Cars stopped on either side of them. A few of the first people that stopped had climbed from their cars. One guy yelled to ask

Lucas if anyone was injured. Lucas yelled for the guy to call an ambulance, even though he counted at least three other people talking animatedly on their cell phones.

Lucas limped across the street to the parking lot where Sully's car came to rest. The entire front of the one-story brick building had collapsed. Glass covered the ground where the plate-glass window shattered. Pages torn from old, used books fluttered through the air like snow in some computer-based realm. Smoke poured from the black car's engine.

Lucas picked his way through the debris and tried to make his way to the driver's side door. He had to push a tall, wooden bookshelf out of the way before he could look through the shattered glass on the driver's side window. Sully's head lolled to one side. The steering wheel had broken his nose, and blood flowed freely from there, and a large gash on his forehead. His car looked like one of those old muscle cars like you would see on the old cop show Chips or something.

Lucas's first thought was Sully was dead. Lucas leaned in to see if he could feel a pulse when he heard Sully groan.

"Sully! Sully!" Lucas yelled.

Sully shook his head to clear the cobwebs. He then looked at Lucas out of the one eye not covered in blood.

"You should have minded your business," Sully said in a raspy voice.

"What do you mean?"

"You should have left me and Simon alone," he said with some effort.

When Lucas saw at the beginning of the chase that Sully was the driver of the car, Lucas thought Sully was trying to kill him to keep him from telling the police about his little crime ring. Lucas thought that was overkill. What did Simon have to do with it? Was he somehow a part of all that, too?

"Did Simon have something to do with this?"

Sully shook his head. Blood fell in drops from his nose as he did. "No, he just said you were messing around in his business, and I felt if you were digging around both of us, you would find something no one would want you to know. So, it was best just to get rid of you."

Lucas furrowed his brow. Sully's voice was weakening, and Lucas did not know how much longer he had until Sully either passed out from the loss of blood or died.

What was so secret that would call for Lucas's death if he knew about it?

"Did Simon tell you to do this?" Lucas practically screamed.

Another shake, more blood falling in drops. "No, man. Simon would never tell me to do such a thing. He's done some stuff for me to get my ass out of trouble before, and I thought it was high time to return the favor."

By killing him? Lucas wanted to ask, but Sully was fading quickly. Instead, he asked, "What is Simon hiding?"

Another shake, this time accompanied by a sad smile. "No bro, it's not him that's hiding something. Check out his lady friend."

"What about his lady friend?"

Sully would never answer that question.

He gasped one last bloody time before his head rolled onto his shoulder.

There would be no more answers. Sully had expired from this world.

CHAPTER SEVENTEEN

A few minutes later, Lucas was in a police car, headed quickly to the Mahoney office complex. Two ambulances answered the call only to find they needed only one of them. The coroner would take Sully and his friend to a mortuary.

Kristen was in an ambulance on her way to the emergency room. She said she would have someone call her aunt, and she knew Lucas had work to do. He promised to come see her as soon as he was able. He felt as bad as he ever had in his entire life when he saw the ambulance doors close on Kristen and zoom off to the nearby hospital.

Guilt overwhelmed Lucas.

Rain splattered on the pavement around Lucas. He barely noticed it.

The paramedics checked Lucas out and recommended he accompany Kristen to the hospital for further tests. He declined and told them he needed to get to his office as soon as he could. At first, they did not want to, but after he told them the situation, and he promised to give the police a full statement of what happened as soon as he could, one officer agreed to rush him to the office.

Lucas knew it sounded self-centered, but he thought about the suit he ruined this morning with Trent's blood. Now, the extra sports jacket he kept in his office looked like something a war refugee would wear. This was not too far from the truth. He needed to go home before he ruined any more of his work clothes.

When the police arrived on the scene, Lucas explained who he was, and why there was a car sitting in the middle of a used furniture store. When he mentioned it was Sully Cavanaugh sitting at the wheel of the crashed car, the officer's eyes went wide. Lucas was sure the police officer knew about Trent's murder from earlier, and Lucas could see them thinking about two of the biggest names in Concord being murdered in the same day.

It really disheartened Lucas to think about what sort of person Sully was when he implicated his best friend's girlfriend with his dying words. Sully could have had everything. Instead, he chose the wrong course in life and ended up dead at an early age. Where Sully went wrong could stem from many things. The money he had could have spoiled him, his choice of friends, or even his broken family life. Lucas did not know. Even though Sully tried to kill him, he could not help but feel sorry for the guy now that he was dead.

When Lucas told the police there was another person riding with Sully, they asked Lucas where the guy was. Lucas pointed at the building a couple of hundred yards down the street and told them to look there. One officer jogged to that spot. He looked around on the ground for a few seconds before he looked at the side of the building. Thankfully, from the angle where the one cop and Lucas were standing, they could not see the thug's body.

The investigating officer immediately threw up on the sidewalk when he saw the body plastered against the side of the building.

Lucas needed to figure out how all this factored in. What did he do to cause Sully to try and kill him and Kristen? Sully thought Lucas had something on him about the string of robberies in the area. Lucas had nothing substantial, but he could have probably fed the police enough to line Sully up in their crosshairs. Was that enough to warrant an attempt on his life? What if it wasn't Lucas that Sully was after? What if Sully decided he would never have Kristen, jealousy took over, and decided if she would not be with him, she would not be with anyone?

Then, the thought struck Lucas. How did Sully know where Lucas was going to be? There was no way Sully was sitting in that car, at that spot, at that time randomly. Sully somehow knew where Lucas would be and when he would pass by. Had Lucas been in Sully's shoes, he would have gone where he figured Lucas Caine would most likely to be. The Mahoney office. Everyone in Concord knew where Mahoney's offices were.

The only plausible conclusion Lucas could come to was Simon tipped Sully off. Simon was the only person who knew Sully that well. Sully admitted he spoke to Simon about Lucas's sniffing around. That conversation had to occur sometime between when Kristen and Lucas met Sully, to their arrival at the Mahoney Estate. Why would Simon tip Sully off? Sully said Simon knew nothing about this. The evidence would suggest he did, and Sully was trying to cover for his friend. Did Simon want Lucas dead too, or just wanted to scare him into leaving the matter alone? Lucas hoped it was the latter rather than the former. No matter what the answer was, the fact was Simon lied to Lucas about something. That or Simon did not tell the full story.

Sully said Lucas should look at Rachel. What did Sully's last request have to do with anything? Until now, Lucas considered Rachel to be nothing more than a peripheral character in the whole matter. What possible reason would she have to kill Trent? That did not make any sense.

For the immediate future, however, Lucas needed to figure out how he was going to mollify the media when he arrived back at the office. Lucas had never done anything like this before. By the time he arrived after Simon's DWI, the media storm was mostly over, and all Lucas had to do was character repair. This was something Lucas never thought he would have to do.

Few things in Lucas's life made his legs shake, but this was one of those situations. Of course, his knees could still be shaking from the high-speed chase.

It was a short distance from the scene where the car chase ended on Church Street back to the Mahoney office complex. They crossed through the light where Copperfield crossed over Branchview. There were several news vans parked on the sidewalk in front of the iron gates at the office.

The rain fell steadily now, and it amused Lucas to see some of the gathered news media were unprepared, not having umbrellas or raincoats.

The officer driving the police cruiser did nothing to allay Lucas's nervousness. He said, "Whoa, that's quite a mess you have on your hands here. How do you want to go about this?"

Lucas craned his neck to see how the reporters were gathered. They did not seem to be trying to beat down the iron bars of the gate at least. In the two streetlights on either side of the gate, a few people waited patiently outside the gate, trying to peer through the bars to see what was going on inside the compound. There was a reporter and her cameraman set up, recording a report off to one side.

"Can you turn on your flashers and pull up to the security box? I'll give you the code so we can get in."

"What if someone tries to get in behind us?"

"The gate will close behind us as soon as we pull through. But I guess if someone gets through, you could jump out and wave your gun around and start screaming at them."

The officer laughed. "No, I can't do that. I'd love to, though. But I'll run the flashers. " He reached over, flipped a switch on the dash, and the lights and siren came on. It was the first time Lucas ever rode in a police car with the lights and siren on. He hoped it would be the last.

When the siren whooped, the journalists milling around the gate drew to attention. As they pulled to the gate, the people standing before it moved to the side. The cameraman filming the reporter turned his camera's attention on the police car.

Lucas gave the officer directions on how to open the gate. When they came to a stop beside the box, the reporters started shouting questions. Lucas stared straight ahead, not meeting anyone's gaze. He would answer those questions in a few moments.

The gate opened, they pulled through, and the gate closed. To Lucas's surprise, no one tried to follow.

"Pull up to the building," Lucas instructed.

Technicians were still active in and around the crime scene despite the rain. Some took measurements of who knew what, while a photographer snapped photos of the ground twenty feet away from where Lucas found Trent's body that morning. To Lucas, that seemed like forever ago. He had to give the crime scene techs credit. They were thorough.

The officer pulled to a stop near the black and yellow tape strewn between two lampposts. Lucas thanked the officer and told him he could get out the same way he came in and climbed from the car.

Carter must have seen Lucas arrive. He was waiting by the main entrance when Lucas got out of the car and stepped over to meet him. He seemed jubilant.

"Man, you wouldn't believe what I found," Carter said.

"What's that?"

"What is today?" Carter asked.

"It's Wednesday. Why?"

He led Lucas inside the building, away from earshot of the investigators.

"After you left," Carter said, "I went back and reviewed the surveillance tapes, and I found every Tuesday the same thing happened."

"What's that?"

"You and Trent are usually the last ones out of the building every evening, correct?" Lucas nodded. "Okay, every Tuesday after you leave, the tapes go blank."

"And not any other day?"

Carter shook his head. "Nope. I went back and checked every day, going back a month, and I found every Tuesday the same thing happened. Once I figured that out, I just checked out the tapes from every Tuesday until I could figure out when all of it started."

"And?" Lucas said, urging him to continue.

"It goes back almost three months. Every Tuesday."

Lucas knitted his eyebrows together. Something in the back of his mind tugged at him, but for now, he could not grasp what it was. "And before three months ago, this did not happen?"

Carter shook his head again. "Not on Tuesday's. I only had time to check out the Tuesday thing. It's possible if I reviewed all the tapes from every day, I might find out something else."

They let the unspoken question dangle: what was Trent up to?

"Another thing I had time to check on was the gate logs."

"And?"

"I found the same thing we saw earlier. Your number would show up exiting the gate, followed a few minutes later by the mystery person using the code to get into the gate. Then later, it would show up again as exiting, followed shortly thereafter by Trent."

"What was the time between the person coming in and then leaving?"

"Usually about an hour."

"Just enough time to . . . well, you know."

If Trent were meeting some shady business contact, Lucas assumed something like that would take only a few minutes to do as they exchanged money or information. What Lucas did not understand was that it was happening every Tuesday. Trent had to be having an affair and meeting some mistress. They set up a regular time for some nookie. He would send the mystery woman a text message or a quick phone call, letting her know when he would be alone, and then she would come in. But why have a secret pass code? Couldn't Trent just let the girl have his personal gate code? Why the subterfuge? Did Trent get off on the cloak-and-dagger stuff?

The security gate was set up a year ago. At that time, Trent had Cody install the backdoor into the system. Was he having affairs at that time? Or, did he have the backdoor put in place on the chance he ever would? After knowing Trent in the time Lucas did, he couldn't see Trent cheating on his wife, but then again, Lucas found in his lifetime some people have a dark private life you would never guess at. It appeared Trent had a darker side to him, and until now, had done a good job of keeping it covered.

There were many questions Lucas was afraid would never be answered.

"Good job," Lucas said, impressed with Carter's thoroughness. But then again, that was why they hired Carter. Attention to detail.

"What happened to you?" Carter asked, just noticing Lucas looked like a refugee.

Lucas forgot he hadn't told Carter about Sully and his friend trying to kill Kristen and him. He quickly related the story. Carter seemed impressed and disturbed at the same time.

Carter asked Lucas about what Sully said at the end. "So, he told you to look at Simon's girlfriend?"

Lucas shrugged. The thing tugged at the back of his brain again, and wished for Lucas to figure it out, but he could not figure out what that thing was.

"Yeah," Lucas answered, "he told me to check out Simon's lady friend. Why? I don't know. I just got done talking to Simon and Rachel, and as far as I could tell, they weren't hiding anything."

"Simon wasn't hiding anything, or Rachel wasn't hiding anything?"

Lucas had not thought to ask Rachel questions. He needed to call Greg, take care of the press outside of the gate, and go try to talk to Rachel in private. He also needed to check on Kristen as soon as he could to make sure she was okay.

"What are you going to tell the press?" Carter asked, reminding Lucas of what lurked outside.

Lucas took a deep breath. "You're right. I really want to go back and talk to Rachel about this right away, but I need to do this first."

Lucas walked back out the door and down the parking lot to the gate. Immediately, the people gathered started shouting questions. Lucas held up his hands and refused to answer questions until the gathered mob was silent.

When they were, Lucas cleared his throat and said, "Ladies and gentlemen, my name is Lucas Caine, and I am the official spokesperson for the Mahoney family. Some of you I have spoken with before, and for those who know me, they know I am forthcoming and honest.

"With that being said, it is a tragic day for the Mahoney family, the city of Concord, the state of North Carolina, and the world. At around 7 o'clock yesterday evening, Trent Mahoney was murdered on these grounds. The police are investigating, and they have a few leads they are pursuing. I am sure the murderer will be brought to justice shortly.

"Now," he continued, "I hope you will be decent people, and let the Mahoney family mourn their loss in peace. Respect their privacy. I promise there will be statements and interviews will be given in the upcoming weeks. The Mahoney family is a private family, but when asked, they have always been more than happy to make public appearances and let some of you into their lives. This will continue in the future, but for now, I ask you to let them alone.

"That is all I have for now, but I do plan on holding press conferences regularly to update you on the situation in the search for Trent Mahoney's killer. I am not going to answer any questions at this time. Thank you and have a good evening."

Lucas waved, turned, and walked away. Immediately, a flood of questions forever left unanswered flooded forth from the mob of reporters.

He walked back to the building. The crime scene people had stopped to watch what he was doing at the gate with the press, maybe hoping they would find themselves on camera on the evening news. They watched him return inside the building before they went back to whatever it was they were doing.

Carter greeted Lucas with a steaming cup of coffee as he walked through the door. "Thanks," he said.

"How did it go?"

"About as well as I could have hoped for. I just told them we had a few suspects, the police were being aggressive in their search, and we hoped to find the killer soon."

"And that satisfied them?"

"No, not entirely. But how could I? I told them I would update them regularly, and to leave the Mahoney's alone for the time being so they could mourn their loss."

"Do you think they will?"

Lucas shook his head. "Absolutely not, but what can I do?"

"Nothing."

"Exactly." Lucas took a deep breath, pulled out his cell phone, and called Greg.

"Are you okay?" Greg asked as soon as he answered. "I just got the word."

"Yeah. I've got a few scratches on me, but I'll be okay."

"God, it's been a hell of a day for you."

"It's been a hell of a day for everyone," Lucas said, closing his eyes.

"So that was Sully Cavanaugh that tried to kill you? Why?"

Lucas told Greg about his suspicions about Sully being behind the crime wave. And how he used that against Sully to get some information out of him about Simon.

"That could be it."

"Yeah, but what bothers me is how he knew where I was going be. Greg, Sully was waiting for me."

"How would he know you would go by there? If he were smart, he could have waited around your office. He would have known you would go by there at some point."

"That's what I thought too. No, I think someone helped him."

"How?"

"Actually, I think Simon helped to set this up. He either wanted me killed or he wanted to scare me into leaving everything alone."

"Simon Mahoney? What's he got to do with this?"

Lucas explained how Simon and Sully were best friends, and how it was Sully that got Simon started down the wrong path.

"But why would Simon conspire with Sully to get rid of you? Wouldn't that be against his best interests? I mean, you're trying to help his family."

"I agree. I don't think Simon has anything to do with Sully's stupid crime wave, but I get the impression Simon is covering something up as well, and maybe they conspired to protect both of their interests. Before I talked with Simon earlier, he was sitting beside his girlfriend, having a hushed conversation on his cell phone with someone, and he hung up almost as soon as I walked into the room."

"Did you hear anything he said?"

"No."

"Do you think the girl knows what they were talking about?"

"I don't see how she couldn't."

"Do you think I need to go over and talk to Simon again? Ask him some probing questions about his personal life?"

Lucas closed his eyes. This was what they hired Lucas to keep from happening: letting the public know too much about the Mahoney's personal lives. He thought again of Trent's dead eyes. Here, however, it might lead the police in the right direction to find his killer. What if Simon was lying about where he was last night and murdered his father? It was the first time the thought had crossed Lucas's mind, and it scared him.

There lies the question, what would be Simon's motive for murdering his father?

"Greg," Lucas answered, "I am afraid Simon, and possibly Sully, could've had something to do with it. The murder. I don't have any solid reasons. It's just a feeling I've gotten in the past few hours. It would explain a lot. It would certainly help explain why Sully was chasing me. If Simon thought I was getting too close to the truth, then it would be in his best interests to silence me."

"Do you know what you're suggesting?" Greg asked.

Lucas took a deep breath. "I know. It's scary."

"Why would Simon kill his own father?"

"I don't know."

"Alright," Greg said, "let me off here. I'll go over there and see what I can find out. Hopefully, it will be a dead end, but I've got to explore all the possibilities here."

"I know, and that's what scares me."

"Me too," Greg said, breaking the connection.

Lucas put the phone back in his pocket and glanced at Carter. He heard Lucas's entire side of the conversation.

"Wow," Carter said.

"Yeah, wow," Lucas agreed.

One of the crime-scene techs came through the door. He was about average height, had a shaved head, and looked tired. Lucas could not blame him. He felt the same way.

He jerked a thumb over his shoulder and said, "There's someone outside the gate wanting to speak with you."

"Yeah, there are lots of people out there that would love to talk to me."

"No, this guy says he's the Mahoney's personal attorney."

Lucas wondered what the attorney wanted. He thanked the tech and returned to the gate, where he was bombarded with a swarm of questions. In between all of them, Lucas saw a tall, older man, dressed in a nice, tailored suit, standing underneath a golf umbrella, waving at Lucas.

He walked to the gate through the rain and said forcefully, "I'm going to open the gate. I want all of you except this gentleman right here," Lucas said, pointing at the nattily attired man, "to step back and do not come inside. If anyone does, I will have you arrested for trespassing and have a restraining order put on you so you cannot come within one hundred yards of this gate or any member of the Mahoney family. Is that understood?"

The reporters acquiesced and backed up a few paces while Lucas punched the code into the gate. The iron bars of the gate opened, the attorney stepped through, and the gates closed again with no incident.

Lucas had met this man on one other occasion. His name was J. Warner Worthington. He had an attorney's name. Lucas wondered if people with a birth name such as J. Warner Worthington were more inclined to be attorneys than, say, go into retail. Lucas figured so.

Lucas took J. Warner's proffered hand, as the questions from the reporters resumed.

J. Warner started to say something, but Lucas told him to hold it until they were back in the friendly confines of the office.

They walked back up the lot and into the building, where Lucas introduced the attorney to Carter.

"Pleased to meet you, Mr. Worthington," Carter said.

"And I you," he said with an Ivy League accent. "Please, call me Jay. " He turned and regarded Lucas in his torn suit and scratches on his face. "You look like hell," he observed.

"Thanks," Lucas deadpanned. "Just trying to go for a tougher image."

"It's a madhouse out there. I had to park down the street and walk up to the gate."

"Yeah, I think the word is starting to spread about Trent, and more people have gathered in the twenty minutes I've been here."

Jay gave a wry smile. "I just found out myself a while ago. I understand you're doing your own personal investigation into Trent's death."

Word traveled fast, Lucas thought. "That's correct."

"Well, I'll just get right to it. I just thought you should know that Carly and Trent bought out a life insurance policy about six months ago."

"Really? For how much?"

"As you can imagine, it's a multi-million-dollar policy."

"Did they have a pre-nup?"

"Yes, they did. It said, basically if they ever got divorced for any reason, Carly would not get a dime."

"Even if Trent committed adultery?"

"Even adultery. If you want to put it that way, it was a pre-nup, which would allow Trent to cheat on Carly as much as he wanted to and get away with it. Or vice versa. It was their way of protecting the family's business and money. I think when they were married years ago, the idea of adultery never crossed either of their minds. Carly knew the trade-offs going in, but she was more than willing to sign it even if it meant no matter how miserable it got, she would have to remain married to Trent if she wanted to have any money."

Lucas wondered if somewhere along the way, Trent remembered his pre-nup agreement allowed him to cheat on Carly without penalty. Did this factor in to anything? Lucas catalogued it in his head along with the rest of the jumbled mess he learned about the family today he did not want to know.

The details of an agreement signed twenty years ago did not concern Lucas as much at the current moment as the one Carly and Trent signed mere months ago. "Did the life insurance policy cover Carly in case something accidental should befall Trent? Such as a bullet to the head?" Lucas asked.

"Yes, accidental death was one thing the policy covered. Even if she breaks all ties with the Mahoney's, Carly stands to be rich for the rest of her life."

"Have you mentioned all of this to the police? To Greg Hanover specifically?"

"Yes, I have. But they didn't take much credence in this being a motive."

"I would call that a big motive for murder."

Jay raised his eyebrows. "That's not for me to say."

"Do you know why they took out the life insurance policy?"

The attorney thought about it for a moment. Lucas knew if Jay said too much, he could violate the attorney-client privilege.

"They did not really give me a reason. All I know is a couple of months ago, they wanted my help in selecting a life insurance policy. I looked over a few. Made some suggestions and they picked one. It was all a simple process."

Lucas knew either Jay could not tell or would not tell him more, so he said, "Thank you for your time."

"You'll receive my bill in the mail," he smiled weakly at what he hoped was a joke and shook Lucas and Carter's hands before leaving. Lucas had one officer escort him out of the gate and back to his car.

"Wow," Carter said again.

Lucas agreed, pulled out his cell, and hit the redial button.

"What's up?" Greg answered midway through the first ring.

"Umm, the Mahoney's attorney just left here."

A pause on the other end of the line. "What did he have to say?"

"He came here to tell me about their life insurance policy. He said he mentioned it to the police, but whoever he spoke to didn't take much credence in it."

"Why not?"

"I don't know. It sounds like a motive to me. Why don't you ask your associate?"

"Did the attorney say who he spoke to?"

"No, he just said the police."

"Give me the attorney's number. I'll call him up and look into this." Lucas gave Greg the number. "Look Lucas, this is good work you're doing. You gave me not one, but two leads in the last hour. I talked to both Carly and Simon earlier and dismissed them. But you come along and somehow find cracks in their stories. Did you ever think of being an investigator?"

Lucas laughed. "No, but right now, my future doesn't look too clear."

"Well, thanks for all of your help. I'm going to go over to the Mahoney's right now and talk to them. I might go see if I can't get a search warrant from a judge before I go to see if I can dig anything up."

"Did you look into the supply company I told you about earlier?"

"Yeah, I called them up and talked to the company president. It saddened them to lose Mahoney's as a client, but they are working out an enormous deal with one of the huge sub shop chains. Their CEO did not seem hurt by the news of Mahoney's and their company parting ways, and I don't figure they would have any reason to kill Trent. Actually, I got the impression they were mad at Trent's assistant more because he screwed up their deal."

Lucas knew Greg was speaking of him. He smiled inwardly. It was borderline unethical what he did to the distribution company.

"Anything else?" Greg asked.

Lucas almost mentioned Sully's dying words about Rachel, but he did not. He wanted to check into that himself. "No Greg. That's all for now. I'm probably going to head back over to the Mahoney estate in a few minutes."

"I'll probably see you there. Alright, thanks again."

Carter heard Lucas's end of the conversation. He filled Carter in on the details that came from Greg's end.

"So, the supply company didn't pan out?"

Lucas shook his head. "No, I thought that was a long shot, anyway."

"Do you think someone from the family could have done this?"

"I'd like to hope not, but I've found out more about them today than I wanted to know. I think Simon had some frustrations with Trent, but not enough so to kill him. As far as Carly goes, Trent had made her rich beyond her wildest dreams. Why kill the goose that laid the golden egg? I don't know how much love was in their marriage, but I know Carly at least cared about him."

"What about Brian or Trent's parents?"

Lucas shrugged. "There was absolutely no reason for Trent's parents to kill him. I simply cannot imagine that scenario ever playing out. Besides, this was too well planned out for either Laura Ann or Quinn to do, anyway. They barely know how to turn on a computer, much less hack their way through a security gate. As far as Brian goes, Brian loved him so much. Trent was his hero. I know Trent pressed Brian to excel in school as much as he could, but not to the point Brian would kill him over it. I think Brian lived his entire life to do nothing but please his father."

"I feel the same way," Carter said.

"Yeah, the only thing I can think of is why did Sully want me to look at Rachel? I can't imagine how she figures into this."

"Let's go ask her."

Lucas raised an eyebrow. "I guess you've been here for a while. Let me call Carly to warn her about what she needs to expect, and then we'll head out."

Carter nodded. Lucas dialed Carly.

She answered quickly. "Lucas, what's going on over there?"

He explained to her how he handled the press. She seemed to like what he did. Then he told her about the visit from her attorney. She was not prepared for that. "Carly, Greg Hanover knows about the life insurance policy. He's going to be on his way over there to ask you another round of questions."

"Why? I've already told him everything I know." She was missing the obvious.

"Well, Carly, think about it," Lucas said matter-of-factly. "You two take out a multi-million-dollar life insurance policy a few months before your husband gets murdered. Now you stand to come out with more money than a person could ever need. They know about your stormy relationship with Laura Ann, and the possibility you want to get away from her."

"But why would I kill my husband just to get away from her? I mean, it's not as if we fight as much as we used to when we first got married. Laura Ann and I can be civil with each other when we need to be nowadays. I think that is due to the boys."

Lucas conceded the point. It did not seem likely Carly would kill her husband because of a long-time dispute. He did not want to bring up this next possibility to her, but it was a real one and one likely to come up in the police's investigation into Trent's death. "Carly, I don't know how to ask this easily. But what if Trent was cheating on you?"

"He wasn't," she said without hesitation.

He did not want to get into an argument with her, but this was a very real scenario he needed to confront. He told her about how Trent had a backdoor put into the gate system with a secret password. She was stunned, but took it in stride.

"Trent would never cheat on me."

"But what if he was Carly? Think about it. He had a secret way into and out of the office's security gate. Carter figured out he had been having these mystery meetings on the same day of the week over the past several months. What if the police found out Trent had been having a woman or women over on those days after everyone was out of the building? Then they piece that together with your having a way out of the family? Doesn't that seem like a likely motive for murder?"

"Oh, no."

"There is a real likelihood they could piece something like this together and put you in their crosshairs. I would call your attorney and have him come when the police are there this time to give you the best advice."

"I'll do that Lucas." She paused. "You don't think I did this do you?"

He hesitated maybe a split second longer than he should have. "No Carly, I don't think you could do this to your husband."

"Thank you."

"You need to be prepared to face some tough questions. If you thought it was hard to face when Simon had too much to drink when he took a drive, then this is going to be light years beyond that."

"I know. I'm ready."

She did not sound confident. Lucas could not blame her.

They were quiet for a minute while he thought of how to phrase his next question. "Carly, you said there were nights where your husband stayed late at work."

"Yes."

"Were these just random nights, or were there regular nights where this seemed to happen every week?" He hoped they were random nights. He had a sick feeling in his stomach she was going to tell him Tuesday nights.

"Hmm," she thought about it, "not really. There was usually one or two nights a week where he came home later than others."

Lucas breathed a sigh of relief.

Unfortunately, she continued, "But it seems like it was mostly on Tuesdays. Why?"

The feeling in Lucas's stomach suddenly felt like a bowling ball. He did not want to fathom the implications of what she just said. All the pieces of the puzzle floating around in the back of his head just came together to form something so sickening he just wanted to quit and let them figure it out for themselves. Earlier, he could see how some pieces fit together but discounted the scenario as being too outrageous.

When he did not answer her right away, Carly repeated, "Why Lucas?"

He took a deep breath before answering. Carter studied him, wondering where he was going with this line of thought. "I don't know, Carly. I'm just trying to put some pieces together, trying to discern a pattern, and make some sense of what happened."

"Okay." She sounded disappointed. The fact was, Lucas did not want to tell her what he thought he knew.

"Are Quinn and Laura Ann still over there?" he asked.

"Yeah, they're in the other room."

"Are they still holding up, okay?"

"I guess so."

"Prepare them for another round of questioning. What about the boys? Are they still there?"

He hoped so. If Simon was still there, then Rachel would surely be there. Lucas needed to think of a way to get Rachel and Simon separated long enough for him to talk to her. He really wanted to get Simon alone in a room and beat the living crap out of him, but that would not get him anything but arrested. What he needed to do was to speak with Rachel. Lucas had the feeling she was the key to unlocking this entire puzzle.

"Yeah, they're in the same places they were when you left."

"Okay, good. Carter and I are going to be there in a few minutes. Tell the boys not to go anywhere."

This caught her off guard. "Why?"

Lucas did not want to explain. He still had said nothing about Sully trying to kill him and Sully's resulting death and a clue. He wanted to keep that last part close to his chest for the time being. If Carly gave Simon any clue what happened, then Lucas suspected Simon would turn evasive, and run. Lucas did not want that to happen. He tried to hide his anger at Simon from Carly. If she got a whiff that he wanted to get Simon one-on-one, she might turn protective, and not let Lucas back into the estate.

"Because the police may have further questions for them as well."

"Okay, I'll hold them here. I don't think they're likely to be heading out this late, anyway. Not today. Not with this rain. But if they do, I'll keep them from going anywhere."

"Thank you, Carly. We'll be there in about ten minutes," Lucas said, and hung up the phone.

Carter looked at him warily. "You're not going to mention anything about your high-speed chase?"

Lucas shook his head. "I just want for her to concentrate on her story. If she gets to thinking her son had something to do with this, then she might try to make it look like she killed Trent just to protect Simon."

"I agree. What if she had something to do with it? You painted a nice motive for her to kill Trent. What if she were fed up enough with the whole situation to blow his brains out? I mean, your story has some legs if you think about it."

"I know. That's what scares me. We will let Hanover investigate that aspect. I'm going to go and maybe rough Simon up and get some answers."

"You really think Simon was in on Sully trying to chase you down?"

"At this point, I can't see how he wasn't. That is the only way I can see Sully waiting for me where he was and when he was."

"What were you getting at when you asked about the nights Trent stayed out late?"

Lucas looked at Carter and shook his head. Thankfully, he did not hear Carly's side of the conversation. "I really don't want to say anything until I know more."

"Why not?" Carter studied Lucas for a second. "Wait, you know, don't you?"

"Know what?" Lucas played dumb.

"You know what Trent was up to, don't you?"

"Maybe," Lucas conceded, "but I really don't want to talk about it until I know more."

"That bad, huh?"

"Worse."

"Aww crap," Carter said, rubbed his chin, and nodded. "What do you want me to do, boss?"

Lucas got an idea and smiled for the first time in a while.

CHAPTER EIGHTEEN

Carter and Lucas walked into the Mahoney's foyer less than fifteen minutes later. The two were soaking wet but did not care. Lucas especially cared less, considering what he had been through today. The rain helped to wash away some of the dirt from his clothes. Greg Hanover had yet to arrive. They had a few minutes to get ready for what was to come.

Carly greeted Lucas with a discrete kiss on the cheek. She shared a brief handshake with Carter. Lucas had the impression from watching her around Carter in the past that she was afraid of him. Lucas could see why. Carter is not someone a person would want to meet in a dark alley late at night.

Carter flashed a wicked smile. "How do you do, ma'am?"

She smiled weakly and did not offer a reply. Instead, she studied Lucas more closely. She wrinkled her brow. "Lucas, what happened to you?"

Lucas told her he had gotten into a car accident after he left there earlier.

She took this in and covered her mouth with her hand. She was empathetic. "Oh dear, with all that's happened today, you had a car accident?"

"Yeah, my car was totaled."

"But you loved that car."

Lucas raised his eyebrows. What could he say?

"Was there anybody else involved? Is the girl you were with okay?" she asked.

"She broke her wrist and possibly her leg. She's in the hospital right now."

"Why don't you get out of here and go be with her?"

Lucas shook his head. "She told me before the ambulance left with her to see this thing through. So that's what I'm going to do."

"If you say so," she said.

"Is everyone still here?" Lucas said.

"Yes, Trent's parents are still sitting quietly in the dining room. The last time I checked, Brian was still ensconced in his room, and Simon and Rachel were still on the same couch."

Lucas thought about a circumstance where he would spend hours on end sitting in the same rooms as this family had done today. He could not think of one, but then again, he had never had to go through anything like this before, and hopefully, never would.

"Did you tell the boys the police were coming?"

"Yeah, they both didn't seem to care. Like I said, I think they're not going anywhere for the rest of the evening."

"Okay, the police should be here any moment. Did you tell Quinn and Laura Ann they were coming back?"

"Yeah, they had the same reaction as the boys did. It has been the longest day of our lives. We are all where we want it to be over. This is just another step towards that end."

Seeing Trent's lifeless eyes now seemed like ages ago to Lucas, when it had been about twelve or thirteen hours since he found the body. This had been one of the longest days of his life, too. First, he found Trent's body, and then prevented Kristen from being mugged. He investigated how someone could get themselves inside of the Mahoney's security fence. He took a nice, long walk with Kristen at Frank Liske Park and then went to eat. He and Kristen met Sully at a Starbucks, trying to get an edge in on Simon. He had been to the Mahoney Estate several times today. The last time he left the estate, Sully nearly killed him. Lucas spoke with the press gathered outside of the office gate, then with the Mahoney's attorney. Now, he was back at the Estate, and it was not even eight o'clock.

"I'm going to go talk with Quinn and get them updated and prepared," Lucas told Carly.

The three of them walked into the dark dining room, where Quinn and Laura Ann were sipping steaming mugs of coffee. They brightened as Lucas, Carly, and Carter entered. Heavy rain poured on the other side of the large bay window.

Quinn stood up, still looking dapper in his tailored suit. He said, "Carly has been keeping us updated with what is going on. I just want to say you two are doing a great job today."

"Thank you, sir," Carter and Lucas said in unison.

"It makes me proud knowing our corporation goes out and hires the best people to work for us. You two are a shining example of that," he said as though he was the emcee at an awards banquet, and he was awarding Carter and Lucas the highest award.

"Thank you," they repeated.

"Now," he said, clapping his hands together, "tell us what the latest is."

They stepped over to the table where Laura Ann sat and took a seat. It felt good to Lucas to sit down and relax for a few moments. He felt sore from the day's travails. They quickly updated the family members on the latest events since he left there a few hours ago. It was the first time they heard about Sully.

Laura Ann shook her head. "I knew that Cavanaugh boy was nothing but trouble." She looked at Carly and shook her head. "You should have never let Simon be friends with him."

Carly shot her an icy glare. It appears the events of the day did nothing to deplete their hatred for each other. The more things changed, the more they remained the same, or so the saying went.

Lucas sighed and rubbed a hand over his face. They saw his angst, and that shut the two up.

Lucas felt angry. He went through hell today, and the last thing he wanted right now was for these two women to argue about someone now dead. He wanted this to end. The thought occurred to him he could just leave, go home, and go to bed. He was not obligated to figure out who killed Trent. He should leave that stuff to the cops. They did not hire Lucas for this. He was frustrated, and he thought it was time to stop being Mr. Nice Guy.

"Look," he said, "you two save the arguing for another time. Right now, I am here to figure out who killed Trent. If you two are going to be arguing constantly, then I'm going home."

That surprised them. He did not think they ever heard him use that tone before. He thought he spoke for Quinn. He sat on the other side of the table with a bemused smile on his face.

"I'm sorry, Lucas," Laura Ann said.

Carly murmured what Lucas thought was an apology.

He stared at the two of them for a bit, as though they were two misbehaving children, before continuing. "Now, I'm going to tell you all something I did not tell the police yet. I could get in trouble for withholding this."

He looked around. They nodded quietly for him to continue. Carter knew what was coming and sat back to gauge the reaction.

"What is it Lucas?" Quinn asked.

"Okay, after Sully crashed through the wall of the bookstore, I checked to make sure Kristen was okay. Seeing she was, I went to see if Sully was still alive."

"Was he?" Laura Ann asked with a hand over her mouth.

"I picked my way through the wreckage. Thankfully, the place was not open, and no one was in the store. When I got to Sully's car, I thought he was dead. Then he moaned and opened his eyes. He told me I should not have messed with his business. Then, because he was best friends with Simon, I asked if Simon had something to do with him trying to kill me." Lucas looked around to gauge their reaction. Unfortunately, he did not see the surprise etched on their faces. He continued, "He said no, Simon did not." They all exhaled in unison. They sucked in their releases at Lucas's next statement. "He said I needed to look at Rachel. He said she was hiding something."

He could tell from their reaction they knew what it was Rachel was hiding.

Carter saw this. He looked at Lucas. "They know something."

Lucas kept his eyes on the three lofty members of the Mahoney family seated before him like a triumvirate of elders looking down in judgment. They looked uncomfortable to be in this room right now.

He could not blame them. He would not take it easy.

"What is it?" he asked in as icy a manner as he could muster.

They looked back and forth between themselves, afraid to speak.

Finally, Quinn spoke first. "Rachel is pregnant."

Somehow, Lucas was not surprised. "What does that have to do with anything?"

"Nothing, I hope," Quinn said.

"But why would Sully tell me to give her a closer look? Where was she last night?"

"Tuesdays are when she volunteers at the homeless shelter," Laura Ann said, and then added, "Such a sweet girl."

"Really?"

"Yeah, she's been doing that every Tuesday since her family moved here sometime last year. It's something her parents encouraged her to do," Carly explained.

That was nice of her, Lucas thought, but there was that tug in the back of his mind again, telling him he was missing something. The pieces began to form a picture, but it was still blurry. He needed some clarification. "Tell us about Rachel's pregnancy," he said.

"There's not much to tell," Carly said. "She came out and announced last week she was two months pregnant."

"Simon's?"

She knitted her brow, offended at the accusation. "Of course, so."

Their thoughts on Rachel's pregnancy were no business of Carter and Lucas's and he did not explore that. Instead, he returned to his first question. "So, what does this have to do with Trent's death?"

Carly and Laura Ann shrugged their shoulders while Quinn said, "I have no idea."

"Again, why would Sully tell me to look at Rachel if she had nothing to do with it?" Lucas was going to pound the table if he had to repeat that question again.

Laura Ann answered, "Lucas, I don't think we know the answer to that. Perhaps you're asking the wrong people."

Lucas looked at Carter, who cocked an eyebrow at Lucas. "You're right," Carter said. "Maybe we should go to the source and ask her."

"I would say that's a good idea, Lucas," Quinn said, "But I don't know what she would have to do with any of this."

"I just don't want to leave any stone unturned," Lucas explained. "Look, I know it's hard, but these are questions that need to be asked, and leads that need to be resolved before we find out who killed Trent. I am going to go talk to Rachel and Simon one last time before I bow out of all of this. After that, I'm done."

"I think that's a good idea, Lucas," Carly said. "You've got to be getting tired. You and Carter have done a wonderful job today, and I think you have had a crazier day than anyone here has. I wouldn't blame you a bit if you just went on home."

The intercom in the kitchen chirped. Lucas recognized that sound as the gate signal. Quinn excused himself and went to answer the call. He walked back a few moments later and announced, "I think everyone arrived at simultaneously. Greg Hanover and Jay both pulled up to the gate at the same time. I'm going to go meet them at the door." Jay, of course, being the Mahoney's attorney Lucas had met a short time ago.

Trent, Carter, and Lucas walked down the long hallway connecting the dining room to the foyer. Trent opened the door to find J. Warner and Greg Hanover conversing. They came in and shook hands all around. Lucas told them he would wait in another room while they talked in the dining room.

When Lucas and Carter were alone, Lucas said, "Ready to do this?"

"Yeah, man. It's just sad these are a couple of kids we're about to play hardball with."

"Simon has been playing grown-up for a while now. He is apparently about to be a father, so let's see if he can act like one. As far as Rachel goes, I wouldn't feel too sorry for her either."

"Why not?"

"I think she's the whole reason this mess happened."

Carter's mouth dropped open. "You know better than I do."

They walked through the other wing of the house and into the sitting room where Simon and Rachel had sat all day. When they walked in, nothing had changed. It still baffled Lucas how someone could sit like that in the same room for this length of time.

Lucas had to maintain his composure. Here sitting was a boy, a boy no less, who two hours ago tried to orchestrate he and Kristen's deaths.

"What's up?" Simon asked, as they entered the room. He looked surprised to see Lucas again so soon. Or was he surprised to see Lucas again, period? Simon made no remarks about Lucas' disheveled look with his dirty clothes and fresh cuts on his face since Simon had seen him last.

Lucas and Carter walked over and sat on the couch across from Simon and Rachel. Seeing Simon so calm, so relaxed, made Lucas angry. He had to keep himself in check.

"Simon, I've got some more bad news for you," Lucas said.

Lucas thought by his being there gave Simon a hint of what the bad news was before Lucas opened his mouth. He kept his fingers crossed Simon had not heard about Sully's death. If Carly, Laura Ann, and Quinn had not heard the news, Lucas figured Simon would not know either.

"Simon," Lucas said, "the police have Sully in custody. They arrested him and the guy with him for trying to kill me and Kristen."

Simon's mouth opened and closed a few times before he could come up with something to say. He raised an eyebrow, and his voice cracked when he spoke. "Why would he try to kill you?"

Lucas looked at Carter. He had the same expression on his face Lucas had. One of 'this guy is a terrible actor.' Any doubts Lucas had in his mind about Simon had nothing to do with what happened to him and Kristen died.

Simon knew all about it.

Carter said, "We don't know Simon. Why don't you tell us?"

"I don't know what you're talking about," Simon protested. He eyed Lucas's cuts and bruises for the first time and asked what happened. He gave Simon a rundown of the entire car chase, leaving out the parts where both Sully and his counterpart died. They lied and told Simon that Sully and his friend were both in custody and agreed to tell the police everything they knew in return for a lesser charge.

Rachel wore a shocked expression. She looked as though she wanted to be anywhere else on this planet right now other than in this room.

"Rachel, leave the room for a few minutes while we have a deep discussion with your boyfriend here."

Thankful for the reprieve, she stared wide-eyed at everyone, got up, and left the room. She was a quiet girl. That was for sure. Figuring out what she had to do with this whole mess had to wait for a later time. Right now, it was time to figure out what Simon had to do with what happened to Lucas.

When she was gone, Simon repeated, "Guys, I don't know what the hell you're talking about. I don't know what Sully said to you or the police, but I guarantee he is lying. He's a pathological liar."

"That may be the case, Simon," Carter said, "but the fact is, he said you had your fingerprints all over what happened to Lucas." Then, according to the script, he turned to Lucas. "I think you should leave and let me talk to Simon. I'm afraid you have too much in this for you to stay unbiased."

Lucas shook his head in frustration, playing by the script, and retorted, "C'mon Carter, I want to hear it from his damn mouth that he didn't try to kill me."

Carter put a large hand on Lucas's shoulder. "Lucas, bud, you need to leave me and Simon alone for a few minutes. Just go see what's going on in the kitchen or something."

"Fine." Lucas stood up and pointed a finger at Simon. "You'd better tell the truth!"

Lucas stormed out of the room, hoping he was a better actor than Simon.

It had all gone according to the little scenario he and Carter concocted in Carter's Jeep on the way over here. The plan was to separate Rachel and Simon so Lucas could talk to her alone. The fear was she would not speak freely with Simon in the room.

Now Lucas had to find her.

CHAPTER NINETEEN

Finding Rachel was easy. She stood by the front door, chewing nervously on a fingernail, staring at the floor. She looked worried, and rightfully so. Her boyfriend could be in a lot of trouble. Lucas supposed she felt as though she were trapped in a difficult situation. In one room were Carter and her boyfriend. In the other room were Simon's parents and grandparents.

She made the choice to be alone.

Somehow, Lucas could not blame her.

She looked up when he walked in. "Oh, Lucas," she said, "Just figured you would be with Simon for a while." She took the half-chewed fingernail out of her mouth. "Lucas, I'm so sorry about what happened to you."

"Why should you feel sorry?" Lucas regretted asking as soon as it left his mouth. The question came out rude, and he did not want her to think he was angry with her.

She sighed, collapsed into an expensively upholstered chair sitting beside the front entrance, and put her hands over her face. "Lucas, I'm no idiot and you're no idiot. We both know it probably wasn't hard for you to believe Sully when he accused Simon of collaborating with him. It would make sense to me if someone were lying in wait for you to pass by on a two-lane country road on the off chance you would pass by waiting to hunt you down. "

Rachel did not know what Sully had told Lucas yet. Somehow, she knew what Sully would say.

"It seemed like a setup," he said. "He said he was just trying to scare me away from getting to close to this investigation. But Rachel, why would he do that if Simon had nothing to do with his father's death?"

She shrugged her shoulders. "Earlier this afternoon, Sully called Simon and told him you two met. He said if he did not tell you what you needed to know, you would tell the police Sully was behind the crime wave. Simon knows his father's death looks bad upon him. He could see how it could all come back and implicate him in his father's death."

"So, he tried to kill me to keep the police from looking too closely at him? Rachel, that doesn't make sense."

"I know it doesn't. But you must keep in mind these are two rich, spoiled kids. They have their entire lives planned out for them. I think they would do anything to keep any hindrance to that from happening. But Sully was supposed to scare you, which is all I heard Simon say."

Lucas loomed over her, looking down at her as she spoke. "But Rachel, he didn't try to scare me. He and his friend were shooting at us, trying to run us off the road. I don't know what your definition of 'scaring' is, but to me, that sounds an awful lot like attempted murder."

She shook her head. "It wasn't supposed to happen like that."

"You realize, of course, by your knowing what they tried and not saying anything, they could charge you with being an accomplice?"

Her mouth opened. She started to cry. "I didn't think about that."

Lucas reached down and patted her on the back. "Rachel, there's something you need to know."

"What?" she croaked.

"Sully and whoever his friend was are dead."

"What? I thought you said they were arrested."

"We said that so Simon would believe it was going to be his word against Sully's." She gasped at the lie. "I talked to Sully just before he passed away. I told the truth when I said he said he and Simon wanted to keep me away from whatever was going on here. When I asked him what that was, he told me to look at you."

She blinked twice in rapid succession. "Did he say why?"

"No, those were his last words before he died."

"Oh, my," she said.

"Yeah, now Rachel, why would he tell me to look at you? What do *you* have to do with all of this?"

She shook her head. "I don't know."

"You don't know? Carly told me you're pregnant. Does that have anything to do with it?" She looked at Lucas in astonishment. "Yeah, they told me. So, I'll ask again, does this have anything to do with Trent's death?"

She sighed and looked at the ceiling. "Because after Simon's parents found out I was pregnant, they went ballistic. His father did, in particular. They couldn't be in the same room together without getting into an argument."

"Were these arguments about you?"

"Sometimes," she said. "It disappointed his parents in my being pregnant, don't get me wrong, but my being pregnant magnified the other problems Simon has."

"Such as?"

"Well, he still likes to party. I dislike him to do that. I do not come around when he is drinking or doing drugs. I *won't* come around when he's doing that."

"Drugs?"

"Yeah, Sully has him into a bit of everything. I hated it, and I hated Sully. I know it's not a Christian thing to say, but I don't care if he is dead. He was the worst influence on Simon."

"So why put up with it?"

She looked around at the elaborate surroundings as though that was all the answer she needed.

It was.

"Good point," Lucas said.

She laughed as best she could. She was still crying, though not as much as before. "But since I told him I was pregnant, he got better."

"What do you mean?"

She wiped a tear streaming down her cheek. "Since I told him, he all but stopped doing things with Sully. He really has matured a lot since he found out."

"I would hope so," Lucas said. "God, Rachel, what do your parents think about all of this?"

"They're furious about the whole thing, but after the initial shock, they seem to have mellowed out. They thought this might happen when I started dating Simon, but even though my parents are all high and religious and everything, they still are like everyone else. They crave money. Now they that know I am going to have Simon Mahoney's child, that if nothing else, me and my child are going to be well taken care of."

Lucas did not envy her. They were quiet for a few moments while he gave her time to think.

"So, Rachel, do you think Simon could have been mad enough at his father to kill him?"

She let out an exhausted breath. "Before Monday, I would have said 'no,' they were just fighting."

"What happened Monday?"

"Trent told Simon he was thinking about canceling Simon's trust fund."

CHAPTER TWENTY

Lucas was stunned. There was the motive to end all motives. It would be as good as a smoking gun in the eyes of the police. If Lucas were to receive a gift of two million dollars two months from now, as Simon was set to get, and was told he would not receive it because of his behavior, Lucas did not know what he would do. Short of a loved one dying, having two million dollars ripped from him would be one of the worst things he could ever think of hearing.

If Simon was as mixed up with Sully as Lucas now believed he was, Simon could be into the same things as Sully. The drugs and possibly the guns popped into Lucas's mind first. If the police thought Simon had a gun, or he could get his hands on one, and were told he would not receive his trust fund, then he would be prime suspect number one.

The thing still nagging at Lucas was, what did this have to do with Rachel? Was she blowing him a smokescreen?

He squeezed his eyes shut. He felt as though he were going round and round in circles. "Okay, I can see how your being pregnant would have something to do with the possibility Trent would cancel the trust fund and then give Simon an excellent motive to kill him to keep that from happening."

She remained silent.

"The question remains," Lucas said. "Why did Sully tell me to look at you?"

She still had no answer.

"Was it because you were sleeping with Trent?" Lucas asked.

All those puzzle pieces that had been moving around in the back of his head all coalesced together to form an appalling scenario. He had this idea before he and Carter returned to the Mahoney Estate, but only wanted to speak of it to Rachel. If Lucas were wrong about this, and told anyone else about his gut feeling, then he would feel horrible. This was a suspicion he wanted to confirm first before telling anyone.

She stared at Lucas, wide-eyed. In that moment, Lucas knew the sickening feeling in his stomach was correct. First, there was Simon saying he saw Rachel almost every day except for Tuesdays. She allegedly volunteered down at the homeless shelter that night. Second, that was the night when Trent most often stayed out late, according to Carly. By Rachel's own admission, she thirsted for power, for the money. She knew even at her age, her extraordinary looks could get her those things. Simon was just her way into this family circle. Simon had influence, but in this small world, Trent was the pinnacle of everything Rachel desired.

"Rachel, my God, he's old enough to be your father," Lucas said, as though it meant anything now that it was over.

She had her face buried in her hands, sobbing. "I know, but God, he was just so much of a man. He was the greatest person I ever met. At first, all I cared about was his money and influence. Then I got to know him, and I'll be darned if he wasn't the best man in the world. He was so nice, so caring. He treated me better than anyone I ever met did. He treated me much better than Simon, or even my own parents."

This reminded Lucas of the Electra complex he studied at college. A Jungian philosophy. The Electra complex held that the girl was jealous of the mother in competition for the father's attention. It is entirely within the realm of possibility Rachel held no respect for her father and transferred that to Simon's father. Freud's more famous Oedipus complex is the one where the boy is jealous of the father in competing for the mother's maternal attention. Here, Rachel was not competing for the attention of her own father, but for the attention of someone else's father.

"How did it happen?" Lucas asked.

Knowing she now had nothing to hide, she told him the entire story, looking around beforehand to see if any family members were near.

About two and a half months ago, on the same night Simon received his acceptance letter to Duke was when it all started. At that point, she had not had sex with Simon. They were fooling around some, but Rachel had not let him go all the way. She was still undecided if she wanted to go that far. She came over that night, not knowing Simon, Brian, Carly, and his grandparents were out celebrating Simon's acceptance to Duke. This was when her parents forbade her to see Simon, so she had to be sneaky about it. When she arrived at the gate, Trent answered and let her through. He said nothing about Simon not being home at that point. She did not call Simon ahead of time to see what he was doing. She assumed he would study as he usually did on a school night.

Rachel admitted since she came to know the family, she looked up to Trent. Even found him attractive.

He let her in and told her he expected Simon would be home any minute. She did not find out until later Trent lied to her at that time. He knew it could be a while before the rest of the family returned. He offered Rachel something to drink while she waited. She said sure. She was thirsty. A few minutes later, Trent brought out a bottle of wine, told her about Simon's acceptance letter, and said he was going to celebrate even though Simon was not home. When he offered her a glass, she accepted.

When Simon did those sorts of things, like drinking or smoking whatever, Rachel stayed away. Rachel did not know. This time, she took a glass of wine. She was happy for Simon, too.

Eventually, the one glass turned into two, then the whole bottle. Looking back on it, Rachel knew Trent was trying to get her drunk, but at that point, she did not care. When he put his hand on her thigh, she did not protest. She returned the affectation. When Trent kissed her, she kissed back. From there, the rest was history. They saw each other most every Tuesday. Rachel invented the story about helping down at the homeless shelter every Tuesday. No one ever checked on that. Why would she lie about helping the homeless?

Lucas stood in shock. His legs got wobbly, and he wanted to sit down, but did not. In all the time Lucas had known Trent, he would have never guessed Trent would do such a thing. There were so many questions to ask, but he knew his time here was limited. Someone could walk into the room at any moment and end the conversation.

"Did Trent ever say why he did it?"

"Yeah," she smiled and wiped a tear from her eye at the memory, "he said I was the sweetest person he had ever met and saw such potential in me as a person who he wanted to be around to cultivate it."

"But what about Carly?"

"I don't know."

That was a line of thought to ponder later. Right now, he had other things he needed to do. "So, who's the father of your child?"

She sobbed uncontrollably.

At this point, nothing surprised Lucas. "Oh, my god. It's Trent, isn't it?"

"Y-yes," she choked out between snuffles. "I believe so. I missed my period the next week, after Trent and I had sex for the first time and took a test as soon as I could. When it came back positive, I told Trent. He came up with what seemed like a simple plan to cover it up."

Lucas did not want to know anymore, but it was like watching a car accident; he could not stop watching. What were the odds a girl would get pregnant the first time she ever had sex?

"What was the plan?"

"Have sex with Simon."

"Trent suggested that?" Lucas asked. He barely believed the entire story, but deep down, he knew Rachel was telling the truth. There was no reason for her to lie.

"Yes, he did. So, I went out, had sex with Simon numerous times, and then at some point, told him I was pregnant."

He stared at her for a second. "Do you realize how twisted all of this is?"

"I know, I know," she cried into her hands. "I curse myself every day for getting into this mess, but there's no way out now."

"Does Simon know about his father?"

She stared at him for a long minute before continuing. "Yes. Sort of. I told him I slept with Trent one time. I told him the story about the night I first slept with his father, and how he got me drunk."

"How did he react?"

"At first, he didn't. He was too stunned." Lucas could imagine. "Then he got furious and yelled at me for a long time. There was nothing to say. I just took it. I felt too guilty."

"Did Simon ever confront Trent?"

She shook her head. "Not that I know of."

"When did you tell him this?"

The tears flowed in a full stream. "I just couldn't take it anymore. The guilt was eating away at me. I didn't want to confess that I saw his dad regularly."

"When did you let him know?" he repeated.

"Monday," she answered. She knew what it meant. Lucas imagined Simon told Sully of Rachel's and his father's betrayal. That was why Sully told Lucas to look into Rachel. Sully knew Simon would tell no one about all of this.

"Who else knew?"

Another shake of the head. "As long as Trent did not tell anyone, we were the only two people in the world who knew about it."

That was a relief. Lucas thought the combination of Simon finding about getting his trust fund canceled and his father not only slept with his girlfriend, but got her pregnant as well, would drive Simon to kill his father without planning an elaborate setup.

"Could he have told Carly about it?" Lucas asked.

She shook her head. "I hope not, but I wouldn't know the answer to that question."

"Okay, let me switch subjects. I know you won't mind."

"Please."

"Tell me about your arrangement."

She told Lucas that Trent gave her the secret gate pass code, for her to be ready, and on Tuesdays after the last person was out of the building, he would send her a text message on her phone. Something innocuous saying if the coast was clear or not. He would send it so that if anyone checked her phone messages, it would show up as a mistaken message. A wrong number. If it said one thing, she knew they were on. If it said another thing, she knew they would have to abort and wait another week to be safe.

It was a simple but effective setup.

"I had the feeling," Rachel said, "that I wasn't the first girl Trent had over like that."

Lucas nodded. That would answer the questions behind why Trent had the backdoor installed into the office gate system before his affair with Rachel began. He thought again about the home setup here. It looked like Renegar's Security could have installed the gate here as well.

"Did he have the same arrangement here at this house?"

"No, just at the office. I don't know if I could have done that here, anyway. It would have been weird doing it in the same bed as he slept with his wife."

"So, how long was this going to go on? I mean, after you have your child, wouldn't it have to end?"

"I don't know. We didn't plan that far ahead."

"What about the times when he told you not to come? What did you do on those evenings?"

"On those evenings, I actually went and volunteer. I did not completely make that up. I had to do it occasionally, just in case my parents ever wanted to go down and check to see if I were telling the truth. It would have been horrible if they went to check me out, drove down there, and the people that worked there had never heard of me."

"If this comes out," he said, "then you're an automatic suspect."

"Why?"

Her youthful innocence was sad in this case. "Because Rachel, if they find out you met with Trent most every Tuesday, in how you're suggesting you did, then you, more than anyone else, would have had the knowledge to pull something like that off."

She saw the validity of his statement. She covered her mouth. "Oh, my God."

"Rachel, I have to ask, did you see him last night?"

This was the moment of truth.

"No, he sent me the message telling me not to come. I may not have gone, anyway. The guilt gnawed at me to where it made me sick, and I felt I had to do something good for someone else. So I went down to the shelter."

"Could anyone down there verify that?"

She nodded. "Yes, I could get the numbers of about three people who saw me there. Also, there's a sign-in sheet for all volunteers showing when I got there."

Lucas hoped that was true. "Okay, three questions. First, do you know when you sent him the message telling him you weren't coming? Second, when did he send you the message? And third, about what time did you make it down to the homeless shelter?"

He asked the third question, hoping she made it to the shelter before the activity at the gate occurred. If that were the case, then she could not have murdered Trent. He could not see that scenario in his head, but he had to look in every nook and cranny.

She pulled a thin cell phone out of her back pocket. After pushing a few buttons, she said, "He sent the message around four yesterday."

That was a good hour before Lucas left the office. "How much notice did he usually give you to show up?"

She looked at the ceiling. "I don't know. Fifteen, twenty minutes. If I did not show up quickly enough, then he would close up shop and leave."

"How often did you not make it in time?"

"Not often. It happened once or twice, when I was stuck in traffic or something. I would let myself in the gate, his car wouldn't be there, and I would leave."

"Simple as that?"

"Yeah."

"Did you two communicate any other times during the week?"

She raised her eyebrows. "Well, yeah. I was over here often. I saw him all the time when I was around Simon. It was easy to find time to talk to him in semi-private. If something happened, we couldn't meet, then he would apologize, and explain why we couldn't see each other."

"Did you two ever... you know, at the house?"

She looked around the room. "Oh, no. Not here, not ever. Too risky. We tried not to let anyone know we even spoke to each other when I was here. He said it kind of came off to everyone here that he was afraid of me, which made it even more far-fetched if anyone ever suspected us of fooling around."

"Okay, back to the second question. Why did he tell you not to come?"

She shook her head. "I don't know. The message he sent was the type that just told me he couldn't see me. That's all. I thought nothing about it. Perfectly normal." She stopped and breathed in. "And I signed in at the shelter sometime between ten after and five thirty yesterday."

"And where is this shelter?"

"It's the shelter in uptown Charlotte on North Tryon."

"How far away is it from the office?"

She bit her lower lip. "About twenty to thirty minutes depending on traffic. Usually when I go, it's around rush hour and I'm pushing every bit of thirty to thirty-five minutes to get there."

Lucas breathed a sigh of relief. Because of the timeline, here was one person he could eliminate.

That left Simon.

Suddenly, they both looked up as they heard a door slam somewhere in the wing of the house where Simon and Carter were. Carter jogged in a few seconds later, looking harried.

"What is it?" Lucas asked.

"Simon left," Carter said.

"He left? Why did he leave?"

"I think he's afraid. He's afraid he's going to be arrested." Carter explained the same picture Lucas painted to Rachel about how Sully died after confessing that Simon had something to do with setting him up, and how Simon now stood to go to prison for it.

Outside the house, they heard a big engine rev and drive away. Greg and Quinn rushed down the hall into the room from the dining room.

"What's all the commotion?" Quinn asked.

"Simon just left," Carter said.

"Where did he go?" Greg asked.

"Don't know," Carter said. "I think he's afraid."

"What is he afraid of?"

"That he will be arrested."

"Why would we arrest him?" Greg asked.

Lucas laid out the story he received from Rachel a few minutes ago to Greg. About how they had been getting into fights, Simon getting into trouble, and how Trent said he was going to cancel Simon's trust fund. He left out the part about Rachel sleeping with Trent. Rachel gave Lucas a thankful look.

"Holy crap," Greg said. He processed what Lucas told him and clasped him on the shoulder. "That's great work, young man."

Quinn held up his hands. "Whoa, whoa, whoa, don't go rushing to judgment on Simon just yet."

"What do you mean?" Greg said.

Quinn shook his head. "I don't know what my son was talking about. He cannot cancel the trust fund. Only Laura Ann and I have the authority to do that. We were the ones who set it up."

"But Simon said his father meant it," Rachel said from where she sat.

Quinn raised his eyebrows. "It doesn't matter if he meant it or not. He had no control over the dispersal of the trust fund."

"I think we're getting caught up in semantics here," Lucas said. "All that matters is if Simon thought his father had that authority. The possibility exists that Simon could have been scared enough to have killed his father."

"I don't believe that for a second," Quinn protested.

"Whether or not you believe it doesn't matter," Lucas said. "Rachel said Simon was into drugs. What if his father broke the news to him, he got all depressed, went out the next day, got high, and killed him?"

"Makes sense," Carter said, rubbing his chin.

"I don't know, man," Greg said. "I've been investigating murders for years, and this is one of the cleanest, best planned out murders I've come across. I was tempted to side with Quinn here by saying that I do not believe that scenario. Not to say your theory doesn't have merit. There is a definite motive there with Simon. But the thought of a *kid* stoned out of his mind, planning and carrying out this murder was far-fetched. I'm not buying it."

"What if he wasn't stoned? What if he was angry enough to kill his father? I think we can all agree Simon is an extremely smart kid. And," Lucas added, "he ran just now."

Suddenly, Lucas turned into an advocate for Simon's arrest. He did not want it to be that way, but that is how it was turning out.

"You're right. We need to go find him." Greg said, and then turned to Quinn, "Quinn, I hate to do this, but I need to call this in and have them on the lookout for Simon."

Lucas could read Quinn's thoughts. If Greg put out an APB on Simon, it would look very, very bad for the family. Things were going to be rocky anyway, and things the Mahoney's did not want the public to know were going to come out. Now it was all about damage control.

That was Lucas's job.

"Greg?" Lucas said. "Hear me out."

"Lucas, you know as well as I do that I need to call this in. Simon is a righteous suspect in this case. We need to bring him in for questioning."

"I know. I understand that." Everyone was now looking at Lucas, wanting to know what he had up his sleeve. "Greg, give us one hour to find him, and bring him in. If we haven't found him by," he looked at his watch, "eleven o'clock then put out your APB."

Greg considered it. "And you think you can find him?"

"No," Lucas answered. Everyone looked at him as if he turned into a giant spider. "I don't think I can find him. I think she can," Lucas said, pointing a finger at Rachel.

CHAPTER TWENTY-ONE

Rachel's red, puffy eyes stared back at Lucas. Everyone's eyes were upon her.

It was now going on ten o'clock on a Wednesday night. A school night. There was a storm going on outside. The booms of thunder echoed through the walls of the house. Lucas did not grow up in the area. He did not know where teenagers hung out at nights. He knew where he grew up in small-town West Virginia, there were several places a teenager could go to get themselves into trouble. They would go to a place and park their cars close together, where they could exchange drugs or whatever else, drink, and just waste the nights away. The funny thing was these places were often public. The police never would go find out what these groups of kids were doing. They figured if they could see the teens, they could not get into much trouble.

Lucas knew there had to be places like that around here. The only question was whether super-rich teenager Simon Mahoney went to places like that.

"Well, where do you think he is?" Quinn demanded of Rachel.

Rachel rubbed her nose, looked at the ceiling, and said, "I can think of a couple of places."

"Where?" Greg asked in a softer tone that would probably yield better answers from Rachel.

A sniffle. "There's a taco place in Kannapolis where he goes sometimes to show off his Range Rover."

Greg nodded. "I know the place. The kids go there to show off their cars and whatnot. The Kannapolis police have made a few drugs busts from there. They've also arrested a few for drag racing."

"Well, Simon never did that. A Range Rover isn't much of a drag racing car." A few nods from Lucas, Carter, and Greg. "There's one other place I can think of where he would go."

"Where?"

"There's a lumber yard off Davidson Road, behind a grocery store some kids go to late at night."

Greg knitted his brow. "You mean the road that circles around to an O'Charley's and Chili's?"

"Yeah," she said. "The owner's son of the lumber yard lets kids in there to do drugs, have sex, and other things at night after the place closes."

"Does the owner know about this?" Greg asked.

"I don't think so," she answered. "I think it's been going on for a few years."

Greg rubbed his chin. "I would have to ask some people I work with if they've heard of this. I haven't."

It was an area off the beaten path where a few small warehouses stood. Lucas had been there a few times to a Habitat for Humanity place the Mahoney Corporation donated some money and supplies. It was just off 29, but it was like being in a different world back there.

"They don't do it every night. It is like its prearranged or something. I know that is where Sully did most of his 'business."

"Was the place going to be open tonight?"

A blank stare. "I don't know. I don't think so. But . . .," she hesitated.

"But what?" Quinn said, getting impatient.

"Simon has a key."

"He has a key?"

She shook her head as if she could not understand why this was a surprise. "Yes, he had a key," she said, getting testy. "He is Simon Freaking Mahoney. The kid who runs the whole setup practically begs Simon to do stuff with him."

The first place Rachel named, the taco place, did not sound like a place where someone who was on the run from the cops would go. The second place, the lumberyard, was more secluded. A place Simon could go to be alone. A place where he could score something to make him forget about his dad's death. Or forget the look in Trent's eyes when he pulled the trigger. Lucas was still furious with Simon for setting him up. He wanted a piece of Simon, and with the possibility he was the murderer hovering around, Lucas could justify beating the crap out of him if the opportunity presented itself.

Carly and Laura Ann joined the small gathering in the dining room. They took up positions behind everyone to listen in. They said nothing, however. For that, Lucas was thankful. The last thing they needed was for these two to complicate matters by getting emotional about the potential downfall of the oldest son.

Lucas noted Brian had yet to come down from his room.

Greg thought it over. His intense eyes focused on Carter. "Okay, Carter, I'm going to call some guys, and I want you to go over to Kannapolis, to the taco place, and see if Simon's there. If he is, try to talk him into going down to the police station with you. Tell him if he comes with you without resistance, things will be less hard on him. I'm sending you over there because you know him and could talk some sense into him. I'm sending my friends with you because you don't have the authority to make an arrest if it comes down to that."

Carter looked like he was itching for some action. He kept clenching and unclenching his fists. "I'll do that."

Greg turned to Lucas. "I know you've done nothing like this. That's why I'm going to ask you to come with me. I'm going to need someone there who knows Simon and knows what is going on. I'm hoping that if there's a familiar face there, he will be more likely to cooperate."

Lucas was tired, beaten, and worn, but for this, he could feel a rush of adrenaline surge through him. This was one of those defining moments in life. A moment when what happens could shape not only his future, but Simon's as well. This might be the only time in his life he was thrust into a position like this. He was determined to see this through to the end.

"Alright, what do you want me to do?" Lucas asked.

"First, I'm going to go run by the police station and grab one of the other investigators to come with us for backup. I'm going to ask you to take another car. That way, if we have to arrest Simon, you won't have to wait for us to take you home."

"I don't have a car," Lucas reminded him. "Remember. Simon tried to have me killed and totaled my car in the process."

Greg tightened the grip on his shoulder. "This is why I'm not going to allow you within ten feet of him. I just want you there to talk to him. I'm out of my element here on this one," he admitted. "You're in a better position to negotiate surrender."

"What about a car?"

Carly spoke up for the first time. "You can use mine. The keys are on the hook by the garage door."

Greg looked at Lucas to see if that satisfied him. The truth was, he had been itching for a chance to drive her Lexus since she and Trent bought matching ones a while back. Trent bought a more contemporary silver edition of the LS 460L edition. Carly opted for the sportier red color. They equipped both cars with the top-of-the-line executive class options, making both cars nearly a hundred grand apiece. They were two of the most beautiful cars Lucas had ever had the privilege of riding in.

He tried to hide his pleasure. "Okay. What now Greg?"

"Go on down to the parking lot of the grocery store, and I'll be there in a few minutes. It's easiest to go through downtown anyway to get over there from here, so it won't be a problem for me to stop and pick up some help."

"I'll be waiting," Lucas said.

Lucas and Carter walked out the front doors into the driving thunderstorm. "What is this stuff falling from the sky?" Lucas heard Greg ask Carter while they walked to their cars referring to the drought in the area.

This left the four standing in the foyer. Well, three stood. Rachel still sat.

Lucas looked at Quinn and let go a deep breath. Lucas felt his pulse racing.

"Lucas," the older man said, "I know you're angry with my grandson, but please, put that aside for now. Let the police sort out everything. Don't feel that you need to take revenge on him. I know he is a contumacious, troubled youth. In some ways, I know we have failed in our raising of him. I can speak for the entire family when I say we hoped that if he went off to school, to Duke, he would grow up and receive some sense of responsibility. But somewhere down the road, he took a wrong turn. Now it looks like he could have killed my only child. How do you think that makes me feel?"

Lucas had no answer.

Quinn continued, "I want whoever murdered Trent brought to justice. Now the possibility exists that the perpetrator of this crime is my grandson. Simon was supposed to be the next one in line to run the business. We failed him in so many ways. Simon had enormous potential. Trent and I saw the potential in him to take our business to another level entirely. We could tell at an early age he could think and figure out things faster than any child we had ever seen before. But somewhere, somewhere down the line, something happened where he strayed from the course. He's been better recently, and I think that has to do with this young woman sitting here."

This drew a rare smile from Rachel.

Laura Ann had her head on Carly's shoulder. Carly's eyes bore into Lucas's, pleading for him to do or say something.

"He's a kid," Lucas said. "I think it's not up to the parents to decide a child's course in life. The only thing parents can do is instill a sense of morals and direction in which a child should govern their lives by. Point them in the right direction.

Ultimately, however, it is up to that child to find out who he is, what he wants to be. It looks like Simon wants to follow the path you all have lined out for him. He was happy when he received that acceptance letter to Duke. I could tell it was something he wanted in his life. That was not something that you could fake. Remember, even though he got into some trouble outside of school, maybe he shouldn't have. Inside the school, he excelled. He wouldn't even try at school if he didn't want to please you all. I think he wanted to please his family. Otherwise, why try? He was just taking a different path in reaching your goals for him, that's all."

Rachel resumed her flow of tears. Laura Ann and Carly did the same. Quinn looked at him hard-eyed. Lucas knew Quinn did not like it, but deep down, he agreed with Lucas.

Simon received two items of horrible news on the same day. Rachel told him about sleeping with Trent. Then Trent told Simon about the trust fund. Lucas would say nothing about Rachel and Trent. He did not want to add gas to the fire by informing Carly that her husband cheated on her with her son's girlfriend. He would leave that between them if it ever came out. If Simon and Rachel kept it quiet, they were the only people besides Lucas who would ever have to know about it.

With that thought in mind, he continued, "We know whether or not Trent controlled it that Simon received devastating news on Monday. Does anyone here know exactly where Simon was last evening?"

Heads shook all around.

"He wasn't here. That's all we know," Quinn spoke up.

"Hopefully," Lucas said, "he has a solid alibi. Just because all the signs are pointing to Simon right now, doesn't mean he did it. If I find him and get him to talk to me, I'll point that out to him. The possibility still exists that was just out blowing off some steam. There may be other suspects out there in this murder. Suspects the police have yet to uncover. It's still early."

Lucas left off the fact if it turned out Simon had nothing to do with any of this, he would still be on the hook for the attempted murders of him and Kristen.

For the first time in a while, it reminded him of Kristen's plight, and felt guilty for pulling her into this with him.

Lucas said goodbye. They wished him luck. A few minutes later, he pulled away from the mansion in the hard rain, driving Carly's car towards the unknown.

CHAPTER TWENTY-TWO

Lucas retraced the path in Carly's Lexus that he took the last time he left the estate, but this time in a different car. Hopefully, minus the suicidal car chase.

A few minutes later, he sat in the parking lot of the grocery store up the street from the lumberyard, waiting for Greg to arrive, pondering his present and future. Rain pounded rhythmically on the roof of the car. The windshield wipers swooshed back and forth. Thousands of drops of rain appeared from the black sky and then just as quickly disappeared into the glow of the lights in the parking lot. There was no end of the rain in sight, which, in the drought, was a good thing. He heard the slosh of water as cars sped by on 29.

When Lucas accepted this job, it was a coup. Of all the jobs he imagined during his time in college, this was better than anything he ever dreamed of. He earned a position of power and authority right out of the gate, working for the richest family he ever knew. This Mahoney family was supposed to be a nice, normal American family, except for having a couple hundred million dollars to their names. They were supposed to be a grounded, down to earth; just like the family you grew up with next door. After a few months of working with them, he found they were like a normal family.

They just were not the Norman Rockwell picture of a wholesome family.

They had problems like everyone else. Brian was an introverted loner. Carly was greedy and selfish. Laura Ann had an assortment of problems, including a lifelong feud with her daughter-in-law. Quinn, well Quinn, was the most stable of the family.

That left Trent and Simon. Lucas knew, to some degree before today, about Simon's problems. He knew Simon abused alcohol and learned today that he also abused drugs. Lucas would have never guessed before today that Trent was capable of the sordid deeds Rachel dropped on him minutes ago. From the time Lucas started his job, he compared Trent's personality and demeanor to his father's personality. His judgment about the two was that the apple did not fall far from the tree. Now, after Rachel's revelation, Lucas did not know what to think of Trent. The investigation from this morning hinted at Trent's secret life. Lucas could not accept that Trent cheated on Carly.

Then things came out about Trent. The first was of him having the secret password designed into the gate. Lucas wondered why Trent just did not give the person he wanted in the gate *his* own password. Lucas thought the answer to that probably was the computer probably could not accept two identically repeated commands. If the computer knows you are supposed to be inside the gate, then another command from the same password asking you to do the same thing would cause an error, or vice versa. Why not give Rachel her own personal password? Then that would start a trail. It would show up in a report somewhere that could be backtracked to Trent. Lucas imagined Trent did not want to leave any trail of his infidelity. More of a trail than he had to. Having the secret password to begin with was telling enough. However, Lucas was sure if it came out, Trent could have explained that away.

Lucas did not know where he would stand with this family after tonight. The person he worked for was dead. He thought he did a great job today. He worked completely out of his training and comfort zone with this investigation. He made it this far in less than a day. Would the Mahoney's appreciate that enough to keep him? If so, would he want to continue to work with them? At this point, he could not honestly answer that question.

Too much remained unresolved.

He thought about Kristen and again felt guilty over what happened to her. He hoped she could forgive him. From the moment they finally met this morning, they seemed to click. He could not think of another person he ever met, let alone another woman, where that happened.

It meant something.

He had had his eye on Kristen for months. He dreamed up imaginary conversations. He imagined what he would say to her in greeting or how to strike up a conversation. Never did he think that once he met her, the conversation between the two of them would flow so well. Would she want to see him again? He hoped he could go over to see her at the hospital as soon as they finished with Simon.

After whatever went down next, he was done with the Mahoney family for the day, possibly forever.

It was the first time he thought about his future in a long while. Since the car accident he was in some years ago, he lived his life one day at a time, grateful to be alive. He had to think about the college he would go to, what he would major in, but never really considered the long-term ramifications of what he was doing. Lucas never considered if business management was what he wanted to do for the rest of his life. It was something he was confident he could excel at doing. He never thought about whether he would enjoy it as a career. After he started working for the Mahoney family, he thought it was a great thing, but he never stopped to think about how far he could go in this company. He thought the answer to that was not much further than where he was now. At twenty-five years of age, he was one of the top men in the company. The other positions he aspired to above him eventually going to be members of the family, namely Simon and Brian. They set the corporation up that way. Lucas hit the proverbial ceiling. He made a lot of money. He wondered if money was necessarily vital to his long-term happiness.

He hoped he was not that shallow.

What was vital to his long-term happiness? He had not considered that question until today. He thought that fifteen, twenty years from now, he would look back upon today as a day that changed his life. He realized after spending much of this crazy day with Kristen that finding someone to spend his time, his life with was important. Before today, he dwelt little on dating. That was due to not wanting to get hurt again. He still wore the emotional scars from what happened between him and Ashley so long ago. Lucas did not have many friends outside of work.

He thought of Brian as withdrawn, but that was sort of like the pot calling the kettle black.

Greg pulled alongside Lucas and rolled down his window. Lucas rolled his down, wondering what Carly would think about having the interior of her car exposed to a downpour of rain.

"Okay," Greg shouted above the rain, "I don't want you in any danger here. When we get there, I want you to wait in your car. If Simon is in there, we're going to go in and try to bring him out. If we cannot get him to come along peacefully, I'm going to call you in to talk some sense into him. You know better about what is going on here than anyone else. I may not have all the answers to this. That's why you're here."

"Greg, there's something else you need to know. Something I could not say back at the estate."

"What is it?"

Lucas took a long breath. "Trent was sleeping with Simon's girlfriend."

Greg was too stunned to speak.

When Greg said nothing, Lucas continued, "Sometime on Monday when Trent informed Simon of cutting off the trust fund, Rachel confessed to Simon that she slept with Trent. She didn't tell Simon that she slept with his father regularly." Lucas then told Greg the sordid details of their arrangement.

Greg stared, speechless. His mouth agape. He kept his opinion to himself.

"I'm ready when you are," Lucas said. "I'll follow."

Greg blinked a few times, gave Lucas a stern nod, rolled up the window, and gestured for his driver to pull away. Greg was obviously stunned by what Lucas told him, but probably more resolved to take Simon in for further questioning.

Lucas dodged a few cars to leave the parking lot, making a left. As he pulled onto the two-lane road, he remembered Kristen saying she knew about some bad things Brian had done. He forgot all about that in the craziness that ensued. She could never tell Lucas what she knew about Brian. It seemed unimportant now in the events that unfolded since then.

He followed Greg's car around a bend in the road to almost a completely different world than what was only a few hundred yards away. Areas of dense, leafy growth surround the narrow, two-lane road on both sides. The lumberyard appeared on Lucas's left a few seconds later. There was a high chain-link fence surrounding the perimeter of the yard. Twin unlit floodlights stood at the top of two poles at either end of the yard.

Lucas came to the end of the road to a three-way stop. There was a small parking area to the left of the lumberyard. In front of Lucas and just to the left were entrances to some warehouses, including the Habitat for Humanity. On the left, in the small parking area, Simon's Range Rover sat by itself. There were no other cars around. The high, chain-link fence separated the parking lot from the lumberyard.

Simon was alone.

Lucas wondered what Simon was doing inside. Drugs? It would be horrible if Greg arrested Simon while under the influence of drugs. For Greg and his friend to find Simon hiding somewhere within the confines of the place, strung out on dope or whatever, would not be smart. If they found Simon high, then they would have to arrest him. Lucas figured unless Simon gave

Greg something to the contrary, that Greg would arrest Simon, anyway. He had the means, the motive, and no apparent alibi. The police found no evidence to connect Simon to the crime scene, but the police faced a lot of heat in just arresting someone to appease the public.

Lucas pulled into the small lot and stopped beside Greg's car. He and his partner got out of the car and came around to Lucas.

Lucas rolled down his window.

"Keep your phone handy," Greg said. "If I need you, I'll call."

"Okay," Lucas said.

"But let me tell you, I really hope that you came down here for nothing. Really, all you are here for Lucas is as a backup plan. You're Simon's voice of reason."

"I hope you're right," Lucas said. He wished them luck and rolled up the window. Lucas watched Greg and his partner slosh their way through the gate, through the falling rain, and creep into the compound.

The rain had not let up since leaving the Mahoney's place. It fell in buckets and the amount of standing water added up.

Five minutes went by, then ten. Lucas could see nothing from his vantage point. He heard no noises. Not that he could hear much through the dull roar of the rain pounding the pavement and the roof of the car.

He was eager to find out what was going on in there. He debated on whether to disobey Greg and go in there anyway. What could Greg do to him? Arrest him? He considered it and decided Greg probably could arrest him on obstruction of justice charges if Lucas ended up interfering with whatever Greg had going.

When he counted fifteen minutes gone by, he decided he could not wait anymore. It was dark, and the area was dimly lit. Lucas wondered if Carly had a flashlight in the car. He hoped she did and dug around trying to find a flashlight. He reached and felt behind the seats to no avail. Then he checked where he should have checked first, the glove compartment.

What happened next blew his mind and changed everything.

CHAPTER TWENTY-THREE

Two seconds after Lucas got out of the car, he was soaked. To this point today, he ruined two expensive suit jackets, two shirts, and now he could safely add at least another jacket to the tally.

He entered through the gate and picked his way between stacks, pallets, and rows of lumber. He had found a flashlight in the glove compartment, and the weak beam cut through the murky darkness. He stopped, straining to hear anything coming through the depths of the compound.

He was about twenty yards in through the gate. The primary structure of the place was in the shape of a huge L. It lay another fifty yards in front of him. He decided that Simon, no matter what state he was in, had to be taking shelter there. Lucas moved in that direction, keeping the flashlight aimed more at the ground than the stacks of lumber. The place had the pleasant smell of wet, freshly cut wood. He could almost feel the large stacks as much as see them. He was afraid of tripping over a stray two by four or something.

He finally eked his way close enough to the building to get under the overhang. Grateful to be sheltered from the rain, he took a few seconds to gather his wits. He still heard no sign from Greg, his partner, or Simon.

Lucas's heart raced from what he found in the glove compartment, besides the flashlight. He tried to make it fit in his head, but it was like trying to shove a square peg into a round hole.

He walked to a set of open, red double doors ten feet away from where he took shelter. He looked inside and immediately heard shouting coming from the corner through the machinery.

"You're not going to take me! You're not going to take me!" Lucas heard Simon scream.

Lucas walked through the opening, and the three came into view. They had Simon backed into a corner. If this conversation was ever civil, it must have changed when Greg mentioned Simon leaving the premises with him.

"Simon," Greg was saying, "all we want to do is talk to you. You're not under arrest. We just need to ask you a few more questions about what happened with you and your dad the other night. He told you he was going to cut off your trust fund, then you find out he slept with your girlfriend. What do you think that leads us to believe?"

"I don't care about the trust fund! That's a measly two million dollars. Someday, I'm going to run this company, and then I'll have all the money I ever wanted. Yes, I was angry and upset about him sleeping with Rachel. When she told me that last night, I left. After what happened today, we talked everything out. We're okay."

"Where did you go?"

"I don't know. I just drove around for a few hours to clear my head."

"Do you have any way of proving where you went?" Greg's partner asked.

Simon thought about it for a split second. "No."

"Then you're going to have to come with us," Greg said.

Lucas stood back during the exchange, hoping it would resolve itself. It almost did.

"No! I told you I didn't do anything!" Simon screamed, and before Greg or his partner could react, Simon attacked Greg, tackling him to the ground.

In the next instant, Greg's partner had his gun out and pointed three inches from Simon's head.

"Don't move!" he yelled. "Get off of him or I'll shoot!"

Lucas knew he had to intervene before Simon got himself killed. He stepped out from where he was hiding, and yelled, "He didn't kill Trent! Don't shoot! "

Greg's friend with the gun wheeled around in surprise at Lucas's voice. With him distracted, Simon leaped up and ran for the only exit.

The one near Lucas.

Simon made it ten feet before the cop fired a shot at Simon's feet, stopping him dead in his tracks.

"Don't freaking move!" the cop yelled, with the gun leveled at Simon's head. "One more step and you're dead!"

Simon slowly raised his hands in the air and kept his position.

Greg got up slowly from the ground and held a hand over his bleeding nose. "What do you mean, he didn't do it?"

CHAPTER TWENTY-FOUR

A few minutes later, they were back at Carly's car, standing by the passenger-side door. Rain pounded them from above.

It took some convincing in the warehouse, but Lucas got Greg's partner to lower his gun and for Greg to humor him for a few moments while he proved Simon did not murder his father.

"Okay, now what?" Greg shouted above the rain.

"Open the glove compartment," Lucas said.

Greg gave Lucas a confused look, opened the door, and did as Lucas instructed.

"Oh, my God," Greg said when the glove compartment popped open. He stood. "When did you find this?"

Lucas explained how he found it while fumbling around for a flashlight.

Greg nodded, reached into his pocket, and pulled out a handkerchief. He bent back down into the car and stood up a moment later, holding a shiny gun by the trigger guard between his fingers.

Simon almost collapsed at the sight of it.

He knew what it meant just as well as everyone else.

Greg held the end of the gun to his nose and sniffed.

"Yup, it's been fired recently." He looked up at Lucas. "Good job."

***

A few members of the police force caught wind of the arrest of Simon Mahoney and arrived a few minutes later with their lights flashing. They hoped to take part in a historic moment in Concord history. There was nothing to see.

After the relief Simon received when he realized he was off the hook for murdering his dad, he cooperated fully with Greg.

When the extra police help arrived, Greg informed Simon that he was arresting him for conspiring to commit murder. Simon was livid. He forgot about that minor detail. He had to be tackled and handcuffed before they shoved him in the back of a police cruiser.

After they took Simon away, Greg asked Lucas, considering finding the gun in Carly's glove compartment, how he thought Trent's murder went down.

"I don't know all the details," Lucas said, "but I would say somewhere down the line, Carly caught wind of what Trent was up to after hours at the office. I can't say if it was before or after they took out the life insurance policy on Trent. I don't know if that was part of her motive or what. Regardless, she knew when she killed him, she had the policy in her back pocket."

"I agree," Greg said.

"Carly knew what Trent was doing after hours on Tuesdays, and somehow got a text message through to Rachel, claiming to be Trent, telling her not to come last night. At some point, she learned how Rachel got inside the gate. Then, after I left yesterday, Carly let herself in the gate. I presume she walked in. If her car sat in the parking lot when Trent exited the building, it would have raised an alarm in him. She hid in the bushes, waiting for him to come out. When he did, she came out from between the bushes and surprised him. They may have argued, I don't know. She could have been so overcome with rage at his betrayal that she just came out of the bushes and shot him."

"Makes sense" Greg said. "We did not find a shell casing at the scene. I imagine she recovered it, threw it away somewhere, and stashed the gun in the glove compartment. She may have been waiting for the whole thing to blow over before disposing of the gun, and that is why it was where you found it."

"The one mistake she made," Lucas pointed out.

"Sometimes all it takes is one mistake to get yourself caught."

"It's such a shame though," Lucas shook his head. "Three members of this family going down in one day. Who would have imagined it?"

"I don't know. Listen Lucas, I know that all of this happened so quickly. You have not had time to think ahead, but if you ever want a job, let me know. You showed me something today. You showed me you have an intuitive sense about you that really helps in this type of police work. I know if you were to join us, you must go through interviews, training and the like. But I think because of the high profile of this case, and the speed with which you solved it, would show to the higher ups you have what it takes."

"Yeah, but I also had some good luck fall my way."

"That's part of the job, Lucas. Every once in a while, it takes a good bit of luck to make things go your way."

Lucas shook hands with Greg. "Well, Greg, I appreciate the offer, and I will consider it, but you're right. It is too soon for me to make any sort of decision about what I'm going to do."

"Take your time," he said.

"I will Greg."

Lucas took a deep breath, and looked around the area, at Simon's abandoned Range Rover, and the warehouse where Simon and his cohorts liked to hang out. It was such a sad, sad thing of what became of the Mahoney family, and of Simon in particular.

Simon's future could have been limitless, but now he will be forever haunted by what transpired here.

"For now, Greg," Lucas said, "I think I'm going to check on someone."

Greg gave Lucas a look of understanding. "Good luck, kid."

Lucas said his thanks, climbed into Carly's Lexus, and pulled away.

CHAPTER TWENTY-FIVE

Kristen looked frail and small, lying in her hospital bed. Her aunt was asleep outside in the ICU waiting room. It was after midnight. Lucas understood why she stayed out there; he could hear her snoring all the way in this room. She probably figured her snoring would disturb Kristen.

Lucas knew had he never met Kristen today that she would not be in this situation. On the flip side, she may have been mugged or worse this morning by Sully's crony, and he couldn't have gotten as far in figuring out Trent's killer without her.

The doctors assured Lucas she would be okay after some rest and rehabilitation.

He kneeled beside her bed and grasped her hand. She had an IV line attached at the wrist injecting who knew what into her body. Air hissed and released from one machine, while another machine beeped and blooped. The room was dark to stimulate rest.

Lucas felt horrible. He was tired, sore, and wanted to do nothing more than to crawl into bed beside Kristen, curl up with her, and sleep for a long, long time.

Suddenly, she squeezed his hand, breaking him from his reverie. Her eyes fluttered open, and she looked directly at him as though she could sense where his eyes were. "Hey," she said in the weakest voice he ever heard.

He smiled, leaned in, and said, "Hey there yourself. How are you feeling?"

She seemed to take an inventory of her body before replying, "Okay, I guess."

"Are you in any pain?"

She shook her head. Lucas thought morphine was one fluid that flowed into her through the intravenous drip. He hoped it would last until her pain went away.

"Am I going to be okay?" she asked.

Lucas did not think she had spoken with her doctor at this point about her prognosis. "You broke your leg, your wrist, and got a nasty bump on the head. But the doctor told me with some healing and rehab, you'll be back to normal in a few months."

She smiled and nodded.

Lucas sat quietly by her bedside for a moment to let her assess what happened. If she could remember anything, that is.

"What happened with Sully?" she asked, breaking the moment of silence.

He took a deep breath. "Kristen, he died."

She closed her eyes. Tears began streaming down her face. He knew she did not care for Sully, but even so, it was still sad to hear that someone you once shared yourself with passed away, even if he were trying to kill you.

"I don't know what you remember, but his car crashed into a used furniture store. I was there when he died."

She looked at him in surprise. "You saw him die?"

Lucas nodded. It was all he could do.

They were quiet for another moment, and then she remembered the other goings on from the day. "Did they ever figure out who killed Trent?"

"Yes," he said, and told her the whole story. He told her how Trent and Rachel were fooling around. About how Trent got Rachel pregnant, and Rachel tried to cover it up by sleeping with Simon shortly after she found out so it would seem to Simon that he would be the father. Then he told her how Trent and Carly had taken out a multi-million-dollar life insurance policy several months ago. When Carly found out Trent was sleeping with her son's girlfriend, she made the plans, got a gun from somewhere, snuck in the gate, and killed her unsuspecting husband in cold blood. By doing so, she stood to receive the full amount of the life insurance policy. No one ever suspected Carly. It was the perfect crime. When they found out Rachel and Trent were sleeping around, it looked like it was either Simon or Rachel who perpetrated the crime. Then Lucas found the gun that Carly used to kill Trent within the glove compartment of her Lexus.

Her mouth formed a perfect O. "So, you solved the mystery?"

He squeezed her hand. "Hey, I had some help. I found the gun, and I just got off the phone with Greg. He said the ballistics from the gun I found matched up with the two bullets in Trent's brain."

"Where did she get the gun?"

"No one knows. We know Sully was into guns, and Simon, by association, may have had one lying around. Maybe she found it one day but didn't say anything about it. Then, when she found out Trent was sleeping with Rachel, she remembered it, and used it."

Lucas saw the gears turning in her head. "That's twisted."

"I agree."

"What's going to happen now?"

"Simon is going to spend some time in probably some minimum-security prison for a couple of years on an attempted murder charge where Sully tried to kill you and me. With Carly, who knows? Possibly life in prison without parole. I don't know. The legal system will sort all of that out. I would say Brian would stay and live with his grandparents until he is of legal age. I feel sorry for the boy. He's bent out of shape about the whole thing."

She shook her head in agreement. "What about you? Are you going to continue to work for the Mahoney's?"

He shrugged. "Quinn has already asked me if I would like to stay on and help to run the company until Brian is ready to take over the reins in the future. Right now, I don't know if I will ever be able to do such a thing. Of course, Quinn also offered me an extremely large raise to do so."

"Wow," she said. "Are you going to do it?"

"I don't know," Lucas said. "I'll have to think about it. I learned today that this family had more problems than I ever thought. In one fell swoop today, Trent dies, and Simon and Carly go to jail. I don't know what this business is going to look like tomorrow. I mean, Quinn could just decide to sell the whole thing and get a place down in south Florida."

"What about us?"

Her question made Lucas smile. Through everything that happened today, she still wanted to seek a relationship with him. Of course, he would like nothing better. She turned out to be a better person than he could have ever imagined during all of those days where he would go to the mall just to catch a peek at her.

"If you want to, I would love to spend a lot of time with you."

That brought a big, weak smile to her face. "I would love nothing more," she said. "But do you think for our first actual date, we could do something normal? Like not getting involved in a murder mystery or car chases?"

He returned the smile, and echoed her sentiment. "I would love nothing more."

CHAPTER TWENTY-SIX

Four months later, Lucas was walking along the sand at Myrtle Beach in South Carolina. The temperature was about sixty degrees. A cool breeze continually hit him in the face. He did not mind. It was not warm enough to walk with a shirt off, but not quite cold enough to require a jacket, either. The sky was blue and partially cloudy above the majestic Atlantic Ocean. The setting sun played hide-and-go-seek with the clouds. The sun's rays shined down on the bluish ocean between the parted clouds.

Four months after Trent's murder, Carly was now at a minimum-security facility, awaiting trial. Even though Lucas found the smoking gun in the glove box of her car, she still maintained her innocence, and pleaded not guilty. Greg Hanover and the police think it is an open and shut case. Lucas was never pleased with the outcome. He thought there had to be more to the story than what they know.

They may never truly know what happened on the night of Trent's death.

Simon was also in prison, awaiting his own trial for helping to plan Kristen's and Lucas's murder. He also pleaded not guilty. Everyone seemed to think he would spend some time in prison.

In exchange for Rachel's testimony against Simon, the police agreed to let her off with probation. Rachel and Simon broke up after Rachel testified against Simon. What choice did she have? She had to think about her still unborn child, a boy, which was due in the next two months. Quinn and Laura Ann were still going to support Rachel and her child, a boy, financially, no matter what happened to Simon.

The child would be their great-grandson, after all. Or so they thought. Lucas knew the child would be another grandson.

Brian had problems of his own. Not of the legal sort. He went into a deep depression since his father's sudden death. He stayed in his room all the time, doing nothing but playing video games. He lost thirty pounds because he would not come out of his room to eat. He did not finish his last semester of school for the past year. Trent and Laura Ann were almost to the point of having him committed to an institution to receive therapy for his depression.

Lucas felt bad for the boy.

Quinn and Laura Ann had to sell their home a few years ago and move in with Trent and Carly, because they were to the point where their health kept them from being able to take care of themselves without help. The two of them did not want home healthcare. They were progressing to that point now that their only son was dead, Carly and their oldest grandson were in prison, and Brian could not even take care of himself, much less two elderly grandparents.

As far as the Mahoney's business was concerned, Quinn was selling it. It tore his heart out to consider such a thing, but with the way the family business was set up, there was no one left to run the company now that Trent was dead, Simon facing jail time, and Brian was not mentally stable enough to run his own life. A group of investors from New York swept in during the weeks following the fallout from Trent's death with an offer that Quinn could not refuse.

No one in that family would suffer for money for many, many years.

Quinn offered Lucas a different job in the company to go along with a much higher salary. Lucas apologized and said he would not be staying with the company. He told Quinn that considering what happened, and with the pending buyout of the company, he felt it would be better for him to move on. Quinn said he understood and thanked Lucas for his role in helping to solve his son's murder. He paid Lucas a full year's salary with the raise he offered. Lucas thanked Quinn, cleaned out his desk, and walked out of the office for the last time.

Lucas kept in touch with Quinn a couple times a week for advice and to see how they were doing. With the money Quinn gave him, augmented by the money he already had in savings, he could stand to take a while off without working, while he tried to figure out where his life was headed.

Something still nagged at the back of Lucas's mind about the night of Trent's death...

"Hey, look down when you walk," a voice said from beside him.

"What?" Lucas asked, coming out of the depths of his mind.

"I said, look down when you walk silly," Kristen said with a giggle. She looked extraordinary walking beside Lucas wearing a pair of gray jogging pants and a Hello Kitty white tank top.

She had a pair of sunglasses perched upon her head as her long, auburn hair fluttered in the slight breeze.

"I'm sorry," he said, bending aside to plant a kiss on her cheek, "I was in my own little world there for a minute or two."

Knowing what Lucas went through in recent months, she said, "I know. That's okay." She smiled and pointed at the ground. "Look."

At this moment, it was low tide. As he looked down at the beach in front of them, in the area between where the tide currently was and to where it reached during high tide, broad pools of shallow standing water reflected the sun's rays. When he looked straight down, he saw the reflection of the clouds perfectly in the thin sheets of water. The sun glistened off the sands of the beach in the reflection.

It made Lucas smile. Something he had been doing much more often in recent months. Although he did not have a job or a career, his future looked bright. Brighter than it had looked his entire life. He had a beautiful girl walking beside him who he swiftly fell in love with, and she loved him in return. He had money in his pocket, and the blank canvas of life ahead of him.

She pointed to the clouds at their feet as the clouds moved across the sand as they walked and said, "Look, it's as though we're walking on clouds."

And it was.

EPILOGUE

What Really Happened That Night...

From the killer's vantage point, Trent looked tired and beaten as he walked the short distance to the primo CEO parking space at the front of the building. The killer did not have to fear any random cars coming into the parking lot, or anyone driving by on Copperfield Boulevard to see the deed was about to be committed. The building was set behind an automatic locking iron gate where you could only get in by inputting a security password. A secret password would allow someone to come into the gate anonymously. This was something the killer found out by being in the right place at the right time, and it was what formed the basis for this plan. The three-story glass structure was set off the road, behind a line of tall, full trees obscuring any view of the parking lot from the road.

The killer knew this and planned upon it.

Trent looked around, as though searching for something or someone. The killer knew whom.

When Trent pushed the button on his keychain to unlock his silver car, the parking lights flashed, the horn beeped, and the killer took that as good a time as any. He pushed through the bushes and came up behind Trent just before he opened the car door.

"Dad," the killer said to get Trent's attention.

Trent turned around in surprise and had a puzzled look on his face. The killer had a feeling that would be Trent's reaction.

"Brian, what are you doing here?" he asked. Brian thought his dad almost looked scared.

He had good reason to be.

Brian looked at the ground for a moment, and then slowly back to his father. "Honestly dad, I've come here to kill you,"

Another puzzled look. "What?"

"Dad, you're a horrible, horrible man."

Trent thought many people would beg to differ with that comment, but said nothing. He especially kept quiet when Brian pulled a gun from behind his back.

"Brian, what the hell are you doing?"

"I told you, I'm here to kill you," Brian said, and pointed the gun in the general direction of his father's forehead.

Trent put his briefcase on the ground next to the car door and took a quick step back with his hands raised.

"Whoa, whoa, Brian. C'mon, you must be joking."

"No dad, I'm not joking. You need to die."

Trent stood, flabbergasted. "Why, son, do I need to die?"

Brian shook his head as though it were obvious. "Dad, as long as you're around, and you have a say in the matter, I'm never going to run the company. You don't want me to. You all picked Simon to be the one to do that. Everyone thinks because I am withdrawn, and I get bad grades I am stupid. That's not true dad."

Trent held out his hands. "That's not true Brian. We never thought you were stupid. Yes, it's true we would prefer your brother to run the company in the future. We want you to have a place in the company as well. We wanted you to run the business at the diner level. There's never going to be a difference in how much money you make, if that is what this is all about."

"Dad, I don't care about the money. No, what I care about is that you're going to give the company to someone who doesn't care!"

"What do you mean?"

"Simon does not care about the business. All he cares about is having money so he can party. He loves the lifestyle that goes with it. Dad, I care," he pointed a finger at his chest with the hand without the gun. "I see what you, grandma, and grandpa did to get this business where it is now. You all are passionate about it. You know that as I have grown up, every time you make a trip out somewhere to tour our restaurants, I wanted to go. How many times has Simon wanted to do that?" A blank stare from Trent. "None, dad, none. He never wanted to go because he didn't care."

Trent recovered nicely. Calm and cool as he was known to be. "Brian, c'mon, we can talk about this. We never knew you were this ambitious. Had we known that we could have planned stuff differently.

We still could, in fact. What do you say we go home, I'll get your grandpa, and we'll all talk about it? Brian, you don't want to kill me. You just want attention."

"You're a liar," Brian came back. "And just because I don't talk to many people doesn't mean I'm trying to get attention right now. If I were, don't you think I would make a more public display? Everyone thinks you're just the most honest person in the world, but I know you're the biggest freaking liar there is."

Trent took another step back. "What are you talking about?"

"You claim you love mom, but I know that's not true."

"What makes you think that?"

"Because you're screwing around with Rachel."

Trent stopped cold, then repeated, "What makes you think that?"

"I heard you talking to her one day at home when you thought no one was around. Everyone was out back on the veranda after dinner, and you two went into the kitchen to presumably get everyone ice cream or something. I came in a few seconds behind you two, and you were talking about her being pregnant with your child. Now dad, I'm not that experienced with women, but I know you have to have had sex with a woman for it to be your child. And you couldn't love mom if you are screwing a seventeen-year-old girl. I don't care about mom either. I think she's slept around on you many times."

"I don't know what to say."

"What can you say, dad? You were screwing your son's girlfriend, and you screwed up and got her pregnant."

Trent took a step towards Brian, trying to assert himself. Brian relaxed his aim slightly during the last exchange, but he countered Trent's move by raising the gun again.

"Brian, you don't want to do this. If they arrest you for killing me, then your life is over, too. Don't you understand that?"

"Yeah, dad, I do. But that's not going to be a problem."

"What do you mean?"

"Because I'm not going to get caught," Brian replied with confidence in his voice. "For one thing, this isn't my gun. I never touched it before today. I found it under Simon's bed a couple of weeks ago, but I did not touch it. I left it there and didn't say anything. I almost forgot about it. Also, as far as I know, there are only four people in this world that know about how to get into and out of that gate with the anonymous password. You, Rachel, Cody, and myself. When this system was being installed, I recognized Cody from when we were in elementary school together. Both of us had a lot in common. He mentioned something about having to take more time with the software for this gate. When I asked him why, he said he couldn't say. When I offered him money, and I said it would just be between us, he told me about your arrangement. I did not think anything at the time, but after I found out about Rachel, I started noticing the evenings where you stayed late here at the office were the same evenings Rachel did not see Simon. I put two and two together, and figured out why you had that put in place. I thought if you had that done before you started screwing around with Rachel, there were probably other women out there you did the same thing with."

Trent did not offer a defense.

Brian continued, "I knew how to get in the whole time the gate has stood. I parked down the street and watched for Lucas to leave. And, in case you're wondering, I sent Rachel a message telling her not to come. I grabbed your cell phone one day and snooped through it. I figured out your little cryptic messages you sent to Rachel every Tuesday. You must think you're James Bond or something with this whole setup. I bet you feel like a real man sneaking around on mom the way you do." Brian stopped and gathered his breath before continuing. "I knew usually you and Lucas were the last ones here every night. After he left, I let myself in and wiped the pad of fingerprints. So after I leave here, I will dispose of the gun, wipe the fingerprints off the exit number pad, drive home, and lock myself in my room."

Trent knew Brian was troubled, but not this deeply. What he was doing required much forethought. This was not a spur-of-the-moment decision. Trent saw Brian could kill him, and probably get away with it barring a confession from Brian. Watching his son's calculating eyes, Trent did not see that happening. He knew if he were to save his own life, trying to reason with Brian would not do it. He would have to either run or get the gun out of Brian's hand.

Trent smiled, took a step forward with his arm extended, and said, "C'mon Brian, just put the gun down. Let's talk about this."

Brian shook his head. "No dad, I'm through talking."

He then raised the gun and fired one shot into Trent's head.

Brian looked at the gun in his hand. The swiftness of the action shocked him. He figured it would be like something he saw in a video game. In those, you shoot someone, or something, some blood spurts from their head, they go down to the ground, and twitch for a few seconds before they die.

When he shot his dad, it was all over instantly. He pulled the trigger, and a spray of blood that reminded him of a red fog blossomed from his father's head. His dad's body hit the ground and never moved again.

Bang, you're dead.

That fast.

Brian had seen many bloody movies and played many bloody, violent video games. Nothing prepared him for reality. The image of the hole forming in his father's forehead was an image that would remain locked there until the day he died.

Brian already knew what he was going to do next. He knew when the body was found tomorrow, the police would look first at his family. He already knew that Simon learned of Rachel being with their dad, and that Simon would not receive his trust fund when he graduated. Brian knew Simon loved money more than anything else, and being cut off from it, and the combination of finding out your dad was sleeping with your girlfriend would be an excellent reason to kill your dad.

On the other hand, if it came out that his mom found out about Rachel and his dad, which would make her angry enough to kill her husband. At least, Brian hoped the police would think that. He was going to plant the gun in his mother's glove box when he got home. The gun may never be found there, but there was always hope that someone other than Carly would find it. Brian knew with those two motives hanging over his mother and brother's heads, it would be unlikely the police would ever look at him. His plan was to keep a low profile in the next day or two, stay in his room as much as possible, and maybe help point someone in their direction to keep any suspicion off him.

He looked around on the ground and found the shell casing from the shot. He put it in his pocket. He walked down the length of the parking lot to the number pad by the gate. Brian's hands shook as he punched in the password to open the gate. Eleven ones and a nine. He took a cloth out of his pocket and gently wiped his fingerprints away from the number pad. He did the same thing upon entering earlier.

As the gate opened, he gazed up at the parking lot, taking one last long look at his father. He felt an emptiness in his stomach, not quite believing what he had just done.

A sense of regret fell over him as the gate opened fully. The only father he would ever have was gone. There would be no bringing him back.

He stepped through the gate and let it close behind him.

It was then, as he walked away, that the cold, hard truth hit Brian: life was not like a video game. If someone died, there was no reset button or extra men.

Only the inescapable reality of what he did.

READ MORE

Be sure to read the next installment in the Lucas Caine Series, Blackbeard's Lost Treasure!

Read Caleb's next mystery, Death on the Boardwalk (Book 1 of The Myrtle Beach Mysteries)!

Enjoy this novel? Please consider leaving a review on Amazon and/or Goodreads.

Learn more about Caleb and his books on his website, CalebWygal.com.

Photo by Pamela Hartle

Caleb is a member of the Mystery Writers of America, The International Thriller Writers. and Southeastern Writers Association, Caleb has authored nine novels. He is a Mystery Writing instructor affiliated with the Osher Lifelong Learning Institution at Coastal Carolina University.

He's also a social media marketer, smoker of meats, amateur woodworker, occasional golfer, and a beach enthusiast known for his knack for not finding shark teeth along the shoreline. In his Lucas Caine Adventure series, Caleb's novels, *Blackbeard's Lost Treasure* and *The Search for the Fountain of Youth,* earned the distinction of being Semi-Finalists in the Clive Cussler Adventure Awards Competition.

Currently immersed in crafting the next installment of the Myrtle Beach Mystery Series, Caleb resides in Myrtle Beach with his loving wife and son. His passion for unraveling mysteries and teaching the art of mystery writing continues to inspire aspiring writers and captivate readers worldwide.